Where There's Smoke, There's Trouble

Debi Graham-Leard

Riverhaven Books

Where There's Smoke, There's Trouble is a work of fiction. Any similarity regarding names, characters, or incidents is entirely coincidental.

Copyright© 2017 by Debi Graham-Leard

Published in the United States by Riverhaven Books, Massachusetts.

ISBN 978-1-937588-73-1

Printed in the United States of America
by Country Press, Lakeville, Massachusetts

Edited by Riverhaven Books
Designed by Stephanie Lynn Blackman
Whitman, MA

Acknowledgements

My sincere gratitude to the following people
for their expertise and support as I created
'Where There's Smoke, There's Trouble'

Pam Loewy and Paula Norton,
Plymouth Writers Group

Det. Lt. Thomas Petersen,
Norton Police Department

Dave Myles, Deputy Fire Chief,
Norton Fire Department

Roger Bryan, Highland Investigations

Ken Decosta, Founder/Director,
RISEUP Paranormal Rhode Island

Deb Ahearn, Investigator
RISEUP Paranormal, Massachusetts

Cover Image: Brennan's Smoke Shop, Raynham, MA

Cover photographer: Robert Sinclaire

Cover Designer & Publisher:
Stephanie Blackman, Riverhaven Books

My sister Jerri Graham Burket, who inspires me daily

Last, but never least, my husband Vinnie
for his unflagging support of my writing efforts

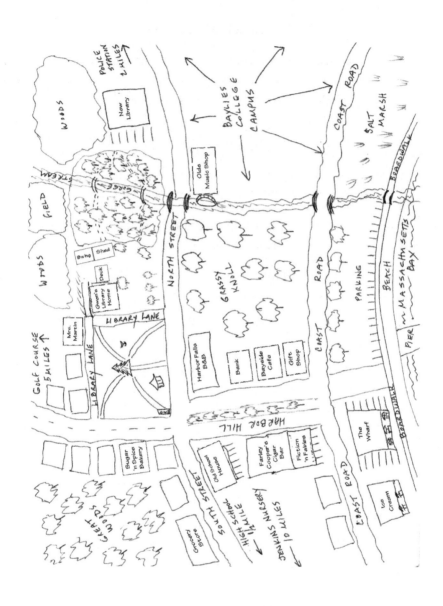

Most people offer warmth and a kind heart.
Others dole out nothing but trouble.

Chapter One... mid-morning Tuesday

With a backward shove of her sneakered foot, Gwen Andrews nudged the heavy oak door closed until the antique latch snicked shut. When she dropped her luggage to the tiled floor, dust motes floated in shafts of sunlight flickering through the stained-glass transom, bathing the foyer in a kaleidoscope of color. She tossed her keys into a carved marble slab, its deep black color belying its benign purpose.

Stepping from the foyer into the open plan of her converted library home, Gwen's acute sense of smell picked up the pungent scent of a closed-up residence. No surprise. She'd been in the Berkshires for more than a month to help her sister Tess transition past her husband's unexpected death and funeral to the beginnings of life without him.

Unfortunately, Gwen was no stranger to the long road of adjustment after the sudden death of a spouse. Almost three years had passed since her own husband Parker had died without warning. Gwen knew too well the pain of loss and the feeling of abandonment. But Gwen had tucked away a secret: Parker's spirit had appeared to her. More than once.

Unsure if he'd discover the trick to show himself to her again, Gwen pushed aside the bittersweet memories and turned right into the dining room. At the far end of her great-great grandmother's maple table, Gwen raised a tall mullioned window. Doing an about-face, she scooted past the foyer entrance to open a second window in the living room. The chilly April air – heavy with saltiness from Massachusetts Bay – swirled inside, dispelling the mustiness with little effort.

A piercing peal disrupted the quietude. Unable to ignore a ringing phone, Gwen sprinted around the fireplace wall and through her music studio to the kitchen with the speed of a much-younger woman. She lifted the receiver before it buzzed a fourth time. "Hello."

"Good, you're home. I've been dialing your cell for hours."

"Sorry, Liz. My battery died. What's so urgent?"

"I'm at my wits end."

During their decades-long friendship, Liz had never let life's challenges get to her. Gwen wondered what on earth had happened now that was beyond Liz's talents to resolve.

"What's going on?"

"You won't believe it, Gwen." In the background, a bell jingled. "Oh, rats. A customer just walked in to pick up her special order. Is there any chance you can come down to the store? I'll explain when I see you."

Here was Liz's Fiction 'n Fables Bookstop near the harbor.

Gwen gazed past the swooping staircase toward the foyer. The contents of her luggage screamed for a spin in the washing machine. Her body ached for a long overdue nap in her gabled bedroom upstairs. *No rest for the weary.* "I'll be right there, Liz."

After making a quick pit-stop in the first-floor powder room, Gwen retrieved her extra cell phone charger from a kitchen drawer, shoved it into her shoulder bag, and headed out the door she'd entered only minutes before. Breathing in the crisp April air, she descended the seven granite steps to her front walkway, deciding a brief walk would be welcomed after spending hours in her car.

She crossed the uneven cobblestones of Library Lane and stepped onto the village green, her favorite feature of Harbor Falls. Despite the distraction of Liz's un-named problem, Gwen took notice of the tulips emerging along the pathways that crisscrossed the village green; the buds on the maple, oak, and beech trees struggling to make an appearance in the next few weeks.

Gwen exited onto North Street and stood tapping her foot until the light stopped traffic so she could cross over to the top of Harbor Hill. She trekked down the sloping grade, admiring the panoramic view below. The boardwalk edging the waterfront. The sailing and pleasure boats bobbing at the wooden pier that stretched toward a gazebo at the far end. Three barrier islands and a rock jetty shielding Harbor Falls from storm surges.

She passed a row of colonial buildings on her right, long ago divided into multiple ground-level retail spaces with offices or apartments above. The enticing aroma of toasting cheese sandwiches tickled her nose from the opposite side of the tree-lined avenue where the Bayside Café occupied the space between a gift shop and the downtown branch of the local bank. Gwen hadn't eaten since the scrambled eggs and English muffin with Tess hours ago. Squaring her shoulders, she ignored her stomach grumbles and determined to eat something after she heard the details of the problem plaguing Liz.

In the final colonial building, and one store up from Liz's bookshop on the bottom corner, a new sign grabbed Gwen's attention. For years, a children's clothing store had occupied this space. But now there was an entirely different shop. The sign read Farley Cooper's Cigar Emporium & Smoking Lounge.

As Gwen registered the oddity of such an establishment in her quiet college town, a man charged out the door and nearly knocked her off her feet. When a pale-blue haze trailed out behind him, Gwen clamped her hand over her nose. Unsettling images of her cigar-smoking Great Uncle Gus roared to the front of her mind. Throughout his summer visit during her pre-teen years, Gwen hadn't been strong enough to escape his depraved groping. His stained fingers. His reeking breath. Gwen shook her head and pushed Uncle Gus to the back of her mind where he belonged.

And then she sneezed. She rummaged in her shoulder bag for a pack of tissues, her eyes closing with each violent *a'Choo*, causing her to stumble down the sloped sidewalk. She managed not to fall, quickening her pace toward Liz's bookstore. When she veered through the door into Fiction 'n Fables, she nearly bumped into an unexpected floor fan whirring away at the entrance.

The bookstore interior reeked with the unpleasant odor of cigar smoke, overpowering the usual woodsy scent of dried herbs and spices from the aromatherapy display in the far corner.

At the register, Liz punched keys to ring up a sale. A female customer – Gwen assumed the one with the special order – shifted from one foot to the other with obvious impatience. Grasping her change, the woman escaped, passing Gwen at a near-run.

When Gwen blew her nose – again – Liz spun around, her features brightening as her deep auburn pixie-cut hair settled around her narrow face as she dashed over. "I'm so glad you're back." Drawing Gwen close, Liz hugged long and hard.

Gwen balled her sodden tissues in her fist and returned the embrace. "On a wild guess, is your new neighbor your problem?"

"Bingo," Liz snapped. "Farley Cooper's Cigar Emporium & Smoking Lounge." She elongated each syllable, her contempt obvious. "His rancid smoke has been leaking through the ceiling tiles into my stock room, my office, and out here in the bookstore. My customers aren't buying books that smell like stale stogies."

"When did this Farley Cooper open his doors?"

"A few weeks ago. And before the opening, workmen hammered and drilled all day, every day. I honestly had no idea what sort of business was going in next door. Now I know that in addition to the children's clothing store next door, that man bought the third storefront on his other side. The empty one that used to be a video store." Liz paused as if she were hearing this news for the first time. "My business is way down. Customers are staying away."

"Why didn't you mention any of this to me? We talked a few times while I was at Tess's place."

"I saw no reason to burden you with my troubles. You couldn't have done anything from the Berkshires anyway."

Gwen laid her arm across her best friend's shoulder and glanced around. "Where's Olivia?"

"I had to lay her off last week."

"Oh, dear. That's a shame. Olivia can convince even the most indecisive reader to buy a book."

Liz snickered. "You're right. I miss her energy. Damn that Farley Cooper."

"Who is he?"

"I have no idea where he came from or why he decided to invade Harbor Falls." Liz took a deep breath, coughing in reaction, waving her hand in front of her face. "Men have been swarming in and out of that cigar bar like bees around a hive."

Gwen strode to the register counter and tossed her damp tissues into the basket below. "A smoking lounge sounds a bit citified for Harbor Falls." Before stashing her shoulder bag on the empty shelf below, Gwen retrieved her charger and plugged-in her dead cell phone. "How did this Farley Cooper open so quickly?"

"Good question," Liz retorted. "The man must have greased a few palms at town hall."

"That's a possibility. It takes time to maneuver the bureaucracy for permits and licenses. Add the construction itself..." Gwen's voice trailed off. Ten years earlier, she and Parker had waited months to obtain the necessary documents before initiating the conversion of the old village library into their unique home. But they'd had to work with the historical commission to make sure they didn't stray from the strict guidelines; Cooper had likely avoided that tedious task.

"Don't get me wrong," Liz went on. "I'm all for free enterprise. But a cigar bar? I don't give a flying fig if Farley

Cooper puffs himself into an early grave, but he has no right to pollute the air in my bookstore."

"Have you talked to him?" Gwen kept her tone level, hoping Liz would follow suit.

"Of course I have," Liz blustered, ignoring Gwen's too-subtle attempt. "As soon as this damn smoke started oozing in here, I walked next door to let the owner know what was happening."

"What was his reaction?"

"He laughed in my face. Said the smoke wasn't bothering him or his customers. Told me it was my problem, not his."

Gwen sneezed again. "Did you go see him a second time?"

Liz snorted. "Of course I did. A few days later, I asked him to check his ventilation system. He laughed at me again. Said he doesn't have one."

"I'm not liking this Farley Cooper. Did you keep trying?"

Liz nodded. "I researched a filtering system to install between our storefronts. I went over there to show him what I'd found and offered to split the cost."

"Generous." Gwen glanced at the now blue-tinged ceiling. "Did he take you up on it?"

"Nope. Said he wasn't about to throw away good money on something he didn't need. I'm embarrassed to admit I yelled at him, but he refused to change his mind." Liz took a deep breath, exhaling noisily. "My bookstore doesn't earn enough to cover the entire expense on my own."

Gwen touched Liz's arm. "I'll lend you the money."

"That's sweet of you, Gwen, but Farley Cooper needs to take responsibility for the problem his cigar bar has created."

The old passive Gwen would have watched from the sidelines while her best friend figured out what to do about the invasive smoke. But after being wrongly entangled in a police investigation the previous fall, Gwen had become more pro-active. "Is there anything I can do?"

Liz fingered a display of postcards near the register, peering at Gwen through lowered lashes. "Well, you've always been more even-tempered and tactful than me. I'm tired of yelling at that man with no results. Maybe you can convince him to accept my offer." Liz paused and added, "Please. Gwen."

The notion of entering the cigar bar gave Gwen the chills. She'd always avoided anything cigar-related, courtesy of good ole Uncle Gus. But she didn't have the heart to refuse Liz's request. Despite her personal revulsion, Gwen agreed to go next door and talk to this Farley Cooper.

But only because her best friend was desperate.

Chapter Two ... mid-morning, Tuesday

Standing on the sidewalk outside Farley Cooper's Cigar Emporium & Smoking Lounge, Gwen squared her shoulders and inhaled fresh air. Unfortunately, she couldn't hold her breath and a conversation at the same time.

As she approached the entrance door, Gwen stopped short. When she'd hurried past a few minutes ago, she'd noticed the new sign stretching above the sidewalk, but not the façade upgrade. The standard glass door had been replaced by a wooden door with the initials *F C* carved into the textured panel. The wide windows on either side now sported frosted glass to discourage peeking inside.

If this new portal was an indication that Farley Cooper possessed the soul of an artist, how difficult could it be to convince him to accept Liz's offer to pay half of a filtering system?

Gwen took another deep breath and stepped inside. The transformation continued. Dark paneling covered every vertical surface. To the right, an arched doorway flowed into the space that used to be the old video store, now filled with card tables and overstuffed chairs.

Down the left side, a gleaming wooden bar dominated a mirror-lined wall. Colorful bottles of liquor decorated the sideboard. Crystal glasses dangled from special racks.

Every detail indicated lots of overtime for the contractor who created this space in such a short time span.

At the bar, three men sat on tall stools, chatting as they sipped drinks and puffed smoke rings into the air above their heads. Gwen nearly choked when their fumes settled around her but vowed to control her recoil until she finished her mission and escaped.

In a windowed chamber at the far end of the room, the fiery glow of cigar tips illuminated the faces of half a dozen men. The haze and dark glass prevented Gwen from identifying any of them. A private room for men who didn't want to be seen on the premises? And why were so many men free during the workweek?

Despite her intent to stifle her reaction, Gwen coughed.

The bartender stopped polishing a goblet and twisted in her direction. "May I help you?" His oversized handlebar mustache wiggled as he spoke, but he wasn't smiling.

"Are you the owner?"

"Not me." He pointed the rim of the glass. "That's the owner over there. He's the one yelling."

Gwen followed the bartender's aim toward a man wearing a black shirt and black slacks. His rough complexion and thin mustache gave him a haggard look. Except for his longish red ponytail, all the man needed was a black hat to resemble the TV western character Paladin.

His flushed face hovered within inches of two men, one older, one younger. "Too late to complain. You should have bought the space when you had the chance years ago. Instead, you opted to rent all this time. And now I own it. Get out of here."

"Hey, Mr. Cooper," the bartender called over. "This lady's asking for you."

Had the bartender purposely interrupted the confrontation? Gwen's respect for the mustached barkeep notched upward.

The older man said nothing. He squared his shoulders and guided his sullen companion toward the exit door.

Farley Cooper gestured with his middle finger at their retreating backs before glancing at Gwen, grinning ear-to-ear, his transformation instant. Waving her over, he paused at a display counter near the archway. He removed his half-chewed cigar from his oversized lips and placed it in a scooped-out black marble rectangle.

Gwen did a double-take. She'd never considered the matching chunk of marble on her foyer table could double as a filthy ashtray. She moved sideways to stand upwind from Farley's smoldering stogy, but the heady smoke drifted in her direction as though she were a magnet.

"Good morning, little lady. I'm Farley Cooper." He extended his rough hand. "But all my new friends are calling me Farley."

Slipping a tissue from her pocket, Gwen wiped her runny nose as she studied him more closely. His receding hairline. The unnatural shade of red hair. The gray tufts around his ears and eyebrows. She avoided touching his hand by tucking her used tissue into her jeans pocket.

"My name's Gwen Andrews, Mr. Cooper, uh, Farley. I have to say I'm impressed with your artistic treatment of this space." She hoped her compliment would soften his reaction when he found out her reason for being there.

"Let me show you my state-of-the-art-humidor." Without waiting for her assent, Farley moved through the archway toward another enclosed chamber at the back of the old video store. He stretched a key ring from his belt, then – finding the door already unlocked – moved aside for her to enter. Wooden boxes – their lids propped open to expose the cellophane cigars inside – lined the floor-to-ceiling shelves on three sides.

To Gwen's surprise, the smell of raw cigars reminded her of earthy potpourri, or a dusty hayfield newly mown in late summer. Apparently, her revulsion was not the cigars themselves, but the acrid smoke created when fire lit the dried leaves.

Another man stood on a tall ladder, pushing aside boxes on the top shelf to make room for new ones.

"Scram, Quincy," Farley ordered, his voice gruff. "You can do that later after I've finished my discussion with this lovely lady."

When Farley swung back to Gwen, the skinny Quincy scowled at his boss's back before climbing down and exiting the humidor.

Farley plucked a cigar from the nearest box. "*Robusto,* the most popular style among aficionados in the USA." He held the stubby cigar against the soft light shining down from pendant ceiling fixtures, admiring the cigar as though it were a wonder of nature. "Would you like a box for your man?"

"No, thank you."

Frowning, Farley laid the cigar in the box, led her out of the humidor, locked the door, and strode through the archway to the main area counter. He retrieved his smoldering cigar from the black marble ashtray, took a puff, and blew the smoke above Gwen's head. "If you're not buying cigars, why are you here?"

Gwen hesitated at his rude manner, then forged ahead to get this over with so she could flee. His smoke settled around her and she stifled a cough. "I'm here on behalf of Liz Phillips next door."

Again, Farley's face flushed, reminding Gwen of Foghorn Leghorn, the cartoon rooster.

"You mean that shrew in the bookstore? She's been over here every other day pestering me about my smoke, trying to brow beat me into paying for a filter I don't need. She'd just as soon see me close my beautiful cigar bar."

Disagreeing, but not sharing her opinion about who was brow-beating who, Gwen made a show of looking around. "I agree you've created a retail space worthy of a magazine spread, but Liz doesn't want to close you down. She only needs you to *contain* your smoke, and she's offered to split the cost of a filtering system. Why don't you be a good neighbor and accept her proposal?"

He banged his fist on the counter, causing assorted matches and business cards to jump in place. The men sitting at the bar spun around in unison to watch the commotion. "I've sunk a lot of money into fixing up this place. No one told me it needed any improvements. And I'm not paying for something I don't need. Tell that to your skinny-assed friend."

Gwen knew when to retreat, and it was now. She backed away

11

until she reached the exit, never taking her eyes off Farley. His outraged face disappeared one inch at a time as the door closed.

***

Entering the safe haven of Fiction 'n Fables, Gwen found Liz pacing near the register.

"Well, what did he say?"

Gwen wiggled her fingers through her feathered hair in a useless attempt to dislodge the cigar stench. "He refused your offer. That man's a piece of work. Do you suppose he's bi-polar? Or maybe has a split personality?"

Heavy footsteps announced a customer. Charles Upton stalked into the bookstore. His tall stature, solid build, and lowered head made him appear more like a raging bull than the police chief.

"How can I help you, Chief?" Liz called over.

As he approached, the acrid smell of burning stogies drifted from his clothing. Had he been one of the men smoking in Farley's windowed back room?

The chief removed his cap, exposing his balding pate. "Was that you next door, Gwen?"

She studied the closed face of a man she'd always considered a friend. They'd shared many lively conversations at Baylies College functions during her decades-long tenure as a music professor.

Despite her confusion, Gwen answered, "If you mean the cigar shop, yes, I was over there. Were you one of the men smoking in that dark room?" Gwen's eyebrows twitched. "Forgive me for saying so, Charles, but during all the years I've known you, I've never seen you smoke. Jumping from nothing to cigars seems rather extreme."

"You sound just like my wife, and I don't appreciate it." The chief pointed toward the reading tables at the plate glass harbor windows. "Now sit. Both of you."

Gwen sat as far from him as possible. Liz did the same.

"All right, that's enough." Chief Upton remained standing.
Liz's forehead crinkled. "Enough what?"

He bristled. "Enough pestering your new neighbor. Farley
opened his cigar bar in good faith, and we all know Harbor Falls
needs new businesses to keep our downtown viable."

"But, Chief…" Liz began.

"Don't *but chief* me. You've been hounding him to pay half
the cost of a filtering system that only benefits your bookstore.
When he refused you, you sent Gwen over to continue the
badgering. I don't blame the man for being aggravated."

Chief Upton glanced from Liz to Gwen and back again. "If I
hear any more complaints from Farley Cooper, I'll charge you both
with harassment. You got that, ladies?" Slapping his hat on his
hand, he reversed direction and strode out, his muscular shoulder
nudging the whirring fan on his way by. It wobbled for several
precarious seconds before re-settling on its base.

Liz jumped up, the legs of her chair screeching across the
wooden plank floor. "I can't believe this. He doesn't care one iota
about Farley's smoke invading my space. And Farley has
obviously convinced the chief it's my problem, not Farley's."

Bruised by the chief's disrespect, Gwen saddened. "He's never
spoken to me so rudely." The memory of the previous September
resurfaced. When Gwen had been suspected in the disappearance
of her uninvited house guest, Chief Upton's demeanor had given
her the impression he'd considered her uninvolved.

But Detective Mike Brown had worked tirelessly to prove
Gwen guilty. In the end, she'd flushed out the real culprit by using
her wits and cunning to track down clues never considered valid by
the detective. Was the chief's pride wounded because she'd been
the better detective? Did that explain his belligerent behavior?

Liz interrupted Gwen's thoughts. "Now what, Gwen?"

"I'm not sure. Apparently the chief isn't concerned about *your*
business sustaining the downtown. Have you spoken to any of the

town officials? Maybe the Board of Health?"

"Not yet. I was hoping Farley would develop a conscience about the filtering system."

"With the chief of police protecting him, I doubt Farley will change his mind."

Gwen paced, then stopped and gestured with her forefinger. "Since the chief's no help, let's go at this from a different direction. Have you mentioned your problem to the Downtown Association?"

"No, I haven't. What are you thinking?"

"Well, if the association helped Farley Cooper maneuver the town clerk, the building inspector, the fire regulations, and the board of health, maybe they'll be eager to avoid exposure and convince Farley to split the cost of your filtering system so you won't take this public. Who's the current president?"

"Aldrich Jones."

"Call him and set up a meeting. This afternoon if he's available."

Twisting sideways, Gwen gazed over at the aromatherapy corner. "Didn't you used to sell candles developed to eat smoke?"

Liz snapped her fingers. "I forgot all about those. When most of my customers stopped smoking, I stashed them in the stock room years ago."

Gwen looked toward the back of the store. "I'll go find them. You make that phone call."

Chapter Three ... late morning, Tuesday

Gwen placed an oversized cardboard box on the first reading table and withdrew three Lord Byron Smokers Candles.

Hanging up the store phone, Liz strolled over. "Oh, good, you found them."

"There are several more cartons back there. And look what else was gathering dust on your shelves." Gwen lifted out three glass hurricane globes.

Liz nodded her approval. "Forgot about those, too."

Ripping the cellophane from three candles, Gwen positioned each on the three reading tables. She lit the wicks, then lowered the glass globes over the flame. "I don't know if these will keep the smoke out of your books, Liz, but the air will smell better."

"Thanks." Liz laid her hand on Gwen's arm. "You're thinking while I'm too busy being angry."

"Did you get through to Aldrich?"

"He's at a lunch meeting. Joanie will text him to stop here on his way back to their office."

Moving to the front counter, Gwen verified her cell phone was fully charged before storing the cord in her shoulder bag and tucking her phone into her jeans pocket. Spying a postcard leaning against the register, she picked it up. "What's this?"

Liz peeked over Gwen's shoulder. "Oh, that's Madame Eudora. She's a fascinating lady. Last week she gave a talk about her latest book. It's called *They're Not Really Gone*."

Gwen flipped the card front to back, not recognizing either the name or the author's photo. An attractive woman, though a little heavy handed with her makeup for Gwen's taste.

When Gwen handed the card back, Liz pushed it away. "Keep it. She's coming this Friday evening to hold a séance."

Madame Eudora suddenly became more intriguing. Gwen hadn't told anyone about Parker's ghostly visits last September. Though she'd tried to call his spirit back several times since then, she'd been unsuccessful. What Gwen wouldn't give to see Parker's pale smile again. "Is the event full?"

"Not quite. Two spaces left."

If Madame Eudora possessed genuine powers, she'd possibly be able to coax Parker's spirit to cross over from the other side. "I'll take one."

"Are you sure?"

Gwen caught herself before spilling her purpose. It would never do for her best friend to think she'd gone loony. "I'm sure."

Liz skewed her face. "Well, the medium did say the connection with the afterworld works better if we have multiples of three, and only seven people have signed up. You'd make eight. I guess I can fill the ninth spot if I have to."

"Then it's settled. What time on Friday?"

"Seven o'clock, after the bookstore closes."

After paying the ticket price, Gwen changed the subject before Liz had a chance to question her interest. "Let me help you bring the rest of those candles from the stock room."

They lugged the remaining cartons to the front counter, where Liz stacked the candles into a pyramid shape. She stood back, tapping her fingers against her chin. "Hmmm. Needs a poster to encourage my customers to buy a few for their homes."

When two older women entered the bookstore, their conversation drifted in with them. "I can't believe your husband spends time over there, Beatrice."

Beatrice made a face. "He comes home stinking to high heaven. I complained about the smell, and asked him over and over not to go back. Told me he'd go wherever he damn well pleased

16

and there was nothing I could do about it. That cigar residue is clinging to every corner of our house." Beatrice sniffed.

"I'm sorry, Bea. Your Frank has always been a sweetheart."

"You don't have to apologize to me, Penelope. It's not your fault that nasty man came to town. Besides, you're the one who lost your store."

Liz drifted over, pausing near the first woman. "Penelope? Is that you?"

"Yes, it's me." She air-kissed Liz's cheek. Thought I'd come downtown and see what's happening with your new neighbor."

Recognizing the sweet little lady who had owned the children's clothing store, Gwen edged toward the group. Although she and Parker had never sired any offspring – not for lack of trying – Gwen had purchased many outfits for the children and grandchildren of friends over the years.

"Oh, hello, Gwen."

"I was so surprised to hear you closed your doors, Penelope," Gwen commented. "I've been out of town so I had no idea about the drastic change."

"Trust me, it wasn't my idea." Penelope hitched her thumb toward Farley's place. "That awful man bought my space and forced me out." Penelope snuffled, but remained stalwart.

"I'm none too thrilled with the man myself," Liz added. "His smoke is ruining my inventory. Luckily, Gwen remembered these smoke-eating candles." Liz pointed to the stack near the register. "I've got a few burning on the reading tables, Beatrice. They should help minimize the stench your Frank is bringing home."

Beatrice strolled to the nearest table and leaned close enough to sniff. "It doesn't have much of a scent."

"That's right," Liz confirmed. "It uses enzymes to exterminate cigarette & cigar smoke."

Penelope stood erect and sniffed the air. "Seems to be working."

17

A man's voice called from the entrance. "Penelope? I thought I might find you here."

A muscular man wearing work pants and a blue chambray shirt with rolled up sleeves stood in the doorway. A pair of heavy gloves rested in his hand. A younger man wearing thick glasses and an identical shirt entered behind him.

"Wade? Billy? What are you doing here?" Penelope called.

In two long strides, the man stood next to her, his hefty arm thrown protectively around her shoulder. The taller gangly Billy moved to her other side.

Penelope waved toward Gwen. "Wade, you know Liz, but let me introduce you to Gwen Andrews. She was one of my best customers. Gwen, this is my husband Wade, and our son Billy."

Wade tossed a fleeting glance in Gwen's direction. "Nice to meet you."

Billy extended his hand. "Me, too, Mrs. Andrews."

"Aren't you working up the coast this morning?" Penelope asked her husband. "I left a note on the kitchen table telling you I was going out with Beatrice."

"I saw it. Read it when I stopped by the house to pick up some tools. I suspected you might be coming downtown. Before I looked for you in here, I went into the cigar bar and gave Farley Cooper a piece of my mind."

Gwen studied both men, realizing why they looked familiar. They'd been the targets of Farley's tirade earlier that morning.

Penelope raised her face, her chin quivering. "It's too late to get my store back, Wade. I don't know why you even bothered. I don't care to see that man's face ever again." She fell against her husband's broad chest and began to sob.

Gwen was reminded of a scene from Beauty and the Beast, albeit a much older couple. Penelope's porcelain skin and delicate structure against Wade's bulk and gentle expression.

Billy stared at her. "Don't cry, Mrs. G. I hate when you cry."

18

Wade tossed a stern look at Beatrice, who had retreated sideways. "Thanks for getting her out of the house, Bea, but next time, go somewhere else."

Between them, Wade and Billy escorted the whimpering Penelope out the door.

Chastised and left behind, Beatrice's flushed face glanced at Liz. "I'll take two of those candles." She paid and scurried out.

Liz gazed after her. "Wade was right to search for Penelope and take her home. Billy seems very protective, too."

"Not many men around like that," Gwen commented, thinking not only of Parker, but of Hal Jenkins as well. She waved toward the pyramid display. "I don't know about selling your books if they smell like cigar smoke, Liz, but you can make a killing on those candles. You'd better order more."

"Good idea," Liz agreed. "I'll have to see if I can find that catalogue." Liz went out to her office and returned a few minutes later to find Gwen looking at a copy of Madame Eudora's book. "Are you hungry, Gwen? I'm suddenly famished."

Gwen's stomach grumbled. "I'll go buy us some lunch at the Bayside Café. Back in a jiff."

***

Gwen queued up in line, belatedly realizing she was standing behind Billy. She called his name, but he didn't respond; she reached up and tapped his shoulder.

He jumped before gazing down at her through his thick lenses. "Oh, it's you, Mrs. Andrews. Sorry, you're on my bad ear side."

So, in addition to poor eyesight, Billy had a bum ear. She grinned in an attempt to help him relax. "You're hungry, too?"

"Wade's walking Mrs. G. to the end of the pier. Asked me to pick up some sandwiches."

"How sweet. An impromptu picnic in the gazebo."

As he shrugged his thin shoulders, his number was called. "See you around, Mrs. Andrews." He retrieved his order and headed out the door.

Gwen thought it odd the way Billy referred to his parents.

Chapter Four ... early afternoon, Tuesday

"Good afternoon, ladies," Aldrich Jones bellowed, his grin wide. He removed his coat, exposing a rotund belly, and stepped aside to let a second man enter. "Bumped into this newcomer outside. Decided to introduce him to a few locals. Jeremy Wakefield, this is Liz Phillips. She owns this delightful bookstore."

Grabbing a napkin, Liz wiped the sandwich juices from her fingers as she approached Jeremy. "Welcome to Harbor Falls. Are you here to stay?"

Jeremy shuffled his feet. "Don't know yet. I'm staying with my cousin for now."

Gwen gathered their lunch leavings and carried them to the basket beneath the counter, never moving her eyes from Jeremy. Although clean shaven, dressed in jeans, t-shirt, and a denim jacket, his face appeared haggard. Gwen sensed he'd not lived a happy life. She guessed him to be in his late thirties, maybe early forties. "I'm Gwen Andrews. Who's your cousin? Perhaps we know each other."

Before Jeremy could answer, Aldrich cleared his throat. "You asked to see me, Liz?"

"Oh, sorry, Aldrich." Liz waved him toward the nearest table.

"Nice to meet you, Mrs. Phillips, Mrs. Andrews." Jeremy headed for the first aisle of books. "I'll just browse around."

Gwen positioned herself at the new arrivals display within sight and earshot of Liz and Aldrich. She didn't know if Liz had purposely placed Aldrich to face the window, but it allowed Gwen to watch & listen without him knowing.

"What can the Downtown Association do for you today, Liz?"

"My bookshop has anchored this corner for decades."

His forehead wrinkled. "I'm well aware."

Liz wrapped both hands around the warm glass protecting the flame of a smoke-eating candle. "Do you know what this is?"

Aldrich parlayed his gaze between the flame and Liz. "It's obviously a candle, Liz. You do know an open flame in a public place is breaking a town ordinance?"

"Of course I do, Aldrich, but this is an emergency with special circumstances. This enzyme candle is trying to combat the cigar smoke seeping in from my new next-door neighbor."

Aldrich swiveled in his chair, his pinched face glancing past Gwen in the direction of Farley's place.

"Oh." He drew out the syllable. "You have a problem with Farley Cooper?"

"So you're aware of him?"

"Only because he joined the Downtown Association."

"Why wasn't I advised about the business going in next door?"

"The Association is under no obligation to notify adjacent shops of new businesses. Our monthly gatherings are intended to meet and greet our members, old and new."

"That's all well and good, but a little warning would have been nice. Let me tell you what's happening." Liz's voice grew bolder. "Farley Cooper's cigar smoke is leaking through the ceiling tiles into my bookstore. Ruining my inventory. Chasing away my customers."

Aldrich stared at her, but offered no comment.

Liz pointed toward the ceiling where a blue haze lingered. "That fan at the door and these candles can do only so much to get rid of the smoke and the stench."

"Did you speak with Mr. Cooper about this?"

"More than once. I even offered to split the cost of a filtering system between our stores, but he refused. I even asked Gwen to have a chat with him." Liz waved Gwen over.

22

Gwen settled in a third chair. "Farley insists he doesn't need to make any improvements."

Tapping the table's surface, Liz took up the dialogue. "Any idea how he was able to obtain his permits so quickly?"

Aldrich fidgeted. "If you're implying the Downtown Association was involved, you couldn't be more wrong. We offer guidance about where to go and who to see for licenses and such." He continued to squirm. "We have no control over the compliance or actions of our members. Perhaps Mr. Cooper paid a surcharge to jump to the head of the line."

Gwen couldn't help but wonder if that surcharge had been above or below the table.

Liz wasn't ready to throw in the towel. "Do you know if the fire chief checked Farley's space for code violations? Was there any discussion of installing a filtering system?"

"I have no idea. You'll have to ask the fire chief." Aldrich stood up. "I'm sorry, but I don't know what you expect me to do."

For a long beat, silence filled the space between them.

Liz's voice softened. "Can you at least speak to Farley?"

Aldrich shook his head. "Sorry. You seem to think I have more clout than I do. I'll stop in again and check on your progress." He shrugged on his coat. "Good day, ladies."

Stomping to the empty cartons, Liz ripped the first one to shreds.

Gwen hurried over. "I thought Aldrich was more influential."

"He wouldn't look me in the eye. I suspect he knows more than he's saying."

"Possible, but I don't know how you'd find out, or what good knowing would do."

They jumped when Jeremy emerged from the fiction aisle.

Liz's hand flew to her chest. "Goodness, you startled me. Did you find anything?"

He held up a book titled *Wild.* "Been wanting to read this one.

23

Heard it's based on a real hiker's experience."

"I'll ring you out." Liz guided him to the register counter.

Gwen followed them. "I haven't read that one. There's a movie as well. Are you a hiker, Jeremy? "

His head wagged back and forth. "Not to this extreme. I can't relate to hikers who trudge along the trails for months at a time. I don't think I'd have the stamina. "

When Liz handed over his change, Jeremy tucked the book under his arm and sauntered out.

"He seems nice, " Liz murmured. Seconds passed before she spoke again. "I don't know what I'm going to do about Farley's smoke. "

"What did Tony say?" Gwen asked.

Liz huffed, the force of her breath lifting her pixie bangs. "My dear husband's fishing the Allagash in Maine with his buddies for three weeks. No cell service. He knew a new store was going in next door, but drove north before Farley's smoke started causing me a problem. "

"Oh, dear." Gwen patted Liz's shoulder. "Never mind, we'll figure out something. Maybe the health department can force Farley to install your filtering system."

Liz flicked her hand. "You're always such an optimist." A stricken expression transformed Liz's face. "Oh, I'm sorry. I've been so busy ranting I haven't asked how your sister's doing."

Gwen hesitated. When Tess had called in tears more than a month ago, Gwen barely managed to decipher her sister's garbled words. Her husband Nathan. Brain hemorrhage. Gone before the EMTs arrived. Gwen had packed her bags and sped west to the Berkshires. Gwen turned to Liz now. "Tess has always been a strong woman, but losing Nathan caught her unprepared. After his funeral, I did my best to keep her occupied."

Liz leaned her forearms on the counter. "Doing what?"

Ticking off their activities one finger at a time, Gwen recited a list. "Browsed antique shops, searched for covered bridges, visited the Norman Rockwell Museum, lunched in out-of-the-way cafes, walked her mountain road. In the evenings, we experimented with recipes and worked on a 1000-piece jigsaw puzzle."

"But how did you two get around your three-day rule?"

Despite the solemnity of the topic, Gwen chuckled. Their mother – not an emotional woman – had raised both sisters on lectures, clichés, and very few hugs.

"Oh, I know the one you mean. *'Fish and relatives stink in three days'.* Tess and I managed our extended time together with no bloodshed. When she kicked me out this morning, I told her to drive over for a visit if she gets lonely."

"What are the chances she'll take you up on it?"

"Can't be sure, but the change of scenery will do her good." Liz frowned. "Wish I had a sister. Being an only child sucks."

"You've got me." With one arm, Gwen circled the taller Liz's waist.

Liz smiled. "Even better."

When a vibration tickled Gwen's thigh, she read the caller ID and beamed. "Hello, Hal."

The rumble of equipment and shouting workers in the background made hearing difficult, an indication Jenkins Nursery was bustling with spring activity.

"Hi, Gwen," Hal shouted. "When are you coming home?"

Touched he'd interrupted his busy day to check up on her, Gwen warmed. "Funny you should ask. I just got back a little while ago. I should have called to let you know I was heading back to Harbor Falls, but my cell phone died during the drive."

"That's not a problem. At least you're safe and sound. How's Tess doing?"

If Gwen had been standing in her own kitchen, she wouldn't have hesitated to answer his question. Although she'd joined the cell phone generation, she considered it rude to have long drawn-out conversations in public places. Even though there were no customers at the moment, she glanced over to see Liz ripping up the rest of the cartons. "It's good to hear your voice, Hal, but can we talk later? I'm at Liz's bookstore."

"Sure. How about meeting me for dinner?"

Although she'd been looking forward to an early evening, Gwen suddenly realized how much she'd missed Hal. "I'd love to. How about The Wharf around six?"

"Perfect. I'll make a reservation. Should I pick you up?"

"Don't bother. I'll meet you there." Rendezvous always made Gwen tingle with youthful excitement. "I'll let you get back to work. See you later." Gwen disconnected and wandered to Liz's side. "I'll carry these squashed cartons out back."

"Thanks." Liz's eyes twinkled with mischief. "Date with Hal?"

"We're just eating dinner. Don't make more of it than it is."

"When are you two going to get serious? You've been spending a lot of time together during the past six months."

"I like our friendship just the way it is."

Liz shrugged as she lifted the carton pieces into Gwen's waiting arms. "It's your life."

"Thank you." Gwen understood exactly why she'd been keeping Hal at arm's length. It had everything to do with Parker's ghostly appearances last September. Gwen harbored a secret hope that one day Parker would again break through the curtain between here and the afterlife. Having a more intimate relationship with Hal would only complicate Gwen's life.

And now there was the possibility of Parker making an appearance during Madame Eudora's séance on Friday evening.

Gwen stopped short. A yellow tabby strolled toward her, its green feline eyes squinting with interrupted sleep.

"Amber, sweetie, where have you been hiding?"

Distracted by everything that had happened in the few short hours since she'd gotten back to town, Gwen had totally forgotten that her pet had taken up temporary residence in the bookstore, much like the cat Agatha in Carolyn Hart's *Death on Demand* series. How appropriate that Amber selected the mystery aisle to make her grand entrance.

Gwen placed the stack of cardboard on the floor and lifted Amber into her arms. As soon as Gwen nuzzled the golden fur, she squealed, "Ewww!" and thrust her cat to arm's length.

Liz rushed down the aisle. "What's wrong, Gwen?"

"Amber smells like cigar smoke." Gwen grabbed the front of her own shirt and lifted it to her nose. "And so do I."

Liz mirrored the cat's stare. "There's nothing more you can do here, Gwen. Why don't you and Amber head back to your place for a bath?"

"Now that," Gwen replied, "is an excellent suggestion. Come on, Amber. Time to go home."

Chapter Five ... late afternoon, Tuesday

Gwen wrestled Amber into the cat carrier, the prison her pet hated the most. All the way up Harbor Hill and through the village green, the cat let loose a constant stream of angry feline mews, making sure her mistress was aware of her objections to her incarceration.

Upon entering her foyer, Gwen sidestepped her luggage and carried the cat past the staircase to the kitchen in the back. For the next fifteen minutes, she battled the squirming Amber through a shampoo and rinse, finally toweling off her pet and lowering her to the floor.

Amber fled to the music studio and skidded to a halt beneath Gwen's Steinway piano, tossing her mistress a searing sidelong glance, licking furiously at her damp coat.

"Sorry, sweetie, had to wash that nasty smoke out of your fur."

Backtracking to the foyer, Gwen flipped open the latches of her suitcases and removed her dirty laundry. When she stood erect, she spotted the black marble slab. The one identical to Farley's. She didn't even remember where she and Parker had bought it. How had she overlooked its use as an ashtray?

Gwen's focus moved to a framed photo of Parker walking Duxbury Beach on their thirty-seventh anniversary, only weeks before his death. He smiled as if to say, '*Missed that one, didn't you, sweetheart*'?

She kissed her fingers and tapped his face. "Don't you start."

Dropping her armful of clothes at door to the basement, Gwen carried the empty luggage up the swooping staircase and placed it near the ladder to the third floor loft. She'd wrestle it up later.

Through her gabled bedroom, she entered the master bathroom, stripped off her smoky shirt and jeans, and jumped into the shower. All evidence of Farley's cigars circled down the drain with the coconut shampoo and vanilla-scented shower gel.

As she towel-dried her hair, Gwen eyed her beckoning bed, fighting the urge to lie down. Vowing not to succumb, she got dressed, seized her stinky clothes and carried them downstairs. She gathered the first pile of laundry at the door and lugged everything to the basement laundry area.

***

The grandmother clock in the foyer bonged quarter to six as Gwen headed out to meet Hal for dinner, opting to again walk through the village green and down Harbor Hill to the waterfront. She never tired of this route, and it wasn't a far distance.

To avoid Farley Cooper's Cigar Emporium & Smoking Lounge, she chose to wend her way down the slope using the sidewalk on the opposite side. Across the street, the cigar bar buzzed with activity. Two men entered and three came out, one with a laughing woman on his arm. What was the attraction? Farley himself or those nasty cigars?

To the left of the cigar bar, Fiction 'n Fables Bookstop sat dark. Liz must have closed up early. Gwen grimaced at Farley's invasive cigar smoke discouraging Liz's usual stream of book-loving customers.

A scene from the movie *It's a Wonderful Life* came to mind. Without George Bailey's big-hearted influence, his unpretentious home town had mutated into Pottersville, a nightmarish collection of cocktail bars, casinos, and gentlemen's clubs. Was Farley's cigar bar the beginning of a similar fate for sedate Harbor Falls? Gwen shuddered at the possibility.

Shaking off her grim ponderings, she waited for a break in the Coast Road traffic before scurrying across to the parking lot of the restaurant. The mild April evening had brought lots of people outdoors – couples strolled hand in hand along the boardwalk that divided the narrow beach from the sand dunes. At the end of the long pier, fishermen cast their lines into Massachusetts Bay, hoping to hook the flounder that schooled each spring. Gwen stood for a moment to watch the activity as she breathed in the salty air.

She entered The Wharf Restaurant and looked around for Hal. Even though it had only been open for less than a year, she considered it a huge improvement over the dilapidated warehouse previously occupying this prime location.

After she confirmed with the hostess that Hal had not yet arrived, Gwen slung her jacket on the back of an empty stool at the bar facing the entrance and ordered Amaretto on the rocks. Not a typical pre-dinner drink, but Gwen's favorite. As it slid down her throat like an elixir, she studied the polished woodwork, colorful liquor bottles reflecting themselves in mirrors, and subtle lighting to create a warm and inviting oasis. Much like Farley Cooper's Cigar Emporium & Smoking Lounge, but without that damned smoke. Had the same construction crew created both spaces?

A movement at the door diverted Gwen's attention. She watched with interest as Hal scanned the area. When he spotted her, he headed her way, coming to a halt within mere inches. The outer edges of his deep blue eyes crinkled as a crooked smile brightened his weathered face.

Hal Jenkins' resemblance to actor Hal Holbrook never ceased to strike Gwen as uncanny. Parker used to tease her that not everybody needed to look like someone else. But Gwen contended there were only so many combinations of face shape, eyes, noses, and mouths. Eventually, everyone would look like someone else. This faux argument had been one of their favorites.

"Welcome home." Placing a paper bag on the adjacent stool, Hal grasped Gwen's shoulders with both hands and planted a juicy kiss squarely on her lips.

When he released her, she nearly stumbled. She'd expected his usual peck on her cheek. Though Hal had never pressured her to be more intimate, his kiss hinted he might have changed his mind.

Was it time to move to the next stage in their relationship? Was Gwen ready to have her love-making talents – and her aging body – scrutinized? Was she ready to risk their easy-going friendship by getting physical? She was undeniably susceptible to Hal's charms. His easy smile. His clever wit.

She caught the spicy scent of Hal's aftershave and blurted, "You smell *good*." Her skin warmed at her uncharacteristic flirtatiousness.

Hal transferred his paper bag from the stool to the floor, sat down, and ordered a scotch. "You *look* good."

Gwen didn't remember what she finally settled on to wear after many changes of outfit. She glanced down. The olive turtleneck to echo her hazel eyes. The pale gold multi-strand necklace and chunky earrings to complement her blonde highlights. Her most flattering jeans to camouflage her ample bottom, though that particular section of her anatomy was out of sight at the moment. Heeled boots to add a bit of height to her short stature. "Thanks."

When his drink arrived, Hal took a sip. The instant he opened his mouth to speak, the hostess arrived. "Your table is ready."

Swallowing whatever he was about to say, Hal retrieved his paper bag from the floor, tucked it under his arm, and carried their drinks to Gwen's favorite window table.

In the harbor, the jetty beacons blinked in the fading dusk, casting their beams across Massachusetts Bay to the shoreline. Night lights conjured magic in the seascape.

"I'm impressed, Hal. How did you manage to reserve this particular table?"

He waved off her compliment. "Easy. The hostess is the mother of Jenna's roommate."

The previous summer, Hal had hired Gwen to fine-tune his

31

granddaughter Jenna's flute-playing in preparation for a music competition. After Jenna won the top prize, she'd graduated early from Harbor Falls High School and was now a freshman at nearby Baylies College.

That competition had marked the beginning of Gwen's friendship with Hal. "We should have invited Jenna to join us."

Hal tilted his head. "Way ahead of you. She's studying for a big test tonight. She'll be in touch as soon as her schedule eases up." He reached over and gave Gwen's hand a squeeze. "So I have you all to myself this evening."

Chuckling to make a joke of his flirtatiousness, Gwen grabbed the menu and perused the specials. When the waitress came to take their order, Gwen ordered seafood. Hal ordered beef plus a glass of wine for each of them.

"How's Jenna adjusting to college life?"

"Loves it as far as I know."

Unprepared to discuss either Hal's sneaky kiss or his romantic mood, Gwen sidestepped into a review of the weeks with her sister. After ten minutes, she took a breath. "Tess kicked me out this morning. I'm not sure I should have left her by herself."

"Tess speaks her mind. She wouldn't have told you to drive back to Harbor Falls if she wanted you to stay."

"Maybe, maybe not."

"I wish I could have gone with you, but spring's a crazy time at the nursery."

"Tess understood. I told her to come for a visit if she gets lonely." Gwen refolded her napkin, unsure where the conversation would go.

Hal took another sip of his scotch. "I was surprised to find you at Liz's bookstore this morning – especially since you'd just gotten back to town. Everything okay?"

Gwen warmed at Hal's gentle manner and thoughtfulness. But the feeling disappeared as she described Liz's troubles with

Farley's cigar smoke: the tainted inventory; the disenchanted customers; Farley's refusal to split the cost of a filtering system; and, finally, Gwen's own failed attempt to convince the man to change his mind.

When she finished, Hal gave her a quizzical look. "But, Gwen, you hate cigar smoke. How'd Liz talk you into going over there?"

Hal had never asked the reason behind Gwen's intense dislike of smoke. She'd never told anyone about Uncle Gus's lewd advances that long-ago summer. Not her sister Tess. Not their mother. Not Liz. Not even Parker. Gwen wasn't ready to share such a disturbing piece of her childhood with anyone. Even Hal.

Forcing recollections of Uncle Gus into the darkness where he belonged, Gwen refocused on Hal's question. "Liz was desperate, so I put aside my revulsion while I tried to reason with Farley Cooper. Without success, as I said."

"What did you think of his place?"

Surprised Hal wasn't more curious about her conversation with Farley, Gwen shared her impression of his retail space. "The décor is impressive, but how anyone can sit in a cloud of revolting smoke is beyond me."

Their dinners arrived, putting their conversation firmly on pause. Gwen ravished her broiled scallops, potatoes au gratin, and roasted fresh asparagus. Hal nearly inhaled his grilled rib eye, baked potato, and green beans almandine. Neither spoke about anything other than the food until their plates were empty.

Swallowing his last bite, Hal crisscrossed his knife and fork to signal the wait staff he was finished. "I need you to keep an open mind while I tell you a story." He leaned down, lifted the paper bag, and placed it on the table between them.

Although the box he withdrew from the plain brown wrapping looked familiar, Gwen couldn't quite place it. And then he rotated it so she could read the label.

Robusto. The type of cigar Farley had tried to sell to her that

33

very morning. Gwen struggled to remain seated. Though she'd discovered that the scent of raw tobacco was not repulsive, she prickled at her reaction to the burning leaves. "Are you planning to smoke those?" She paled at the prospect.

"Oh, I doubt it."

"Then, why…" Gwen stuttered, "…why did you buy them?"

"I didn't buy them. Let me tell you what happened."

Gwen stiffened. Was Hal about to reveal something she didn't want to hear? Up to this moment, she'd thoroughly enjoyed their time together. Impromptu walks in nearby woodlands. Snowy hikes in the state parks during the winter holidays. Dinners just like this one, either at a restaurant or in one of their homes.

He interrupted her pondering by launching into the promised story. "When I was a young man, my dad's foreman introduced me to cigars while he was teaching me the ropes as a nurseryman. When I dated Claire back in the late '60's, she made me choose between her and the cigars. She won, and I haven't smoked one since, even after she passed away."

Hal's wife, gone now for twenty years, had been as precious to Hal as Parker had been to Gwen. She understood his loyalty.

Hal cleared his throat and continued. "This morning, my foreman Oscar Haze and I were making plans for the nursery over coffee at the Sugar 'n Spice. Oscar – he's the son of my dad's original foreman – mentioned a new cigar bar near the harbor. He knows I used to smoke and suggested we check it out."

"You and Oscar went into Farley's place?"

"We did. Having a look around wasn't going to hurt me."

Gwen folded her arms, not certain she wanted to hear the rest.

"Oscar chatted with Farley, who busted me because I gave up cigars for a woman. He shoved that box into my hands. Told me if I decided to man-up, I could pay him later."

"Farley Cooper is a nasty, selfish man. You could take those cigars back."

Hal half-nodded. "True."

Gwen glanced out the restaurant window into the night. Darkness had descended over Massachusetts Bay. A light fog dimmed the lights of the buoys. No moonlight offered a glimmer of brightness as Gwen digested Hal's tale with as much calm as she could muster. Was he being truthful about not smoking the Robustos? Or was he only saying the words he sensed she wanted to hear? Would he hand the stogies back to Farley and extinguish the temptation of his youthful habit? Why would Hal keep them if he didn't intend to smoke them?

Her mind swirled with questions. Was she about to lose Hal to Farley? If those wretched cigars became a fixture in Hal's life, what would she do? Push him away to avoid the cigar stench and the disturbing memories of Uncle Gus? Unable to envision her life without daily contact with Hal, Gwen sagged.

And then she shifted her thoughts to Farley. Why was that man causing so many problems for the good folks of Harbor Falls? First, he'd bought two of the three retail spaces in Liz's building and forced Penelope to close her shop. He'd somehow managed to obtain his permits from town officials in record time. He'd convinced Chief Upton to put a stop to Liz's complaints about the rampant cigar smoke. Farley's words to Beatrice's husband had caused a rift in their previously-smooth marriage. And now he'd shoved a box of cigars into Hal's hands, knowing full well Hal had given them up years ago.

Was Farley simply accustomed to forcing his will on others? Whatever the man's background, Gwen sensed he would bring nothing but trouble to her tranquil college town.

As if reading her mind, Hal tapped his finger on the wooden box, interrupting her brooding. "I promise you, Gwen, these cigars are no threat to us."

Chapter Six ... early evening, Tuesday

The shrillness of an alarm stopped Gwen in mid-swallow of her last sip of wine. Diners at nearby tables dropped their forks, the clatter echoing off the elegant walls. Wait staff froze in place with trays aloft, seemingly unsure of what to do.

With one hand, Hal reached for Gwen's, his forehead creased with concern. With his other, he picked up the paper bag concealing Farley's cigars. "Let's get out of here. I can't tell if there's a problem inside the restaurant or somewhere nearby."

He quickly pulled out his wallet, leaving enough cash to cover their meals and drinks as well as a healthy tip.

Gwen grabbed her jacket and purse, letting Hal guide her through the crowd and out the restaurant door.

The smell of pungent smoke filled the evening air, a stark contrast to the pleasant scent of the brick ovens inside The Wharf. Two fire engines roared into view at the top of Harbor Hill. As the huge machines flew down the sloping avenue, their rotating lights shot red fingers into the trees lining the thoroughfare. At the bottom of the hill, airbrakes hissed to a stop.

Gwen quickened her pace across Coast Road until she was close enough to see the flames were not licking at Liz's bookstore on the corner. Instead, they were leaping through the left side frosted window of the cigar bar. Farley paced on the sidewalk.

The fire chief jumped from the first truck and shouted above the noise of the engines, "Who owns this store?"

Farley rushed over. "I do."

Two police cruisers, their blue lights flashing, squealed to a stop at the curb. Patrolmen jumped out and eased Gwen and Hal –

along with a gathering crowd – away from the Colonial-style building and onto the median strip planted with majestic birch trees. Camera flashes lit up the storefront and the faces of the onlookers.

The fire chief kept after Farley. "Anyone inside?"

Farley shook his head. "Nobody now."

"Good. Step aside so my men can put out your fire. No sense in losing the entire building."

Two firemen rushed forward holding the business end of a hose, waiting for the other men to connect it to the hydrant halfway up Harbor Hill. When the stream of water erupted, they fought to control the bucking ferocity. When they aimed at Farley's frosted window, the glass shattered, allowing the water entrance to extinguish the flames.

Drifting the hose to the left, the firemen doused the front of Liz's bookstore. Gwen looked on, cringing when she witnessed Liz's window glass shattering under the impact of the pressurized liquid.

Gray smoke swirled into the darkened sky. Black soot floated in the air, landing on the sidewalk, the pavement, and the gawking onlookers. Gwen brushed at several ashes, but only succeeded in smearing them into the fabric of her jacket.

Three additional firefighters, wearing protective gear and masks, rushed toward the elaborately carved door, their axes raised.

"Hold on there," Farley barked, running forward to block their advance.

The fire chief intervened. "My men have to make sure the fire didn't spread."

Farley huffed. "No need to destroy my expensive door. It's not locked."

The first fireman in line lowered his axe arm and reached for the handle with his other hand. When the door opened with ease,

37

he grimaced, then rushed inside, followed by the other two men.

Above the noise of the engines and the murmur of the crowd, Gwen could hear the firemen stomping around, yelling to each other. She gripped Hal's hand, calmed by his responding squeeze.

"Damn it," Farley swore at the fire chief. "Why did it take you boys so long to get here?"

"We arrived in record time," the fire chief shouted back, his jaw jutting forward. "Do you know how it started, sir?"

Farley extended his hand and shouted, "Sorry, Chief. We haven't met. I'm Farley Cooper."

When the chief ignored the hand, Farley shifted his weight and lowered his arm. "Some fool must have dumped an ashtray into the wastebasket instead of the sand bucket. I tried to put it out myself, but my damned fire extinguisher wouldn't work. Shoddy piece of crap."

Without responding to Farley's diatribe, the fire chief warned, "You can't re-enter your store until the building inspector clears it for occupancy."

Farley's brash voice rose above the commotion. "You can't keep me out of my own place."

Checking his watch, the fire chief again ignored Farley's challenging words. "I'll contact the inspector tonight, but it's getting late. He might not get here until tomorrow morning. Let's hope the damage is minimal, both for your shop and the bookstore next door. Give me your cell phone number."

A black Ford Explorer arrived, its siren adding to the cacophony. Police Chief Charles Upton emerged and strolled over to Farley and the fire chief. When they shifted their bodies to face away from Gwen, she couldn't hear their words.

Headlights announced a vehicle barreling up Coast Road from the south. The onlookers shifted their gaze from Farley's drama to a red jeep as it screeched to a halt. A woman jumped out and ran beneath a street lamp. Recognizing Liz, Gwen tried to push past the officers controlling the crowd, but was held back to watch helplessly from the sidelines.

When Liz rounded the corner of the building, she stopped short and stared at the gawking crowd, the fire engine, the ladder truck, the firemen. She hurried toward the door of her bookstore, halting abruptly at the sight of her damaged window. Glass shattered. Diagonal wooden mullions broken. Water dripping from the sill to the sidewalk.

The fire chief hurried over, his voice raised. "Sorry, ma'am, but you can't go in there."

"Why not? I own this bookstore."

"There's been a small fire next door. My men have put it out. I need you to let them into your shop to make sure there are no embers on your side of the common wall."

Liz fumbled through her key ring until she found the right one, inserted it into the lock, and stepped aside for two burly firemen to enter. They emerged in less than a minute, nodding their heads at the fire chief.

When Liz made a move to go inside, the fire chief stepped forward and inserted his arm between her and the entrance. "I'm sorry, but you can't go in until it's been cleared for safety. Give me your cell number to pass along to the building inspector. He'll call you, most likely in the morning."

Scowling, Liz removed a business card from her shoulder bag and handed it over. Sidestepping the fire chief, she marched up to Farley, who stood with his arms crossed.

"Next door would be you, Farley Cooper. Did your filthy cigars start a fire? I should have known you were a reckless beast. Now look at what you've done," she hitched her thumb, pointing toward her damaged window. "You're going to pay for this."

Police Chief Upton stepped between Liz and Farley. "That's enough, Mrs. Phillips. I'm sure the fire was an accident. You need to calm down."

"Calm down?" Liz shouted. "Farley Cooper has been nothing but trouble since he stepped foot in Harbor Falls. I'm not going to calm down until he's gone."

Gwen winced at Liz's angry words.

The patrolmen seemed to forget all about their crowd control duties and headed toward Liz.

With the blockade withdrawn, Gwen moved to step off the median curb. She felt a tug on her sleeve and swiveled to see Hal holding her back.

"Wait, Gwen. I know you want to rescue Liz before her temper gets her into hot water, but the police will stop you." He pointed at the fire trucks. "Look. The firemen are rolling their hoses. They'll all be gone in a few minutes."

Gwen had to admit Hal was right. Although the officers were no longer paying any attention to the onlookers, they'd surely notice her approach and wave her off.

When the firemen with axes exited the cigar bar, they murmured a short conversation with the fire chief before they climbed aboard their trucks and drove off. After exchanging a few words with Chief Upton, the police officers drove off in their patrol cars, followed closely by Chief Upton.

As soon as the taillights disappeared, Gwen crossed the street and rushed toward Liz, who was staring into the crowd, her gaze moving from one inquisitive face to the next. When she locked eyes with Gwen, Liz's hand flew to her mouth, her eyes widening. "I'm so embarrassed." She seemed to lose her energy and would have collapsed if not for Gwen's sturdy support.

Hal appeared beside them. "Gwen, why don't you take Liz to the restaurant for a glass of wine? I've called Oscar to bring plywood and a few of my crew to board up her broken window. I'll meet you there when we're finished."

Gwen sent him a thankful glance. "Good idea." She threw her arm around Liz's waist and guided her toward The Wharf.

***

As soon as Gwen re-entered the restaurant, she remembered that she and Hal – along with the many other diners – had rushed out when the alarms blared more than a half hour ago.

"Sit here, Liz, I need to take care of something." Gwen lowered the shell-shocked Liz onto a padded bench at the entrance.

Gwen caught the attention of her waitress and asked the young woman for a copy of their bill. She wanted to make sure to reimburse Hal for her half as was their custom. When they began spending time together, Gwen had insisted on paying her share no matter where they went or what they did. It had taken Hal some time to adjust, but he'd come to accept her wish to pay her own way. Gwen reviewed the bill and considered how she'd offset the expense of Hal's plywood and his men's overtime. She'd check with him later to be sure all his expenses were covered.

Gwen hurried back to the bench, ignoring the stares of other diners who must have witnessed Liz's public meltdown in front of the bookstore. Guiding her best friend to the far side of the bar, Gwen ordered two glasses of White Zinfandel before settling them both in a corner table away from scrutiny.

Liz downed a grateful gulp. "Thanks for rescuing me."

"You're welcome."

Shaking her head, Liz whined, "I'm still dealing with Farley's lousy cigar smoke, and now I've got the added bonus of wood smoke, a broken window, and water damage."

"Don't worry," Gwen promised. "I'll help you through this."

Sipping their wine, the two women rehashed Farley's disruptive presence until Hal slid in beside Gwen twenty minutes later. "Liz, your window's boarded over."

"Thanks, Hal. You're a lifesaver."

"Taking care of your window was the least I could do. What comes next?"

Liz swirled her remaining wine. "For one, I'll call my

insurance agent to meet me at the bookstore tomorrow. I've owned my section of that building for so many decades I can't recall my exact coverage. That is, if the building inspector gives me the okay to go inside."

"That's a good start." Hal signaled the barman and ordered his second scotch of the night.

Seemingly unaware of what she was doing, Liz wet her finger in her wine and circled the rim of her crystal glass, creating a high-pitched ringing. "And I'll need to contact a clean-up company. I have no idea how long they'll take."

Gwen reached over and lowered Liz's hand. The ringing stopped. "I'll help you figure out a solution to this mess. There must be an official somewhere in Harbor Falls with enough clout to force Farley to install a filtering system. Otherwise, as soon as he repairs his damage and re-opens, you'll have to deal with the same smoke invasion problem."

"By the way, Liz," Hal interjected. "Why did you show up at the bookstore tonight?"

"Simple. I received a text from my smoke alarm."

Chapter Seven ... early morning, Wednesday

After a long night of little sleep, Gwen threw off her covers and placed her feet on the thick area rug beside her bed.

A loud feline protest yipped beneath the comforter. Amber slid out and jumped off the queen-sized bed, landing with a thud. The cat flew out the half-open door to the mezzanine hallway, no doubt heading for her feeding station downstairs.

"Sorry for disturbing you, sweetie," Gwen called, knowing the cat would ignore the apology.

After she showered and dressed, Gwen exited her gabled bedroom and paused at the railing. Across the mezzanine opening, in the sitting room that spanned the entire rear wall of the old library, the rising sun streamed in through a bank of windows. Memories of Parker's curses during their ambitious conversion project brought a melancholy ache to Gwen's belly.

And then Liz's misfortune flew forward in full force. The smoky bookstore, the pulsing water from the firefighters' hoses, Liz's paled expression at the sight of her damaged window, and her unmitigated fury when she confronted Farley.

Provoked by his invasive cigar smoke, Liz had surged directly to outrage after last evening's fire. Given the police chief's warning not to harass Farley, Gwen could only hope Liz would take heed and keep her distance. Despite Gwen's promise to help, she wasn't sure how much help she could actually provide.

In the kitchen, a preoccupied Gwen filled Amber's food and water bowls before glancing out the oversized bay window above the sink. She marveled at the swiftness of the seasonal change. So many weeks ago, before she'd driven to Tess's in the Berkshires, the rear gardens still held the charm of a winter wonderland. Now, the last of the snow had melted. Delicate crocuses and sturdier daffodils poked through the detritus. Spent remains of last fall's perennials and dry leaves sprawled atop the flower beds, new shoots not yet evident. Lofty grasses bent halfway. Time for spring clean-up, And soon.

***

"Good morning, Tess."

"I didn't expect you to be checking in on me so soon."

Gwen softened her tone. "Just want to ask how you're doing."

"You don't need to worry about me, Sis. I'm fine."

How much of Tess's claim was true, and how much bravado? Gwen was well aware of the depth of agony Tess was suffering after Nathan had been ripped from her life. The desolation and loneliness could be nearly unbearable.

Sure, Tess would be fine – eventually – but she would always nurture an empty hollow in her heart for Nathan. When Gwen had grieved for more than two years after Parker's death, his ghost had appeared to her, releasing the last dregs of her anguish. Or so she'd thought.

Gwen spoke into the mouthpiece. "I know you'll be fine, Tess. Remember my invitation. Whenever you need to get away, hop in your car and drive to Harbor Falls. My guest room will be waiting for you."

"Thanks, Gwen. I won't forget. Though, after what happened to your guest last fall…"

Tess didn't finish the sentence, but Gwen instantly picked up on the reference. The Henrietta Incident still reared its ugly head every once in a while. "Well, Tess, she was *uninvited*. You, on the other hand, are welcome any time."

The sisters talked for a few more minutes before Tess mumbled a good-bye.

Gwen set a cup of tea to brew and wandered down to the basement, bringing up another load of yesterday's laundry. As she folded her clothes, her cell phone vibrated in her jeans pocket.

"Gwen?" Liz's tone sounded no less desperate than it had the night before. "Do you mind if I stop over for a few minutes?"

Gwen checked the kitchen clock. Nearly nine on a Wednesday. Liz would normally be opening her bookstore by now. Perhaps the inspector hadn't yet made an appearance to let her inside.

"No need to ask permission, Liz. Come on over."

Two seconds later, the front doorbell chimed. A distraught Liz stared at Gwen. Her red Jeep was parked at the curb, Gwen lifted her eyebrows at her best friend. "You were standing on my doorstep when you called my cell phone?"

The two of them burst out laughing.

Despite Liz's strained expression, she doubled over, finally straightening up and taking a deep breath. "Oh, that felt good. "I haven't laughed for weeks."

Holding the heavy oak door wide, Gwen waved Liz in and led her to the kitchen. Liz stood at the island countertop, her cell phone clutched in her hand. "I can't stand this waiting. Until the building inspector clears me to go into my store, I can't set a time with my insurance agent."

When Liz's cell buzzed, she lifted her hand and glanced at the caller ID, her face lighting up as she pushed the green button. "This is Liz Phillips."

Gwen fixed a second cup of tea, listening as Liz set up a time to meet the inspector.

Disconnecting the call, Liz took a cautious sip of the hot liquid, and dialed again, this time to her insurance agent.

Gwen asked, "Is there anything I can do?"

"Would you come to the bookshop with me? If I see Farley, I'm sure to lose my temper again and make a bad situation even worse."

Gwen reached for Liz's nearly full cup and placed it in the sink. "Let's go."

***

Belted into the passenger seat of Liz's jeep, Gwen held on for dear life as Liz raced around Library Lane.

Waiting with little patience for the North Street light to turn green, Liz zoomed across the intersection and down Harbor Hill before squealing into her bookstore's parking lot.

Gwen hopped out and tried to keep up as Liz made a beeline toward a man pacing the front sidewalk, holding a clipboard, and checking his watch.

"Mr. Thorndike?" Liz called.

The man made an attempt to straighten his thinning hair. "Mrs. Phillips?"

"Yes, that's me." Liz withdrew keys from her shoulder bag as she approached the door.

Mr. Thorndike spoke. "No one answered the cigar bar's cell phone, so I guess I'll inspect your place first."

Liz twisted her key in the lock and pushed the door open. When she reached inside and flipped on the light switch, nothing happened.

Thorndike retrieved a flashlight from his pocket. "You stay out here while I have a look."

Sensing Liz's disappointment, Gwen moved closer. "Any idea how long this will take?"

Mr. Thorndike shook his head. Nearly fifteen minutes later, he stuck his head out the door. "Come inside, Mrs. Phillips."

When Gwen attempted to follow, he held up his hand. "Sorry, but I'm only responsible for the owner."

Liz tossed Gwen an apologetic look before following the inspector inside.

Not to be outmaneuvered, Gwen stepped to the window on the

46

left of the entrance, this one not broken by the pressurized water from the fire hoses. She cupped her hands against her cheeks, touching the glass to block the light so she could peer inside.

Cloaked in dimness, the bookstore gave off an air of melancholy. Even the light streaming through the harbor-facing windows couldn't put a dent in the gloom.

She watched the inspector lead Liz around the interior, making notations on his clipboard as his flashlight shone onto the broken window, the singed common wall, and the stained ceiling tiles. Through the window glass, Gwen could barely hear every other word. The inspector and Liz moved toward her office and the stockroom at the back, out of Gwen's sight and earshot.

Soon re-emerging into the main bookstore, Liz gestured for Gwen to come inside.

The inspector ripped off the top copy of his report and handed it to Liz. "Give this to your insurance agent. I found no structural damage. Feel free to come and go. Good day, ladies." He half-saluted and strolled out to the sidewalk.

Liz sank into a chair, her eyes traveling over his written comments. "All these repairs are going to take days, if not weeks." She looked up. "I need a big favor from you, Gwen."

"Something to do with that report?"

Placing the document on the table, Liz shook her head. "Not directly. But there's no way I'll reopen by Friday evening."

"What's so special about Friday?" Gwen asked.

"You forgot? The medium is holding a séance after hours."

"Sorry, Liz. It slipped my mind. What's the favor?"

"Can you host her event at your place?" Liz sat up, suddenly energized. "Think about it, Gwen. Your old library's the perfect spot to communicate with the dearly departed."

Gwen straightened. If Liz only knew the accuracy of her statement. Parker's ghostly appearances last fall suggested the old library was indeed the perfect location for a séance. But after

47

keeping quiet all these months, Gwen wasn't about to blurt it out now. Still, there could be unexpected issues. "I've never attended a séance, Liz. What do I need to do?"

"You don't need to do anything. Madame Eudora will lead the group. I'll call her and the other women who signed up to let them know about the new location. I'm sure she'll be thrilled."

Chapter Eight ... mid-morning, Wednesday

"Hello. Anyone in there?" A suited woman with frizzy brown hair peered from the doorway into the darkened bookstore.

"Over here, Fannie." Liz waved the woman inside.

"Why's it so dark in here?"

"Melted wires. One more thing needing repair, I'm afraid."

"I've been out of town. What happened?"

Gwen sat at harbor side table to give Liz and Fannie some privacy, but could still hear every word.

"Did you know a cigar bar opened up next door?" Liz asked.

Fannie waggled her head. "No clue. I didn't write their policy."

"Well, last night, someone caused a fire over there, and it did some damage over here."

"Oh, no." Fannie's tone revealed genuine concern as she gazed around. "At first glance, it looks like your repairs are minimal. You were very lucky. I've seen flames destroy these old colonial buildings."

"The inspector just left. Here's his report." Liz extended the piece of paper.

Fannie perused the notes. "This is quite a list. Broken window. Water damage. Smoke blemishes. Stained ceiling tiles." Her voice trailed off as she murmured the last item.

"Will my insurance take care of the repairs?" Liz asked.

Fannie opened her briefcase and removed a file folder. "As soon as you called, I grabbed my copy of your policy." Fannie flipped the pages, speed-reading the various sections.

"Unfortunately, Liz, you have a hefty deductible to keep your premium low. You'll need to submit the costs of repairs equaling your deductible before your coverage kicks in."

"Damn." Liz dropped her head into her hands.

With no warning, the building inspector rushed through the open bookstore door. "Can I borrow someone's phone? My cell isn't getting a signal, and the land line next door isn't working. I need to call 911."

Gwen reached into her pocket and placed her cell phone in his hand. "What's going on?"

Before answering, he dialed the three digits and held the phone to his ear. "It's not good, ladies. When I left you, I called the cell phone I was given for the owner. No answer. I knocked on the door. No response. I knocked again and called out. Still nothing. When I tried the handle, I found the door was unlocked, so I went inside. A man is lying on the floor behind the counter. His head's bloody. I assume he's still alive, but I'm no expert."

***

Once more, the sound of sirens filled the downtown harbor area. Gwen, Liz, and Fannie hurried out to the sidewalk to watch the drama unfold.

An ambulance arrived, then a police car. Two patrolmen emerged. One entered the cigar bar with the EMTs. The other engaged Mr. Thorndike in conversation.

Gwen whispered to Liz, "Do you think it's Farley?"

"He wasn't supposed to go inside his store until the inspector cleared it for safety, just like me," Liz answered.

Fannie leaned closer. "So why was his door unlocked?"

Chief Upton's black Ford Explorer squealed to a stop at the curb. He jumped out and glanced at the three women before disappearing into the cigar bar.

A few minutes later, the EMTs emerged with a stretcher topped by a large body, the face angled away, a red ponytail in plain view. They slid him into the back of their ambulance, slammed the doors, and drove off at breakneck speed, siren blaring.

50

Chief Upton posed in the cigar bar doorway and glanced around, then made a beeline for Liz, ignoring Gwen and Fannie. "I'm glad you're here. Saves me the trouble of tracking you down."

"Why would you need to track me down, Chief?"

His expression remained grim. "You'd better have a damn good alibi for where you've been since you threatened Farley last night."

"What are you implying?"

"The man is seriously injured, and I don't know anyone madder at him than you."

Liz backed away. "You can't be serious."

"Don't leave town." Chief Upton pivoted on his heel and joined the police officers hovering at the cigar bar entrance. Seemingly satisfied the scene was under control, the chief got behind the wheel of his SUV and sped off.

Wide-eyed, Liz faced Gwen and Fannie. "I can't believe this. Now he assumes I'm the one who attacked Farley."

The color drained from Liz's face as she realized the gravity of the situation. Eyelids fluttering, she folded to the sidewalk.

***

"Liz?" Gwen straightened the office daybed's pillow.

Fannie closed the mini-fridge, her hand grasping a bottle of water. "She awake?"

"Not yet." Gwen raised her voice. "Liz?"

Liz's eyes opened and drifted to Gwen. "What happened?"

"You fainted."

"I never faint."

"Well, you did today."

Liz raised herself on one elbow. "How did I get here?"

"Fannie and I carried you in from the sidewalk."

"You did?"

"Sure. You might be tall, but you don't weigh much." Gwen accepted the water bottle from Fannie, unscrewed the cap, and held it out. "Here, take a drink."

Struggling to a sitting position, Liz downed the entire contents. "I don't care what the chief thinks, I did not attack Farley."

When Gwen didn't comment, Liz stiffened. "You believe me, don't you?"

"Of course, of course." Despite Liz's volatile temperament, Gwen couldn't imagine her best friend doing harm to another person. Even someone as nasty as Farley Cooper. But the chief seemed to think Liz was capable.

Fannie reached out for the empty bottle. "Liz, maybe you should call your attorney."

Liz jerked her head and stammered, "But I don't have an attorney."

In one smooth movement, Gwen pushed herself from the daybed and pulled out her cell phone. "I'll call Ernie and ask him what we should do."

Ernie Maguire had been Parker's best friend, golfing buddy, and attorney. Gwen had enlisted his legal counsel during the Wickham Incident the previous fall. Bizarre that Liz now found herself in a similar circumstance – the threat of arrest for a crime she hadn't committed.

Fannie patted Liz's shoulder. "I'll leave you two to sort this out. Send me the estimates for the repair costs, and I'll open a claim with your insurance company."

Liz watched Gwen dial. "Can Ernie help us?"

"He'll at least give us some direction."

When Ernie's answering machine picked up the call, his lilting Irish voice spoke into Gwen's ear:

'The good news is I've finally retired. I'm enjoyin' a cruise on the Mediterranean with my lovely wife Fiona. The bad news is,

I'm not in the office to take your call. Please leave your name, number, and a brief description of your legal need. When we return, I'll refer you to another attorney who can best handle your problem.'

Gwen did a double-take, then mentally kicked herself for not staying in touch with Ernie and Fiona. At the buzz, she stammered, "Ernie, this is Gwen. Congratulations and never mind why I called. Let me know when you're back in town and I'll have you and Fiona over for lunch."

"That didn't sound very encouraging," Liz commented, her expression anxious.

"It wasn't. Ernie's retired. He's on a cruise with his wife. He'll make a referral when he gets back."

"When is he coming home?"

"His outgoing message didn't say."

Liz sprawled across the daybed. "Now what? Do you know any other attorneys?"

"Afraid not. Ernie's the only one."

"Let's look in the yellow pages and see who else is listed."

"I don't know, Liz. An unknown lawyer? We won't know if he's good or a waste of time." Gwen stared out the window. "We're two intelligent and resourceful women. We can surely figure out the best course of action."

"You're right. Got any ideas?"

Through the bookstore's plate-glass windows, Gwen gazed across Coast Road and past The Wharf Restaurant, drinking in the peaceful harbor scene. She willed it to provide a spark of inspiration. In short order, she snapped her fingers.

Liz jerked to a sitting position. "What?"

"When Farley wakes up and points his finger at his attacker, you can stop worrying about being arrested."

"Duh," Liz blurted. "We should have thought of that earlier.

How do we find out if Farley has opened his eyes?"

Gwen's love of mysteries kicked in. "I'll contact the hospital." She googled the local medical facility on her cell phone and tapped the phone number to dial.

"Memorial Hospital," a nasal voice answered. "Where can I direct your call?"

"I need to know the condition of a patient brought in by ambulance this morning."

"Are you a relative, ma'am?"

Gwen was caught short by the question. "He's my neighbor." Liz made a face and smacked her forehead.

The woman on the other end snipped, "Hospital rules allow updates to relatives only."

The warmth of a blush radiated up Gwen's neck. She thanked the operator, disconnected, and faced Liz. "Sorry, I wasn't fast enough to claim I was related to Farley. How about you call back and say you're his sister?"

Liz strode into her office and picked up her business phone and winked at Gwen. "Just in case the hospital has caller ID. What's the number?"

Scrolling to her call history, Gwen recited the digits as Liz punched the buttons, then listened as Liz asked about her brother's condition. Within seconds, she slammed the phone down.

"They no longer give out status on the phone because anyone can claim to be a relative. That woman says I can come to the hospital and prove my identity. Can you believe her?"

"She's only obeying the rules." Gwen snapped her fingers. "Don't worry about hospital guidelines, Liz. I know someone at the police station who might tell me how Farley's doing."

In an instant, Liz was on her feet. "I'll go with you."

Gwen shook her head. "I wouldn't recommend you go anywhere near the chief."

"Good point. Besides, I need to organize this clean-up."

"Plus, you have to call Madame Eudora and the séance attendees. I'll be back as soon as I can, hopefully with good news." Liz reached for the receiver. "Good luck, Gwen. And thanks."

Chapter Nine ... mid-morning, Wednesday

Unsure if she'd be able to discover Farley Cooper's condition, Gwen trekked up Harbor Hill and through the village green to retrieve her car for the drive to the police station. She'd done enough walking for one day.

Heading north, she passed Baylies College, the new library, the fire station, and the town offices. The next building, a two-story structure of gray stucco with white trim, housed the Harbor Falls Police Department. She eased her Sonata into a parking spot.

As she entered the lobby, a uniformed officer behind the plate glass window gestured to a metal box set into the adjacent wall.

She leaned close and spoke. "Gwen Andrews to see Detective Mike Brown."

Gwen and the detective shared a complicated history. Last September, he'd suspected her of foul play when her uninvited guest disappeared under mysterious circumstances. After she'd flushed out the real culprit, their mutual distrust had evolved into mutual respect. She could only hope his appreciation of her sleuthing instincts remained intact.

After enduring the alarming interrogation within these walls, Gwen still found the station creepy, but didn't see any alternative if she wanted to learn Farley's status. Was she naïve to think Detective Brown would tell her simply because she asked?

The desk sergeant picked up his phone, punched some keys, and mumbled a few words. Hanging up, he motioned her to the left-side door, which he buzzed open seconds later and waved her through. "Mike told me to bring you up to the detective unit. Follow me."

Up the elevator to the second floor and through a maze of hallways, the sergeant led her to an open area with windows looking out onto the rear parking lot and the woods beyond. Four desks and multiple filing cabinets filled the space. Gwen recognized the middle-aged Detective Brown right away. He hadn't changed since their encounter last year. The same buzz haircut, the same muscular shoulders atop his short frame.

A second officer sat with his back to her. Something about him seemed familiar, but she couldn't quite place him.

"Here's your visitor," the sergeant called out.

Mike Brown scrambled to his feet. "Thanks, Bert."

As the sergeant's footsteps faded, the detective waved at his side chair. "Have a seat, Mrs. Andrews. How have you been?"

"Well enough." Gwen lowered herself onto the hard, wooden surface, obviously fashioned to keep suspects uncomfortable.

"What can I do for you today?"

Getting to the point would work better than boring the man with an extended tale about Liz's predicament. "I'm hoping to find out Farley Cooper's condition."

Despite his confused look and penetrating stare, Brown called to the officer at the desk against the window. His back was still to them, his head down. "Hey, Snowcrest, what can you tell me about Farley Cooper?"

Snowcrest grabbed a folder and rolled his chair the few feet to Brown's desk. "Not much, Mike. The file's pretty slim." He held it up in confirmation.

"Detective Benjamin Snowcrest," Brown waved toward Gwen. "This is Gwen Andrews."

Snowcrest offered his hand.

Gwen found herself gazing into an older version of a familiar face from long-ago. The detective's thick white hair plus his name confirmed their connection. As she released his hand, the memory flooded back. Decades before, when she and Parker lived south of town, long before they'd converted the old library and moved to the village green, she'd taken a spill off her bicycle on Coast Road. She'd been righting herself when a younger Officer Snowcrest cruised by. He'd made sure she and her bike were not damaged before driving off. In the years that followed, whenever he'd passed her, he'd stopped and said hello.

Snowcrest's bland expression now implied he didn't remember their encounters. Deciding she must have aged beyond recognition, Gwen gave his memory a nudge. "Nice to see you again."

He cocked his head sideways. "Do I know you?"

She gave him a nod, waiting for his recall to engage.

The detective's face lightened. "Of course. The bicycle lady. Haven't seen you in years."

Gwen stifled a grin. "After my husband and I moved, my biking route changed."

"Well, you don't look any worse for wear, as they say. No more spills off your bike?"

"None that left any marks."

Snowcrest moved his gaze to Brown. "What do you need to know about Cooper?"

"Mrs. Andrews here asked about his condition."

Snowcrest refocused on Gwen, his demeanor serious. "Why?"

The bare facts would be least likely to entangle Gwen in another police investigation. "I was next door at the Fiction 'n Fables Bookstop when Mr. Cooper was taken away in an ambulance a few hours ago."

"So you're just curious?" Snowcrest suggested.

Gwen was beginning to regret her brilliant idea to come here seeking an update on Farley. Her expectation of a quick and private conversation with Detective Brown had vanished when he'd deferred to Detective Snowcrest. Wrapped up in Liz's panic, Gwen had ignored the fact that the police would be charged with finding the attacker.

Snowcrest's gaze studied her face as he waited for an answer. She echoed his question. "Yes, just curious."

He removed the only document in his file and shared what was written. "There's not much to tell. Mr. Cooper's out cold at the hospital. One witness after the fact. The building inspector. No weapon found." His eyes traveled down the report before refocusing on Gwen. "Are you here because you know something about this crime?"

Watching him, Gwen reasoned that the paltry file meant no conversation with Chief Upton, who would have surely shared his suspicion of Liz. Gwen needed to get out of there, and fast.

She glanced at her watch and rose to her feet. "I'll leave you to your other cases. Thank you for your time, detectives."

She half-expected one of them to shove her back into the chair and grill her, but as good fortune would have it, Snowcrest's desk phone began to ring.

He rolled his chair backwards, yanked the handset from its base, and listened. After barking a few words, he slammed it down, the echo bouncing off the bare walls. He retrieved his badge and gun from a drawer. "Gotta get to the hospital, Mike. Cooper's awake. Hope to get some details about his attacker." Snowcrest rushed down the hallway toward the elevator.

Gwen ordered herself not to fist-pump the air. Farley waking up would be a great relief to Liz. As soon as he told Detective Snowcrest who'd attacked him, Liz would be off Chief Upton's proverbial hook.

Chapter Ten ... noontime, Wednesday

At the bottom of Harbor Hill, Gwen turned right onto Coast Road and immediately pulled into Liz's harbor-side parking lot. She walked around the corner to the main entrance of the bookstore, stepping over hoses that snaked their way through the door from a huge panel truck covering half the front sidewalk. A noisy motor rumbled in its back cavity.

Inside Liz's shop, two men in overalls with headlamps clamped in place shone their beams into the shadowed areas near the broken front window. The roar of wet/dry vacs was deafening as they sucked up standing water and glass shards. The workmen's shouts back and forth added to the commotion.

Skirting strange barrels blocking the aisles of books, Gwen made her way to the office and knocked on the doorframe.

Liz hung up the phone. "Sorry about the noise, Gwen." Liz waved toward the retail area. "The clean-up company."

"They got here fast." Like Liz, Gwen increased her volume.

Standing up, Liz closed the office door, making only a slight dent in the roar of the machines. "Did you learn anything?"

"Can we go outside so I don't have to yell?"

"Sure. Let's walk down to the harbor and find a quiet spot."

The pandemonium dropped perceptibly as the two friends put distance between themselves and the grumbling truck. After crossing Coast Road and passing through the parking area of The Wharf Restaurant, they stepped along the boardwalk and sat down on the first bench, facing eastward toward the bay.

"Okay, Gwen," Liz began. "You've kept me in suspense long enough. Who did you see at the police station?"

"Detective Mike Brown."

"Was he willing to share information?"

"Not Brown. Another detective, Snowcrest, is handling Farley's assault. While I was sitting between them, Snowcrest got a phone call from the hospital."

"And?" Liz demanded, her impatience evident.

Gwen squeezed Liz's hand. "Farley Cooper woke up."

Liz jumped to her feet. "Great news!"

Gwen reached out and eased Liz back onto the bench. "Too soon to celebrate. We don't know if he saw his attacker. And if he did, whether he knows who it is."

"Oh, don't be such a Debbie Downer. Let's just assume he'll finger the guy, and I can get back to repairing my bookstore without worrying about being arrested."

Liz smiled for the first time in days.

***

"Mrs. Phillips?" The cleaning company foreman approached as soon as the two women re-entered the bookstore. "We've finished vacuuming up the water and glass shards. When you're done with those barrels, call the office and we'll pick them up. Keep your floor fan running to move the air until everything has thoroughly dried. Good luck with your repairs." He tipped his logoed hat and walked out, his crew trailing behind him, their arms loaded with hoses, mops, and rags.

With the machines gone and the shouting ended, the bookstore eased into quiet, the silence palpable.

Liz released a huff of air. "I'm so glad they're gone. I could hardly think with those machines, but it was a necessary evil. Did I thank you for chasing down Farley's status?"

"Not directly, but it's the least I could do. Now forget about Farley for a few minutes and tell me what I need to know about hosting Friday night's séance."

Liz picked up a copy of *They're Not Really Gone* from the display beside the register and waved Gwen toward the office.

From her desk, Liz lifted a piece of paper and handed it to Gwen. "Here's a list of the attendees. I've spoken to most of them about the change of location and left messages for the others."

Gwen ran her finger down the page, not recognizing any of the names. Not that it mattered. She folded the séance list and tucked it into her jeans pocket.

Hearing footsteps, they leaned sideways for a view of the entrance. Chief Upton stormed in, swearing when he bumped the floor fan. Three other men followed him. A state trooper, a local patrolman, and a man carrying a satchel emblazoned with the BCI logo of the Bureau of Criminal Investigation.

"Uh, oh," Liz mumbled. "This doesn't look good." When she met the police chief halfway, he shoved a piece of paper at her.

"Elizabeth Phillips, this is a warrant to search your bookstore."

Liz stood ramrod straight, her hands down at her sides, not reaching for the document.

Another voice called from the entrance. "Chief Upton?"

"Snowcrest, great. You got my message to meet me here."

The detective tossed a quick nod at Gwen as he moved past her. He spoke to the chief in a lowered voice. "Cooper slipped into a coma before I reached his bedside. I need to interview the doctors and nurses. Maybe he spoke to them when he woke up."

Gwen's sharp ears caught every word. If Farley had told anyone on staff the name of the person who attacked him, Liz would be cleared. Until that name was uncovered, the chief's suspicion of Liz would not diminish.

Snowcrest glanced down at the paper in Upton's hand. "Didn't realize you requested a search warrant, sir. Can I take a look?"

When the chief handed over the document, Snowcrest read a section out loud, "*Any blunt object that appears to have been used as a weapon.*" He passed the copy to Liz.

Gwen couldn't imagine they'd find any such weapon in the bookstore, but wasn't about to let Liz endure their search with no moral support.

"Where's the light switch?" Chief Upton demanded.

Liz's laugh held no amusement. "There *is* no light. At least not until the electrician makes repairs to my melted wiring tomorrow."

"Go get your heavy-duty lights," the chief barked at the patrolman and state trooper.

In less than a minute, the two officers hustled in with bulky flashlights. They worked their way up and down the aisles, tilting novels from the shelves, scattering copies of Madam Eudora's book from the check-out counter, sending business cards and bookmarks tumbling to the floor.

The crime scene tech bided his time near the entrance. Detective Snowcrest stood beside Chief Upton, their voices low as their eyes followed the movements of the searchers. Gwen could hear none of their words from her position near the windows.

From the wall beside the register, the patrolman lifted the fire extinguisher from its hook and checked behind it. When he leaned down and squinted into the open shelving beneath the check-out counter, he shouted, "I've got something."

Chief Upton hurried over and peered into the space. "I want pictures from every angle before you move that evidence."

The photography finished, the tech lifted a black marble ashtray with his gloved hand and peered at a stain on one sharp corner. "Looks like blood," he commented. "And there appear to be more than a few fingerprints."

Chief Upton strode toward Liz. "I'm charging you with assault."

Liz backed away. "But that ashtray isn't mine. I've never seen it before."

Gwen moved to shield Liz. "Chief, I noticed that same ashtray on Farley's display counter yesterday."

"That doesn't mean Mrs. Phillips didn't use it as a weapon."

"But, Chief," Gwen reasoned as she pointed at Liz. "Look how skinny she is. How could she have possibly overpowered Farley Cooper? He's a big man."

"And you think I'd hide the weapon in my own store?" Liz added, her defiance palpable.

"Save your breath." The chief stretched to his full height.

Snowcrest broke in. "If I could make a suggestion, sir?"

Chief Upton didn't look pleased with the interruption. "What is it, Snowcrest?"

"If Mrs. Phillips never touched the ashtray, then any fingerprints lifted won't match hers. The county sheriff's department has been trained in digital fingerprinting." Snowcrest waved the tech forward to stand beside them. "Do you have the new equipment with you?"

"My name's Peter Quinn," the tech supplied. "I was just about to bring that up myself. And to answer your question, yes, the new software is loaded onto my laptop. Give me a minute to set it up." He removed the laptop from his satchel and went to work.

Chief Upton threw his hands in the air, but didn't say anything.

Snowcrest focused on Liz. "All we need, Mrs. Phillips, is your permission to take your prints. Unless they're already in the system."

"They are not," Liz blustered. "I've never been suspected of any wrong-doing, never arrested, never anything. I'm not in anyone's system."

Liz tugged at Gwen's arm, but spoke to the detective. "I need to talk to my friend first."

Snowcrest waved them off, but didn't move from his position near the door.

Liz pulled Gwen to the window tables before speaking. "What do you think, Gwen? Should I let them take my prints?"

Gwen shrugged, uncomfortable with giving advice that could

thrust her best friend into more trouble. For her own piece of mind, Gwen needed to confirm Liz's claim of innocence. "You told the chief you've never seen that ashtray. Is there any chance you might have touched it during one of your visits to Farley's place?"

Liz assumed a puzzled look, but Gwen could see she was rewinding the mental video of her multiple visits next door.

Finally, Liz shook her head. "Not a chance. You told him you noticed it on Farley's display counter?"

"That's right. Near the archway. Were you ever in that section?"

Again, Liz shook her head. "Nope. I stayed near the bar, close to the exit."

"I've heard of fingerprints being planted."

"Oh, Gwen, you read too many mysteries and watch too many TV cop shows."

"I hope you're right."

"I am right," Liz confirmed, her head bobbing up and down.

"I'm no lawyer, Liz, but it sounds to me like there's little risk if you let them take your fingerprints for an immediate comparison."

Liz thumped the tabletop. "I agree with you. The quicker I give them my prints, the quicker the tech can say mine don't match the ones he dusted on that ashtray."

Breaking away, Liz strode toward Detective Snowcrest and Chief Upton, her arms crossed in a defensive gesture, her chin raised. "Despite my irritation that you think I attacked Farley Cooper, I'm giving you permission to take my fingerprints because I've never touched that ashtray. When you're finished with your silly comparison, you can search for the real criminal."

She stretched her hands toward the tech who was dusting the ashtray, digitally photographing the emerging prints and downloading them into his laptop. He brought up another screen and instructed Liz to place each finger and thumb onto the appropriate squares.

Gwen stood in silence and watched the proceedings. Completing the task in short order, Peter Quinn lifted his laptop and headed for a secluded reading table, saying over his shoulder, "My analysis won't take very long."

The chief conferred with Snowcrest, the patrolman, and the state trooper.

Gwen and Liz stood side by side, staring out the windows without seeing the coastal landscape, speaking little as they waited.

In less than a half hour, Peter Quinn carried his laptop to the register counter. "All right, folks, let me explain my findings." He angled the screen, pointing from one fingerprint to another, pointing out the swirls and ridge details that distinguish one person's prints from another's.

"Unfortunately," he announced, "my comparison of the partial prints from the ashtray to Mrs. Phillips' prints is inconclusive. I'll have to transfer these details to the state lab. Their equipment is more sophisticated. There are also larger fingerprints we need to compare to the database."

Chief Upton scowled.

Gwen squeezed Liz's hand.

Snowcrest and the two other officers remained somber and unemotional.

"Then take everything to the state lab," the chief barked. "And tell them to put a rush on it. We need to confirm Farley Cooper's blood and identify those partial prints."

Peter Quinn tucked the ashtray into an evidence bag and his laptop into his BCI satchel, then headed out the door.

Chief Upton strode to Snowcrest. "Meet me at the station." He stared at Liz. "Like I told you earlier, don't leave town."

Snowcrest glanced at Gwen and shrugged a suggested apology. His apparent discomfort at Chief Upton's suspicions could be a ploy, Gwen mused. The old good cop, bad cop routine. On the other hand, Gwen's status as the credible 'bicycle lady' might imbue her with some slight influence. If she got the chance, could she convince Snowcrest that Liz had nothing to do with Farley's injury and send the detective off to look elsewhere for the culprit?

When the bookstore emptied of the various law-enforcement officers, Gwen rushed to Liz's side. "I hope that wasn't a mistake."

Liz glared at Gwen. "But I never touched that damn ashtray. There's no way they're going to match my fingerprints. Listen, you don't need to babysit me, Gwen. Why don't you go on home? I'm sure you still have plenty of catch-up chores."

Still uneasy, Gwen forced a smile. "Well, all right, if you're sure."

"I'm sure. Now get outta here." Liz gave Gwen a gentle shove along with a faux grin.

Chapter Eleven ... mid-afternoon, Wednesday

Safely ensconced in her library home, still uneasy about Liz's predicament, Gwen peered out the bay window above her kitchen sink at the winter-weary flower beds. Liz was right. There was a lot of catching up to do. The weeks spent in the Berkshires consoling Tess had delayed Gwen's annual spring clean-up. Not that she would dream of blaming her sister.

Changing into her yard work sneakers and grabbing a pair of garden gloves from the basket near the French door, Gwen headed out to the potting shed at the edge of the woods. She retrieved the best tools for the tasks to be done and hauled them to the closest flower bed. With long-bladed shears, she trimmed the ornamental grasses nearly to the ground and tossed the bare stems into a lightweight fabric barrel. The clippers made short work of removing the dried stems of peonies, sedums, and Dusty Miller. Each time Gwen filled the barrel, she emptied it onto the compost heap behind the shed.

Careful not to disturb emerging shoots of Japanese painted ferns, coral bells, and bleeding hearts, she gently raked maple and oak leaves held captive in the beds around the lower deck. In the wide expanse of side lawn, she picked up scattered sticks and small branches, breaking them into lengths to fit her two-sided fireplace before storing them in the shed to dry.

Moving to the front yard, she trimmed the climbing roses along the cast iron fence. From the flower boxes hanging beneath the front windows, she removed brittle evergreen boughs left over from the holidays, making a mental note to buy pansies at Hal's Garden Center to add spring color to the façade.

Absorbed in her sprucing project, Gwen didn't notice the hours ticking past. The impending dusk robbed the landscape of color, making it difficult to distinguish details. She stored the tools and fabric barrel in the shed before inspecting all four sides of the old library. The tidy appearance provided her with a deep sense of accomplishment.

However, the time spent with Mother Nature had not passed without worry about Liz hovering just beneath the surface. Was her friend being too cavalier about Chief Upton's suspicion? Would the fingerprint analysis identify the person who attacked Farley Cooper and force the chief to move his spotlight off Liz?

Questions with no answers. At least not yet. Gwen retreated to her kitchen, boiled elbow pasta, assembled a pan of macaroni and cheese with ham chunks, and slid it into the oven.

Feeling the brush of fur against her ankle, Gwen looked down. "Amber, sweetie. Have I been ignoring you? Where have you been napping?"

When the cat made a yipping sound, Gwen hauled her chubby tabby into her arms and buried her nose in the feline softness, inhaling the clean scent of cat shampoo.

The scratching of a key in the front door brought Gwen to full alert. Seconds later, the doorbell chimed. Lowering Amber to the kitchen floor, Gwen strode toward the foyer. The heavy oak door swung inward and a brown-haired head sprinkled with gray popped into view.

Jumping back, Gwen squealed, "Tess?"

Her sister's matching squeal echoed throughout the first floor. "Gwen, you scared me."

Gwen stared into Tess's alarmed face. "You're the one who scared me."

"Sorry."

"Why didn't you let me know you were coming?"

"You invited me to drive over if I got lonely. So here I am."

"Don't get me wrong. I'm glad you came. I just wasn't expecting you this soon." Gwen waved Tess into the foyer so she could close the door. "Get yourself in here."

For a brief moment, the sisters embraced until Tess stepped away, her expression sheepish. "After you left yesterday, I wandered around my house. Didn't know what to do with myself. No one to talk to."

Removing a tissue from her sleeve, Tess wiped at her eyes. "I miss Nathan more than I imagined possible." Tess handed the tear-soaked tissue to Gwen. "Don't mind me. I know I'm preaching to the choir. You had to deal with these feelings when Parker died."

Again, Gwen debated whether to tell Tess about Parker's ghostly visits. During all the months between then and now, Gwen could have shared this other worldly news with her sister, but the timing never seemed right. Now that Tess had lost Nathan, Gwen wondered whether telling Tess would either help her find comfort in the possibility of a spiritual reunion with her husband or if she'd declare Gwen had tumbled over the edge. In the end, Gwen decided to keep it to herself for the time being.

Tess tilted her head, sniffing the air. "What are you cooking?"

"Mac and cheese, but it won't come out of the oven for a while yet. Let's get you settled in, and then I'll tell you what's happened in Harbor Falls while I was with you in the Berkshires."

Gwen carried Tess's luggage to the second-floor guest room while Tess re-parked her Prius beside Gwen's Sonata in the driveway. Meeting up in the kitchen, Tess removed her green jacket and hung it on the back of an island stool.

Amber glared at them with feline indignation, emitted a loud meow, and strolled to her feeding station.

"Poor starving kitty," Gwen teased, filling the food and water bowls. "You know, Tess, every time I take Amber to the vet, he says she needs to lose weight. Have you ever tried to convince a cat to eat less?"

The sisters chuckled when Amber devoured the food as if she was coming off a ten-day fast.

"Can't say that I have. Nathan and I kept several outdoor cats over the years, but they stayed slim chasing mice."

When the stove timer dinged, Gwen slipped on oven mitts, removed the oversized rectangular Pyrex pan, and placed it on wooden trivets positioned on the granite countertop.

"Wow, you made a lot." Tess leaned over and inhaled. "Your mac and cheese has always been one of my favorite comfort foods. Are you ever going to share your secret ingredient?"

Gwen eyed her sister. "What do you mean? It's no secret."

"But you've never told me."

"Because you never asked."

"Well, I'm asking now. So what is it?"

Gwen smirked. "A pinch of dry mustard in the cheddar sauce. All from scratch. No boxes."

"That's it?" Tess smacked Gwen's arm in a playful manner.

"That's it." Gwen scooped generous helpings onto two plates.

Tess lifted her fork and carefully inserted a steaming bite into her mouth. She chewed, moaned, and swallowed before speaking. "Oh, this is so good."

The sisters had always been careful not break another of their mother's rules: *Don't speak with your mouth full.* And so, they finished their meal without talking. Eventually, Tess squashed a belch and broke the spell. "You promised to tell me what's been going on around here."

Wiping her mouth with a napkin, Gwen began. "I'm not sure where to start." She launched into a retelling of the upheaval instigated by Farley's cigar bar, ending with the discovery of the ashtray in Liz's bookstore and her precarious position with the police chief.

Tess squinted at Gwen. "I hope you're not planning to get involved."

71

"I'm not planning anything, Tess. But if Liz needs my help to prove she's innocent, I'll do whatever I can."

"Sorry, Gwen. Of course you will. You and Liz have been friends for decades. There's no way you'd leave her to fend off the authorities without coming to her rescue. How long will it take the state lab to process those fingerprints?"

Gwen shrugged, "No idea. Depends on how many other cases are ahead of this one."

"I hate to ask this, Sis, but have you considered Liz might not be so innocent? If this Farley Cooper guy pushed her far enough, would she have snapped?"

Gwen would never admit this disturbing idea had already reared its ugly head. "It's true: Liz has a quick temper. She was really pissed at Farley Cooper. But I can't bring myself to believe she attacked the man."

"Then you should go with your gut instinct." Tess tented her fingers against her chin. "Can we visit Liz's bookstore?"

Gwen glanced at the kitchen clock. "She's probably gone for the day – no electricity and no natural light at this hour. Let's walk down tomorrow morning. She'll be supervising her repairs."

"Sounds good." Tess placed their dirty dishes in the sink. "What else is going on in peaceful little Harbor Falls?"

"There's one more thing. Liz scheduled a séance on Friday night, but there's no way the bookstore will be re-opened by then. She asked me to host the event here."

Tess's expression darkened. "Did you agree?"

"I couldn't say no." Gwen took a chance she wouldn't upset her sister with her next suggestion. "I don't know if the timing's wrong for you, Tess, but there's one more seat if you're interested."

Tess lifted an eyebrow. "I'm not sure I believe in the hereafter, but count me in. It could make for an interesting evening. I need all the distraction you can provide."

Chapter Twelve ... early morning, Thursday

As Gwen shifted sizzling bacon strips around the frying pan, the front bell chimed. She lowered the burner temperature and hurried to open the door.

"Good morning, Mrs. Andrews."

"Detective Snowcrest? What are you doing here?"

"I need to ask you a few questions." He held up yesterday's slim manila folder.

After her clumsy visit to the detective unit, and her presence at the bookstore during the afternoon search, she shouldn't be surprised that he wanted to talk to her. She stepped aside to let him enter. "I'm fixing breakfast. If you haven't eaten, you're welcome to join me and my sister Tess." Gwen could not justify rudeness.

"Thanks. I haven't had a home-cooked meal in ages."

As Gwen led him to the kitchen, his statement struck her as odd. What policeman would begin his day without a proper breakfast to keep him energized? Perhaps his wife didn't like to cook. Or maybe he was divorced. Or widowed. Or a confirmed bachelor.

Pushing aside her irrelevant speculation, Gwen spoke over her shoulder. "Would you like a cup of hazelnut decaf coffee?"

"Sure. I take it black."

Gwen filled a sapphire blue mug emblazoned with *Baylies College Music Department* and handed it to him.

He took a cautious sip. "Hmmm, good. What's your secret?"

What was it with secrets? First Tess accusing Gwen of holding out on her secret ingredient in mac & cheese. Now Detective Snowcrest tasting a secret additive in her coffee. And then there was Gwen's secret about Parker's ghost, but that didn't count. Did

73

it? Gwen sensed her face warming at the detective's compliment.
"I sprinkle cinnamon on top of the grounds."

Tucking his thumb through the handle of the mug, Snowcrest
stepped to the French doors and peered out. After a few sips, he
swung his scrutiny to the open floor plan. "I didn't realize this old
building was a private home."

Gwen cracked eggs into a bowl and whipped them to a bubbly
froth. "The village library had been abandoned for years by the
time my husband Parker and I bought it from the college more than
a decade ago. He was an architect and designed the conversion."

"Interesting layout. Is he here?"

Startled by the question, Gwen took a moment to answer. "I'm
a widow."

Snowcrest cleared his throat. "Sorry, I didn't know."

At the sound of feet racing down the staircase, he pivoted.

Tess stopped at the midway landing and stared at him. "I didn't
know we were expecting company this early."

Gwen picked up on her sister's insinuation that a polite person
would not stop by uninvited. The detective didn't seem to notice
the dig. "Tess, this is Detective Snowcrest. He's investigating the
Farley Cooper attack. I invited him to join us for breakfast."

Snowcrest nodded toward Tess as she descended the remaining
steps. "Nice to meet you, Tess. Sorry to horn in on your meal. That
wasn't my intention."

Tess did not take her eyes off him. "So why *are* you here?"

Gwen smirked at Tess switching to protective big-sister mode.

Snowcrest shifted his weight. "I need to ask your sister a few
questions."

Tess moved to the cabinet, grabbed three plates, and placed
them at Gwen's elbow near the stove. "I'm not sure she knows all
that much." As Tess slid oatmeal bread into the toaster, she pointed
her chin at an island drawer. "Grab some forks and knives, would
you, Detective?"

He did as he was told, adding paper towels for napkins.

Dividing the bacon strips and scrambled eggs onto the plates, Gwen transferred them to the island counter. She poured two more mugs of coffee and handed one to Tess. Choosing the closest stool, Gwen waved the detective to the opposite seat. Tess sat at the other end of the island.

Gwen knew why Snowcrest had appeared on her doorstep. He wanted to know why she'd asked about Farley Cooper's condition yesterday. If Chief Upton had shared his suspicion of Liz, the detective would ask Gwen's connection. Would he question her while they ate or grill her after they finished breakfast?

Snowcrest shoveled the bacon and eggs into his mouth like a man who hadn't eaten for weeks. In record time, he pushed his plate away. "That was delicious. Thank you." His grey-eyed focus moved from one sister to the other before coming to rest on Gwen. "Now, tell me all you know about Farley Cooper."

Gwen cautioned herself to choose her words with care. "Not much. I only met the man two days ago."

Snowcrest removed a small notebook from an inside jacket pocket along with a pen. "Can you remember your conversation?"

Was he commenting on her age? Did she appear to be senile? Based on the lines around his eyes and mouth, Gwen figured he couldn't be more than a few years younger. In fact, he probably could have retired by now if he'd wanted to.

Putting aside his possibly unintended insult, Gwen mentally rewound her abbreviated conversation with Farley, debating if anything she said would inadvertently implicate Liz. Did Snowcrest – who could easily pass as a white-haired version of the crafty TV detective Columbo – agree with Chief Upton's opinion of Liz's guilt? Or was the detective simply collecting information for an unbiased analysis? For a split second, Gwen debated the wisdom of inviting him to breakfast.

Tess leaned across the counter. "Excuse me, Detective, but I fail to see how my sister's limited time with this Farley Cooper person can add much to your file."

"The smallest detail is sometimes the biggest clue." Snowcrest favored Tess with a chiding glance.

Tess swung her focus to Gwen. "I don't see any harm."

Respecting her elder sister's advice, Gwen recounted Farley's patronizing greeting, his pressure to buy cigars, his anger when he found out she was there about splitting the cost of a filtering system to keep his smoke from seeping into the bookstore, his calling Liz her *'skinny-assed friend'*, and his unwitting impression of Foghorn Leghorn, the cartoon rooster.

That last comparison drew a lop-sided grin from the detective.

"I can't imagine that any part of my brief encounter with Mr. Cooper is going to help you find the real attacker." Gwen's message that it hadn't been Liz was none too subtle.

Snowcrest leaned against the stool back, crossing one ankle over his knee, toying with the lace of his shoe. "Indirectly, you've provided substantial facts. Farley Cooper didn't like to be challenged and was quick to anger. There could be others who had a less than pleasant interaction with him."

Gwen relaxed. "So, you're looking in all directions?"

"Chief Upton is convinced that your friend Liz bashed Farley on the head with that ashtray. My job is to investigate and find the real evidence."

Tess interrupted. "So what are you going to do next?"

Snowcrest pushed away from the island and peered at his watch. "I need to ask Mrs. Phillips a few questions. Thank you for your time. And for breakfast."

Gwen wasn't about to let Liz face this detective on her own. "Tess and I are walking down to the bookstore in a few minutes. Why don't you come with us?"

He grinned. "Sure. I could use the exercise."

Chapter Thirteen ... mid-morning, Thursday

As Gwen, Tess, and Snowcrest made their way through the village green and down Harbor Hill, they chatted about frivolous topics. Seagulls squawked overhead, floating on an imperceptible spring breeze from the bay.

Toward the bottom of the hill, they reached Farley Cooper's Cigar Emporium & Smoking Lounge. Bright yellow crime scene tape crisscrossed the fancy door and stretched left to include the broken window.

"I wonder what will happen to the business," Tess mused.

Gwen followed Tess's gaze. "I have no idea if Farley Cooper has a wife or children. I don't even know if the man is married."

As they passed Farley's and approached Fiction 'n Fables Bookstop, Liz exited her shop and gazed away from them toward the harbor.

Gwen called out, "Liz, is something wrong?"

Liz whipped around, her hand flying to her chest. "Goodness, you startled me. No, nothing more is wrong. I'm just taking a break."

Liz noticed Tess and opened her arms for an embrace. "I'm so sorry about Nathan."

"Thanks." Tess disentangled herself. "I don't know if I could have made it past his funeral if Gwen hadn't stayed with me."

Snowcrest moved to their side. "I didn't know. My condolences."

"Thank you," Tess murmured, not offering any sad details.

Liz shifted her attention to the detective. "I didn't expect to see you this morning."

Gwen intervened. "He stopped by to ask me about Farley Cooper. When he mentioned he was coming here to talk to you, I invited him to walk down with us."

"Do I need to be concerned, Detective?" Liz's question included a hint of wariness.

He shook his head. "I'm interviewing you as a witness. If this was an official interrogation, we'd be down at the station. I don't consider you a prime suspect."

"But a suspect just the same?" Liz challenged.

Snowcrest lifted one shoulder. "Everyone's a suspect. But I can't see you attacking Farley, no matter how – let's say feisty? – you may be. You have no criminal record."

"Feisty?" Liz snorted. "Me?" She raised one eyebrow. "If you don't think I'm the one who attacked Farley Cooper, how do you plan to change Chief Upton's mind?"

Snowcrest suppressed a lop-sided grin. "By finding the person who actually did it."

Liz twisted toward Gwen. "Should I talk to this detective or find myself a lawyer?"

Gwen again questioned her instincts about Snowcrest. Was her trust of him skewed by his helpfulness when she tumbled from her bicycle long ago? By his friendly greetings whenever he'd passed her on Coast Road way back when? Was she foolish to believe he considered Liz innocent simply because he stated he was searching for the real culprit?

"Sorry, Liz," Gwen said. "I can't make that decision for you."

Liz studied Snowcrest. "Tell you what, Detective. I'm not sensing you're trying to railroad me. Let's sit inside."

She led them into the darkened bookstore. "Sorry. Still no lights until the electrician's finished." Liz gestured toward a craggy man standing atop a ladder against the right-side common wall. His tool-laden work belt tugged his pants much too low on his hips, exposing wizened body parts best hidden.

Liz waved in the opposite direction toward the tables at the windows facing the harbor. "Have a seat, Detective. At least we have some light over here."

Gwen slung her shoulder bag on the back of a chair and sat down. Tess took the next seat. Liz tossed them both a half-worried look as she settled next to the detective.

Snowcrest plucked his notebook and pen from his pocket. "Mrs. Phillips, I need to understand the sequence of recent events. When did you first become aware of Farley Cooper?"

"I met him a few weeks ago after he opened his cigar bar."

"In here?"

"No, at his place. When I smelled cigars and saw the blue smoke drifting through my ceiling tiles, I high-tailed it next door. Saw his fancy sign. Realized I'd found the source of the smoke."

"You weren't told about the cigar bar ahead of time?"

"No, I wasn't. And I gave Aldrich Jones from the Downtown Association a piece of my mind for the oversight. He probably didn't want me to raise a stink." Liz smirked. "Forgive the pun."

Snowcrest scribbled in his notebook. "Who was there besides Mr. Cooper?"

"The place was mobbed. Men at the bar, men playing cards in the old video store, all puffing away. There was a bartender and another guy re-stocking the shelves."

"What was the gist of your conversation?"

Liz huffed. "I explained his smoke was causing problems in my bookstore. When he laughed at me, I didn't know what to say, so I came back here to stew about his reaction."

"Did you go over there a second time?"

Liz nodded. "A few days later. Asked him to check his ventilation system for leaks. He laughed at me again and said he didn't have one."

"Can I assume you didn't give up?"

Liz passed her hand along the edge of the table. "After I did some research, I approached him a third time and offered to share the cost of a filtering system between our storefronts."

"What was his reaction?"

"Not only did he refuse, but he turned beet red and started yelling. He scared me, so I left."

Gwen suppressed a comment. Liz had said she'd yelled at Farley at the end of that third encounter. Not a fact Detective Snowcrest needed to know. It would only bolster the chief's suspicion of Liz's guilt.

"I didn't waste my time going over there again and waited for Gwen to come home."

"For what reason?"

"Like I told her, she's always been more tactful than me."

Snowcrest focused his attention on Gwen. "So that's why you went into the cigar bar?"

"Yes. But I wasn't any more successful than Liz."

He made a note. "Let's skip to Tuesday evening. What time did you close after the fire, Mrs. Phillips?"

"Let me clarify. I had already closed up and gone home. A few hours later, a text message appeared on my phone that my smoke alarm had gone off. I drove back to see if it was real. The firemen had finished putting out Farley's flames by the time I arrived."

"You're fortunate your bookstore suffered only minor damage."

"You're telling me. But I'm afraid I lost my temper and yelled at Farley."

"Chief Upton told me about that. How long did you stick around?"

Gwen scooted her chair closer. "Let me answer that one. Hal Jenkins suggested I take Liz to The Wharf Restaurant for a glass of wine while he boarded up her broken window."

Snowcrest wrote Hal's name and flipped to the next page. "Did you return to the bookstore that same night?"

Liz drummed her fingers on the tabletop, her face a study of concentration. "No, I didn't."

"Did this Hal Jenkins lock your door before he joined you at the restaurant?"

Liz sat up, a panicked look transforming her face. "I didn't think to ask him. I had opened it for the firemen to check for embers. I don't remember locking up after that."

"So you didn't go back to the bookstore?"

"No. I went home and crawled into bed. The next morning, I drove here to meet the building inspector. I turned my key in the lock, but I didn't notice whether it was locked or unlocked."

"Can anyone confirm you were at home all night?"

Liz's head jerked up. "I need an alibi?"

"Just dotting my i's and crossing my t's," Snowcrest commented, his pen poised. "Everyone I talk to needs an alibi."

"In that case, Detective, I have none. My husband's in Maine fishing."

"Did you speak to him on Tuesday night?"

Liz shook her head. "No cell service in the Allagash."

Gwen's concern deepened. The fact that Liz couldn't prove she was home all of Tuesday night did not help matters.

And why hadn't he asked Gwen for her whereabouts? She didn't plan to remind him of his omission, because she'd been alone with her cat. No alibi either.

Liz stood up, her chair toppling backwards. "I'm finished talking to you, Detective. I don't appreciate you pretending to believe I'm innocent, then making me sound guilty."

Snowcrest also got to his feet. "That's not my intention, Mrs. Phillips. If I don't follow investigative procedures, Chief Upton will question my results. Let me ask you this," he continued, pointing to the shadowy area above the entrance door. "How many more security cameras do you have?"

Chapter Fourteen ... late morning, Thursday

Liz's angry expression eased as understanding dawned. "There are several others, Detective. The monitoring equipment's in my office. Come this way."

Gwen and Tess followed, pausing at the office door.

When Liz flipped a switch, a bank of miniature TV screens atop a filing cabinet blinked on, tossing a bluish light on the walls and ceiling.

"I thought you had no electricity?" Gwen called over.

Liz spoke over her shoulder. "The security system has its own battery back-up."

Snowcrest leaned closer. The top left monitor focused on the area at the front of the register from the ceiling camera he'd noticed a minute before. The top right monitor highlighted the harbor-side parking lot. The bottom left monitor provided a view through the stockroom to the back-alley door.

"What section is this one supposed to cover?" He indicated the bottom right screen, apparently focusing on ceiling tiles.

Liz pointed to a label of tiny letters. "The connecting door."

"What connecting door?" His tone was incredulous.

Gwen was equally surprised. During all the decades since she'd moved to Harbor Falls after college and met Liz, she'd never seen or heard about a connecting door. How fascinating.

Liz answered the detective's question. "Halfway down the inside wall."

"Show me," Snowcrest prompted.

"Hang on." Liz opened a file cabinet drawer and withdrew an oversized flashlight.

Gwen and Tess trailed behind as Liz escorted Snowcrest to a bulky drape suspended from brass rings on a heavy-duty rod. After pushing an upholstered reading chair to the left, Liz slid the curtain aside and aimed her beam at an antique door.

"I've never used this door, and neither did Penelope."

"Who's Penelope?"

"Penelope Grainger. She owned the children's clothing store in the middle section."

"By the middle section, you mean the space where the cigar bar's located now?"

"Exactly," Liz confirmed. "Farley also bought the old video store on the far side."

Snowcrest pointed up. "Any idea how long that camera's been misdirected?"

Liz blushed a deep shade of rose. "Sorry. I've had very few theft problems, so I rarely think to check. I don't remember the last time I switched on the monitors."

"I'm surprised you bothered to install the system," Snowcrest commented.

Liz snorted. "A slick rep with a great sales pitch."

"Why's this door even here?" His disbelief was obvious.

"From what I was told when I purchased my third of this building years ago," Liz answered, shining her flashlight on the door, "when the original colonial building was converted into retail space, the first merchant owned all three sections. After he died, it was split into three separate stores. Instead of replacing the doors with walls, they were simply locked from both sides. I'm embarrassed to admit I forget it's here most of the time."

When Liz reached for the doorknob, Snowcrest grabbed her wrist. "Fingerprints," he warned.

"Fingerprints?" Liz asked.

Without making further comment, the detective tugged a pair of latex gloves from his jacket pocket and snapped them onto his

83

hands. Avoiding the doorknob, he moved his fist a few inches above the latch plate and gave the door a mighty push. It bounced against the doorframe and popped the antique lock. The door swung toward them, revealing a second door. Snowcrest gave it an equal shove, and it opened to reveal Farley Cooper's cigar store. "This old hardware wouldn't prevent anyone from moving between Farley's place and your bookstore." Snowcrest retrieved his cell phone and snapped a few pictures.

Liz's eyes got huge. "Are you saying the person who attacked Farley snuck through this door and hid that damn ashtray beneath my counter?"

"I'm not saying anything. I prefer not to speculate until I have all the facts."

Gwen glanced down and noticed gouges in the floorboards. She was no expert about scratches, but were there two sets of fresh marks? One made by Farley's attacker and the other by Liz just now? "Detective, if prints on that doorknob match the ashtray, will they be enough to clear Liz?"

"Don't get ahead of yourself. Peter Quinn needs to dust this entire area and this camera, plus collect any evidence left behind on the floorboards. We don't know yet if there are any readable prints." He gently pushed the door until the old latch caught. "I have a few more questions, Mrs. Phillips. Let's go back to the table so I can take notes."

Releasing the heavy drape to camouflage the door, Liz traipsed after him, with Gwen and Tess close behind.

Snowcrest retrieved his notebook before once again taking a seat. "Did anyone from Farley's construction crew approach you about replacing that old door with a fire door?"

Liz shook her head. "Never met any of the crew."

Gwen leaned in. "We were speculating the other day about Farley's permits. Wouldn't the inspector have insisted on a fireproof door, given the type of business Farley was opening?"

"Hard to say. But your question brings up a related topic. Have you heard any rumors about the cause of Tuesday's fire?"

"I did," Gwen offered, appreciating her ability to eavesdrop. "Farley told the fire chief someone must have dumped an ashtray into the wastebasket instead of the sand bucket."

Snowcrest's pen moved across the page. "I'll check on that." Closing his notebook, the detective tucked it into his jacket pocket.

The bookstore door opened. Wade Grainger looked around the dark interior, his eyes coming to rest on Liz. He strolled toward her, acknowledging Gwen with a nod. Billy trailed behind, pushing his glasses up on his nose.

Liz focused on the newcomers. "Is there something I can do for you, Wade?"

"The question's can I help you." He pointed to the logo on his chambray shirt. "I don't know if you're aware, but I install windows and doors." He waited a beat to let his words sink in. "I see your front window's still boarded up from the fire."

"Actually, Wade, your timing's perfect. Can you give me a quote?"

"Sure. My pad's in the truck."

"I'll get it." Billy zipped out the door.

"Thanks, Son," Wade called after him. "Liz, if you want to replace that old connecting door with a fireproof version, I can handle both with a discount."

"You know about that door?" Detective Snowcrest asked.

"Sure. Penelope has a matching one on her side." Wade hesitated. "I mean she used to."

Liz put up one finger. "Hang on a sec, Wade." She swiveled to face the group. "Sorry, but there's no avoiding this. I have to replace my window. Are we through here, Detective Snowcrest? I'm sorry I was a little terse with you earlier."

He waved off her apology. "Your reaction was not unexpected, Mrs. Phillips. Don't let anyone touch that door until we've collected whatever evidence was left behind."

"I'll wait until you give me the okay to replace it," Liz promised.

"I may have more questions for you," he added.

"Call or stop by anytime."

Detective Snowcrest nodded at Gwen and Tess before walking out.

"Tess and I will help wherever we can, Liz."

"Thank you both." Liz tossed a grateful glance at the sisters.

"No time like the present," Tess commented. "Is there anything I can do for you right now?"

Again, Liz held up one finger, signaling she'd be right back. She marched up to the electrician. "What's your best guess about how soon I'll have power and lights in here?"

The old man hemmed and hawed, poking his hand into the exposed wall and moving the wires around. "About another half hour should do it."

"Great." Liz walked back to the table and pointed toward the aisles. "After the police search, I found more than a few books on the wrong shelves. As soon as the lights come on, you could re-sort them alphabetically by author. Otherwise, my customers won't find what they're looking for."

"I can re-organize them," Tess offered. "It'll make me feel useful,"

Liz glanced at Gwen. "It's not a big enough job for both of you."

Gwen grabbed her shoulder bag from the back of the chair. "In that case, I'll leave Tess with you and head back home."

Liz hugged Gwen. "Thanks for suggesting the detective walk down here with you. I wasn't nearly as nervous talking to him as I would have been without your support. But now I need to make arrangements with Wade. I'll see you soon." Liz threaded her hand through Wade's arm and led him toward her office.

Tess tapped Gwen's sleeve. "I shouldn't be more than an hour or so."

"Hang on a second." Gwen dug in her purse and held out a miniature flashlight. "If you want to start working before the lights are restored, you'll need this."

Tess reached for the flashlight and disappeared into the stacks.

As Gwen approached the outer door, Billy nearly bowled her over on his way in, quotation pad in hand.

"Sorry." His skin reddened as he righted his glasses. "I should watch where I'm going."

"No need to apologize, Billy."

He touched the brim of his Red Sox baseball cap and moved past her.

When Gwen stepped onto the sidewalk, Detective Snowcrest pushed himself off the front of the building. "Can I walk you home, Mrs. Andrews?"

After a few seconds of befuddlement, Gwen caught up with his reason for asking. "That's right. Your car's parked at my place. Let's go."

Chapter Fifteen ... mid-day, Thursday

As Gwen and Snowcrest hiked up Harbor Hill, she increased her shorter steps to keep pace with his longer stride. When they reached the steepest section, he placed his palm against the small of her back, giving her a welcome boost up the grade.

"Thank you, Detective."

He grinned at her, giving him the appearance of the younger officer she'd met all those years ago, despite his full head of white hair. When they reached the North Street light, he glanced at his watch. "Let me buy you an early lunch at the Sugar 'n Spice. My treat to repay you for breakfast."

"Sure." Gwen agreed without hesitation. Although she wasn't hungry, the detective had provided perhaps her only chance to uncover his game plan where Liz was concerned. Based on his reaction to that connecting door, Snowcrest seemed open-minded to the possibility of an intruder. Was Gwen indulging in wishful thinking, or was the detective truly searching for a more likely suspect?

No sooner had the two of them carried steaming bowls of creamy clam chowder and freshly baked bread to an empty table when Hal entered the café with Oscar Haze at his side. Gwen had bumped into the foreman several times at Hal's nursery, but had never warmed up to the man. His ever-present cloud of cigar-smoke reminded her of the character Pigpen in the Charlie Brown cartoon series, not to mention the unwelcome reminders of Great Uncle Gus. Whenever Oscar was in the vicinity, Gwen worked hard to keep her distance.

As if a spotlight was trained on her, Hal glanced her way, his eyebrows arching. He murmured something to Oscar before moving toward her table, his mouth set in a straight line.

"Hi, there, Gwen." Hal dropped into the adjacent chair and flung his arm across her shoulders. "Mind if we join you?" His eyes narrowed. "Oscar's ordering my lunch."

Locked in Hal's possessive grip, Gwen got the message. He wasn't pleased to find her lunching with another man. She hurried to make introductions, counting on Hal to revert to his easy-going self. "Detective Snowcrest, this is Hal Jenkins."

Snowcrest rose halfway to his feet and extended his hand. "Glad I bumped into you, Mr. Jenkins. Saves me the trouble of tracking you down."

When Hal ignored the detective's gesture, Snowcrest dropped his arm and resettled in his chair.

"Why would you need to track me down?"

"To ask you a few questions."

"About what?"

"The fire at the cigar bar on Tuesday evening, and anything you know about Farley Cooper."

Hal released his grip on Gwen and leaned both forearms on the table. "Why Farley?"

"He was attacked late Tuesday night or early Wednesday morning."

Hal's forehead wrinkled. "Cripes! How badly is he hurt?"

"He woke up briefly at the hospital then slipped into a coma. Doctors can't say when or even if he'll come out of it."

Hal's shoulders relaxed. "And you think the fire and his attack are connected?"

"Hard to say. At this point, I'm simply collecting statements."

Grateful to see Hal was back to his normal amenable self, Gwen listened with rapt interest. If the detective was still interviewing witnesses, Farley hadn't named his attacker during his brief time of awakening. This did not bode well for Liz.

89

Before Gwen had a chance to confirm her assumption, Oscar Haze arrived at their table with a loaded tray. Cigar fumes wafted from the man like heat from a hot summer tarmac.

Gwen grabbed a napkin and covered her nose, blocking a sneeze seconds before she would have sprayed all over the detective. When she sneezed again, she surged to her feet and reached for her shoulder bag and jacket.

"Excuse me. I'm allergic to cigar smoke." Whether her allergy was real or self-imposed didn't matter. She glanced at Snowcrest. "Thanks for lunch."

The detective again rose halfway. "Uh, you're welcome, Mrs. Andrews."

Escaping outside, Gwen sucked-in a lungful of fresh air before charging along the sidewalk that rimmed the village green. With each step toward her home on the northwest corner, she replayed the scene in the café. How discouraging to have her fact-seeking lunch with the detective interrupted by Hal and Oscar, only to be chased away by the foreman's lingering cloak of cigar-smoke.

As she drifted around the village green, Gwen revisited Hal's possessive reaction when he found her with the detective. Had he mistakenly judged Snowcrest as unwelcome competition? She harbored no doubt that Hal's urgent kiss on Tuesday evening signaled his desire to deepen their physical bond. If Gwen continued to resist Hal's advances, would he no longer settle for her friendship with*out* benefits?

Reaching her front door, she hurried inside and dashed upstairs to change into some gardening duds. At this rate, she was going to run out of clean clothes in no time flat.

She'd barely zipped up a fresh pair of jeans when the front door chime sent her racing down the wide staircase. She opened the door to reveal the detective.

Snowcrest held out a bag labeled Sugar 'n Spice. "You forgot your leftovers."

"Thanks." She reached for the bag. "Actually, I don't think I'd taken even one bite before Hal and Oscar arrived."

From behind his back, the detective withdrew a matching second and third bag.

Gwen couldn't help but laugh. "You didn't eat your lunch either?"

"After you rushed out of there, I didn't stick around very long."

"So you didn't take Hal's statement?"

The detective's white head moved imperceptibly. "Better to speak to him alone. I'll catch up with him on another day."

"That's probably best." Gwen looked from her bag to his. "If those are your leftovers, why don't I reheat our chowder and we can eat it now?"

"Terrific idea. Thanks."

Gwen mentally cheered as he followed her to the kitchen. Their interrupted meal had been reinstated through Snowcrest's thoughtfulness. She now had a second chance to query him about his investigation into Farley's attacker.

She transferred their chowder into ceramic soup bowls and tucked them into the microwave.

"What can I do?" Snowcrest asked, setting the third bag on the granite countertop.

"Grab some spoons and knives from the top drawer." She pointed with her chin.

Above the clatter of gathering the utensils, the detective spoke. "Hal Jenkins wasn't too pleased to see you having lunch with me."

Gwen had no intention of discussing Hal with Snowcrest. "What's in the third bag?"

Snowcrest opened it, stuck his nose inside, and rolled his eyes. "Pastries. I couldn't resist."

Gwen couldn't decide which cartoon character he mimicked, but his lighthearted manner didn't escape her notice. Was he playing games as part of his investigation? She didn't know him

91

well enough to venture a guess.

When the timer dinged, she transferred the bowls of chowder to heat-absorbing place mats. "Let me know if you want this hotter." She reached into a cabinet and placed a shaker of thyme between them.

He tried a spoonful. "This is heated just right. Thanks."

Gwen eyed him as she stirred the thyme into her own bowl of chowder before dipping her spoon for a taste. She hesitated to ask Snowcrest if he was truly investigating beyond Liz. What would he say if he wasn't?

Before she got up the gumption to broach the subject, the detective cleared his throat. "Actually, Mrs. Andrews, this worked out perfectly. There's something we need to discuss."

Her spoon slipped from her fingers. Chowder splashed. "There is?" She grabbed a paper towel and wiped at the mess.

"There is," he repeated. "I wasn't assigned to work your case last fall, but Mike Brown reminded me of your initiative and resourcefulness. You out-maneuvered him and proved you weren't involved in the disappearance of your house guest."

Gwen would never forget those horrific days and nights, but she didn't want to dwell on that unpleasant chapter of her life, thankfully over and in the past.

Snowcrest kept talking. "You uncovered relevant information from witnesses Mike didn't consider useful. May I remind you that you nearly lost your life in the process? For my peace of mind, I don't want you or your sister trying to prove Mrs. Phillip's innocence. Let the police department do the investigating."

Gwen opened her mouth to protest but then closed it. It would be a waste of time to argue. She was already planning to do whatever snooping she deemed necessary to clear Liz, and she didn't need Detective Snowcrest's approval.

"Listen, Mrs. Andrews," he went on. "I can see by the look in your eye that you probably won't take my advice. But take a moment to think about it. Someone was upset enough to bash-in Farley Cooper's head. Anyone looking for that person will be in equal danger."

"Anyone would include you, detective."

"But that's my job." He pushed his jacket aside, exposing his policeman's gun.

As Gwen stared at the sinister weapon, the ceiling light bounced off the gun's gleaming surface. Something niggled at her subconscious, but she couldn't quite put her finger on it.

He released his jacket to fall over the revolver before reaching for the third take-out bag. Unrolling the top, he reached inside and dangled a cinnamon bun for her inspection. "My lecture's concluded. Want to split this with me?"

Gwen's mouth watered at the tantalizing whiff of sugar, but she stayed strong and shook her head. "Thanks, but I'm trying to avoid sweets."

When she caught him glancing down her body, he blushed. "Sorry. But I have to say, you look fine to me."

Gwen opted to avoid a discussion about her extra pounds and wasn't about to ask if he was flirting with an old lady, although Snowcrest wasn't much younger. That would make him a dirty old man. For a split second, she again wondered why he hadn't retired from the police force.

The cinnamon bun thunked when he dropped it back into the bag. He rolled the top tight and stood up, bag in hand. "I'd better get going. Thanks for reheating my lunch. If you remember any more details, or come across anything that could be related to Farley's attack, give me a call." He slid his hand into a pocket and handed her a business card from the Harbor Falls Police Department, Detective Unit. "My direct line is printed there."

After walking Snowcrest to the door and watching him ease into his unmarked car, Gwen replayed his parting words. Had he given her unofficial permission to dig up whatever clues she could on Liz's behalf? Or had he uttered his casual instruction without considering how she might misinterpret his meaning?

Gwen chose option one.

Chapter Sixteen ... mid-afternoon, Thursday

As Gwen came up the basement stairs with the final basket of clean laundry, someone shouted from the rear deck. "I'm back."

Tess came through the French door.

"I didn't expect to see you so soon."

"Not so soon, Sis. For one thing, it took me quite a while to re-organize Liz's books."

"And the second thing?" Gwen asked, half-teasing.

"The de-smoking barrels." Tess's eyes widened.

"Is that what those are? Liz didn't have a chance to explain."

"It's a fascinating system. Volcanic rocks line the bottom. Above them, a shelf where we fanned her books to expose the smoky pages. She'll switch out her inventory until they're all de-smoked. It'll take days, but Liz thinks it's worth the time and effort. I want to go back tomorrow and see if it worked."

"Sure. We'll probably be down there every day until she's cleared of Farley's attack. Did you eat lunch?"

"Yep. We ordered sandwiches from the Bayside Café across the street." Tess plopped onto an island stool. "Liz's electricity is back on, and she's calling around to find a wallboard guy. What have you been doing?"

Gwen set the kettle to boil and dropped tea bags into two mugs for a sisterly chat. "For one, Detective Snowcrest walked with me from the bookstore and invited me to lunch at the Sugar 'n Spice as a thank you for breakfast."

"He did? Wasn't that a bit awkward?"

"Not at all. I welcomed the chance to find out more about his investigation. And then Hal and his foreman Oscar walked in."

"I sense they created a problem?"

"Hal acted like a teenager when he saw me having lunch with another man."

"You mean Hal was jealous? What did he do?" Tess asked with a barely disguised snicker.

"For one thing, he sat down next to me and captured my shoulder in a very tight grip, and he was rude to the detective."

The kettle began to whistle, giving Gwen a moment to ponder Hal's reaction. During all her years with Parker, never once had her husband shown any sign of jealousy when he'd seen her having a meal with another man. She'd often shared lunch with other men during her tenure at Baylies College, although those meals most often took place in the college cafeteria. Visiting musicians, other professors, a student's father. The list had been endless.

"Are you going to bring this up next time you talk to Hal?"

Gwen filled the two mugs and placed one in front of Tess. "I just don't know. I've never had to deal with a jealous man."

"Well, I hope you can smooth it out with Hal. Maybe you just need to convince him you're a one-man woman."

"Hmmm," Gwen murmured, not committing one way or the other. Hal's tight clutch had made her feel confined, captured, trapped, bringing back disturbing memories of Uncle Gus. Gwen hadn't appreciated the reminder one bit and didn't look forward to it happening again.

But Gwen had never told Tess about their great uncle's behavior and had no plans to confide the details all these decades later. "Hal backed off when Snowcrest mentioned Farley's attack and his need to ask Hal about the fire."

"What a relief. So did the detective ask his questions? Did Hal's answers match yours?"

Gwen shook her head. "Oscar arrived at our table with their lunches. He reeked of cigar smoke. I started sneezing, so I left."

Tess dunked her tea bag. "So you never had a chance to grill the detective?"

"As a matter of fact, Tess, I didn't realize I hadn't eaten my meal until Detective Snowcrest showed up with *my* lunch, *his* lunch, *and* a bag of pastries."

Tess raised her eyebrows. "He delivered your leftovers?"

"It wasn't out of his way. If you remember, he parked his car out front this morning."

"Oh, yeah. I forgot."

"But our dear detective had an ulterior motive for delivering my lunch."

"He did?" Tess chuckled. "What was it?"

"He's aware I solved the Henrietta mystery last fall and warned me off his official investigation of Farley Cooper's attacker."

"Should we take his advice?"

Gwen reached over and laid her hand on Tess's arm. "Well, here's the thing. Just before he left, he said, and I'm paraphrasing, *'If you find anything important, give me a call at the station'.* I take that to mean he's giving me permission to snoop."

"Oh, gosh, Gwen, do you think that's what he really meant?"

"How else could I interpret those words?"

Leaning sideways, Tess tossed her tea bag in the trash. "It does sound like he'd be interested if you unearth a clue. We've both got an appetite for mysteries, but it's a lot more dangerous in real life than in the pages of a novel." Tess stared into her tea. "There might be a connection between the fire and the attack."

"I've been thinking along those lines, too. Even Hal brought it up when Snowcrest mentioned both events in the same breath. If the fire was set on purpose to harm Farley, the arsonist might have come back later to finish the job." Gwen slid the sugar bowl closer and measured a serving into her mug. When the overhead kitchen light reflected off her teaspoon, she bolted upright. "Flashback!"

Tess jumped. "What?"

"I just remembered what I couldn't quite grasp when that light bounced off Snowcrest's gun."

"His gun? He showed you his gun?" Tess's eyebrows moved halfway up her forehead.

Gwen waved off her sister's concerns. "He was only making the point that he's a trained professional and I'm not."

"So, what did you remember just now?"

"Flashes. At the fire Tuesday evening. Someone was taking pictures. If there *was* an arsonist, he might have joined the crowd to watch his handiwork. Maybe he's been caught on camera."

"Probably a bystander, don't you think?"

"Maybe. But it could have been a reporter from the Gazette," Gwen countered. "Why don't we find out if anyone from the newspaper was at the fire?"

"Do you know anyone who works there?"

Reaching back into her memory, Gwen lit upon a reference. "After Parker died, a reporter came to see me about a tribute to his architectural projects, including his conversion of this old library. But I haven't bumped into her since."

Gwen opened an island drawer, withdrew a legal pad and pencil, and wrote Shirley Knapp at the top of the blank page. "I'll call the paper as soon as we finish our tea."

***

"I'm sorry, but Shirley's out of the office. Would you like to leave a message?"

Gwen requested a call back and disconnected.

"Do you think she'll call you?"

"Hard to know, Tess. Depends on how many stories she's chasing I guess."

"We need a plan for when she does. I've read more mysteries than you, Gwen, only because I'm two years older. The key to chasing clues is subtlety."

"I agree. If Shirley finds someone on staff who snapped pictures during the fire and asks why I want to see them…" Gwen paused and tapped her chin. "I'll say I'm helping Liz with her insurance claim and didn't think to shoot photos on Tuesday night."

"Perfect. Now we just wait?"

In answer, Gwen's cell phone buzzed, jiggling its way across the countertop. She grabbed it before it dropped off the edge, making a face when she read the caller ID. "Hello, Hal."

"Hi, Gwen. I'm sorry for the way I acted at lunchtime. When I saw you sitting with that white-haired man, I lost it. I apologize."

Relieved Hal was not only aware of his uncustomary rudeness, but was willing to make amends, Gwen relaxed.

Without giving her a chance to respond, Hal kept talking. "I'll square it with Detective Snowcrest when he takes my statement. Do you know how soon he'll contact me?"

She decided against telling Hal about Snowcrest delivering her leftovers and finishing their lunches together in her kitchen. No sense in poking a hornet's nest. "I have no idea. I guess the detective will let you know when he's ready."

"You're probably right. Listen, can I fix dinner for you tonight to make up for my bad attitude?"

Gwen considered his invitation and decided to ease up. "Why not? You're a decent cook."

"Hey," he retorted with mock insult. "If I recall, you're crazy about my meatloaf."

Gwen's spirit flooded with optimism until the tinkle of notes diverted her attention. In the music studio, Tess toyed with the keys of Gwen's baby grand piano. "Oh, rats, Hal. I can't have dinner with you tonight. Tess is here for a visit."

"Oh." His disappointment echoed in his voice.

Tess rose from the piano bench and held up one finger.

"Hang on a sec." Gwen placed her hand over the mouthpiece.

"Go ahead and make your plans with Hal. With Liz's husband out of town, she'll probably be happy to have dinner with me."

"Are you sure, Tess?"

"I'm sure."

Anxious to smooth the waters, Gwen removed her hand from the mouthpiece. "Tonight's fine, Hal. What time?"

"How about six-thirty?"

***

An hour later, Gwen answered a second call.

Shirley's raspy voice barked, "May I speak to Gwen Andrews?"

"This is Gwen. Thanks for getting back to me, Shirley."

The other woman hesitated. "Is my voice that recognizable? Never mind. Are you the Gwen Andrews who lives in the old library on the village green?"

"I am."

Shirley chuckled. "When I saw your name on the message slip, it rang a bell. I didn't think there would be two Gwen Andrews in our little college town. The article we wrote together about your husband was one of my best. How are you holding up, Sweetie?"

Shirley had not only recalled Gwen's name, but also her status as widow. "I'm keeping busy."

"An understatement for sure. First, your husband's death. And then that nasty Wickham woman last fall. Another reporter wrote the article about her, but I was impressed with your cleverness. What can I do for you today?"

Gwen forged ahead. "Did you or someone else from the paper happen to take pictures of the fire on Tuesday evening at the new cigar bar near the harbor? My friend Liz could use them for help with her insurance claim."

"Sorry, I wasn't there. But tell you what. I'll check with the other staff members and our apprentices. Why don't you stop at the Gazette office in about an hour?"

"Thanks, Shirley. I'll see you then."

100

Gwen glanced at Tess. "If you're not too tired, want to come with me? Two heads are always better than one."

"Try to stop me," Tess snorted.

Chapter Seventeen ... late afternoon, Thursday

From the other side of the reception area, Gwen recognized the raspy voice that called out, "Hello there."

Gwen and Tess pushed up from the chairs in the *Harbor Falls Gazette* reception area. A short woman with cropped gray hair, wearing a shapeless wool suit, scurried across the well-worn black and white floor and approached the sisters.

After a brief hug, Gwen introduced Tess.

"You're in luck, Gwen," Shirley Knapp said. "One of our apprentices happened to be strolling the boardwalk Tuesday evening. She always carries her camera and snapped some pics."

"Any chance we can have a look at those photos?"

"Sure, sure. Follow me."

As they entered the cavernous newsroom, the smell of ink and paper took Gwen back to her college days. Although her major had been music history, she'd minored in journalism and had landed a weekend job at the Boston Globe. What path would her life have taken if she'd pursued a career as a reporter instead of a music professor? Great movie concept, but she thought it had been done.

Shirley stopped at the first in a line of well-worn desks. "Annabelle?"

The young woman jumped to her feet, spilling a cup of coffee in the process. "Sorry, sorry," she stammered, mopping up the liquid with wrinkled napkins from Burger King.

Shirley continued talking as if the girl's clumsiness was a common occurrence. "This is Gwen Andrews and her sister Tess. Have you made copies of those fire pictures?"

Annabelle dropped the soggy mess into her wastebasket before grasping a stack of photographs from the elevated shelf above her desk. She handed them to Shirley.

Shirley carried the bundle to the adjacent desk and arranged a dozen or so across its surface in a two-tiered grid, dropping the last few onto a side chair. "They're in order by the time stamp." She reached for the first photo in the top left corner and held it up. "Is this what you're looking for?"

Gwen studied the image of Farley's place, the firemen pointing their hoses toward flames licking at the window left of his door.

"These look promising." Gwen took a quick survey of the other images: the water from a fireman's hose breaking Farley's left side window. Water streaming into the cigar bar through the broken window. The water dousing the front of Liz's bookstore, though her sign wasn't visible. Liz's window glass shattering, the shards reflecting the whirling lights of the fire trucks. Farley preventing the fire fighters from axing his door. Farley talking to the fire chief. Liz pointing her finger at Farley as Chief Upton looked on. Gwen leading Liz away. Firemen rolling up the hoses, smoke swirling up the face of the building.

Sliding the pictures into a single pile, Shirley extended them to Gwen. "Here you go."

"What do I owe you?" Gwen asked, reaching for her wallet.

Shirley waved away the offer. "My treat. I have a feeling I'm going to get another story out of these photographs."

Gwen didn't comment one way or the other except to offer a slight smile. "Thanks. These will be a great help." She eyed the photos discarded on the chair. "What are those?"

Shirley glanced down. "Orientation shots. The surrounding area, our fine citizens standing around gawking. You want them?"

Gwen resisted the temptation to explain why she was asking about the pictures – to identify the people watching the fire, one of them a possible arsonist, if indeed the fire had been set on purpose. "Only if you don't need them."

Handing over the other half dozen pictures, Shirley said, "They're all yours. We've got the digitals for our article. You let me know if anything news-worthy comes of your interest."

"I will." Gwen glanced at Annabelle. "Nice photography."

Annabelle pointed at a bystander in the top photo. "Is this you, Mrs. Andrews?"

"You can call me Gwen. And yes, that's me. I'm good friends with the bookstore owner."

"That's one of my favorite places to browse. Was her store damaged very much by the fire?"

"Melted wires, broken window, water damage," Gwen answered. "She's contacting service companies to help with the clean-up and repairs."

"Well, I hope she's able to re-open soon."

"Thanks, Annabelle. I'll share your hopes with Liz."

Annabelle blushed. "Let me get you something to hold those." She opened her desk drawer and handed over a manila folder.

Shirley's voice rasped, "I confess, I have another reason for wanting to see you in person, Gwen."

A second person with an ulterior motive. "You do?"

"This morning, I got a call from a Madame Eudora. She's looking for someone to record her séance tomorrow night and asked if any of our staffers have experience with low-light photography. Annabelle here has connections with a local ghost-hunting group and can borrow the special equipment."

Opting to let Shirley reveal her ulterior motive at her own speed, Gwen waited.

Shirley filled the silence. "Madame told me the event was originally scheduled at the bookstore, but because of the fire, it'll be held in your home." She waved at Gwen's manila folder, implying an exchange. "If you don't mind, I'm going to tag along with Annabelle. I've always wanted to witness a séance."

Gwen tucked the folder under her arm, squeezing it to prevent the photographs from falling out. "I don't mind at all, Shirley. The séance is scheduled to begin at seven, so you two should arrive earlier to set-up your equipment."

Shirley flushed a rosy pink. "We'll be there around six-thirty."

Leaving Annabelle at her desk, Shirley escorted Gwen and Tess to the reception area. "Is there a link between these photos and the assault on Farley Cooper?"

Gwen didn't need to fudge a response. The truth would suffice. "As far as I know, the police haven't made that connection." The fact that Gwen and Tess *had* was irrelevant.

Shirley nodded, seemingly satisfied.

***

When the sisters exited the *Gazette* building, gathering clouds obscured the sun. Settling into the driver's seat of her Sonata, Gwen held up the manila folder. "I'd like Liz to take a look at these. Find out if she can identify anyone else in the crowd."

Tess glanced at the clock in the dashboard. "When is Hal expecting you?"

"Six-thirty. We have time."

"Shouldn't you tell Detective Snowcrest about these pictures?"

"I'll call him later. More helpful if we identify the majority of the people first."

Tess shrugged. "Well, all right. I just don't want you to get on his bad side."

"I'm not sure the detective has a bad side."

Tess gave Gwen one of her classic big sister looks. "And I'm not sure I want to know what you mean."

Gwen scoffed. "Don't read anything into my offhand remark. I was only referring to his gentle manner, his level-headedness, and his chivalry to deliver my lunch."

"If you say so, Sis. By the way, thanks for inviting me to tag along today."

"Well, when you showed up on my doorstep last night, you said you needed a distraction. I'd say chasing clues qualifies."

***

In the now brightly-lit bookstore, Liz sorted through the array of photographs. "Did Shirley ask why you wanted these?"

"Not directly. I hinted that these would be useful for your insurance claim. But Shirley didn't ask, so we didn't have to lie."

"Might not have been a lie, Gwen. Never hurts to have visual proof of damage. If I hadn't been so angry at Farley, I would have taken pictures with my cell phone."

Liz peered closely at the faces captured on film. "Geez, I don't know what to tell you. Some of these people are customers. Others are casual acquaintances. The bank clerk. The waitress at the Bayside Café. The others I don't know."

Gwen retrieved her legal pad and pencil. "Why don't you tell me the names of the people you do recognize?"

"Well, all right." Liz pointed to one person at a time. "You know some of them. There's Wade and Penelope. You and Hal, of course. And over there Billy standing next to a man who looks familiar, but I can't quite place him."

Liz slid the photo back to Gwen and pointed at the man in question.

Gwen squinted. "Isn't that Jeremy Wakefield?"

"Who?" Liz asked.

"The newcomer Aldrich introduced to us on Tuesday morning."

Liz bent down for a closer look. "You're right. Now I recognize him." She tapped the picture. "See? He's still carrying the book he bought about hiking."

"Hmmm," Gwen commented. "He must have hung around the harbor for the rest of the day."

Moving from one face to the next, Liz provided first and last

106

names of customers who charged on a regular basis, first names only for repeat customers who paid cash. Gwen wrote them all down, along with any details Liz offered.

"Are you going to show these to Detective Snowcrest?" Liz wanted to know.

"Yes. He told me to let him know if I find anything relevant, or at least he said words to that effect."

"You think he was giving you permission to snoop?"

"That's my interpretation."

Liz shrugged. "I hope you're reading him right. I'll accept help from anyone who can get me out from under Chief Upton's suspicion." She waved at the photographs. "What inspired you to chase down these snapshots in the first place?"

"Let me explain," Tess said. "This afternoon, Gwen remembered a flash going off during the fire, so she called the newspaper and asked if any reporters were in the area." Tess waved at the pictures and beamed. "This is the result."

"Do you think the fire's connected to the attack on Farley?"

"It's one possibility. Tess and I are just gathering details that could be useful in solving the crime."

Before Liz could comment further, Gwen snapped her fingers. "Almost forgot to share an update on the séance. Madam Eudora asked Shirley if anyone on staff at the paper could record the event. One of the apprentices, Annabelle, can borrow the special cameras from a local ghost-hunting group, so both she and Shirley will be there tomorrow night."

"If Madame Eudora requested them, it's fine with me as long as it's okay with you."

"Oh, I don't mind at all. Like Shirley, I've never attended a séance. It'll be useful to have a recording we can watch later."

"Liz?" Tess moved closer. "Gwen has plans with Hal tonight, and since your husband's out of town, I'm wondering if you'd like to go to dinner with me."

"I'd love to. There's a restaurant up the coast I've wanted to try. It's called The Lucky Lobster. What's a good time?"

While Liz and Tess finalized their plans, Gwen sorted through the crowd photos, but no other faces jumped out at her.

When the bookstore bell jangled, Wade and Billy walked in.

"You have an update on my window?" Liz called over.

Wade headed toward her. Billy lagged behind. "Explain it to her, Son."

The document in Billy's hand quivered as he pushed his thick glasses up his nose. "Your front window's an unusual size. Not in stock. It's on order."

Liz moaned. "Not the news I was hoping to hear. How soon will it be delivered?"

Billy shrugged but didn't say a word.

Wade took over. "If you'll trust us with a spare key, we can install it when it arrives without bothering you if it's off hours."

Liz seemed to consider his offer. "Good idea. Follow me."

Billy wandered to Gwen and peered over her shoulder.

"Hi, Mrs. Andrews. What's ya got there?"

She couldn't fault Billy for being curious. He was simply waiting for Wade to come back with Liz's spare key.

"These are pictures a Gazette reporter snapped during Tuesday's fire next door."

His expression brightened. "That's cool. Can I see?"

No harm in letting him look at the photographs.

***

Sitting at her great-great grandmother's dining room table, Gwen located the detective's business card hiding in the bottom of her shoulder bag and punched his cell number into her phone.

"Detective Snowcrest, this is Gwen Andrews. My sister and I found something that might be of interest to your investigation." She surveyed the photos covering the table's maple surface.

"You did? Want to tell me now or keep it a secret?"

In the background, car horns blared. "Excuse me?"

"I'm sorry," Snowcrest apologized. "I'm stuck on Route 128. What did you find?"

Gwen tamped down her curiosity about why he was driving the always-crowded highway skirting around Boston. Maybe he'd been visiting the state lab for an update on the blood and fingerprint analysis. Based on his cranky mood, she assumed the tests weren't completed. She answered his question. "Photographs taken during the fire on Tuesday night."

"Why do you think those will help clear Mrs. Phillips?"

Gwen didn't want to out-maneuver Snowcrest, so preceded with caution. Asking a question would put the detective in the superior position. "Don't arsonists sometimes attend their fires? Farley's attacker might have been standing in the crowd."

Snowcrest paused. "Interesting theory, but there's no evidence connecting Tuesday's fire to Farley's attack. At least not yet. We don't even know if the fire was intentional or accidental."

Gwen blanched. Despite her conviction that there *was* a connection, she might have let her imagination jump the gun.

Snowcrest's tone changed to one of interest. "How many photos do you have?"

"More than a dozen. But only three of the crowd."

"Did you recognize anyone?"

"Several. And Liz identified a few others."

"Tell you what, Mrs. Andrews. Your hunch might not be wasted. If we do find evidence of arson, your photographs could become important. Make a list of the names matching the faces, and anything you or Mrs. Phillips know about that person."

Gwen stopped herself before saying she'd already created such a list with Liz's input.

Snowcrest kept talking. "I'll come by around ten tomorrow morning and we'll have a look. That'll be late enough so you won't feel obligated to feed me breakfast again."

Gwen couldn't hide a smile. Despite her caution around the detective, she couldn't help but like the man.

Chapter Eighteen ... early evening, Thursday

At dusk, thickening clouds created a shrouded sky with only the barest glint of moonlight.

At the entrance to Jenkins Nursery, a huge sign announced opening day on Saturday. Gwen's headlights guided her up the dirt lane toward the security lights fronting the garden center. Circling around the back, she parked in front of Hal's farmhouse. She knew the layout of the nursery after many visits over the past months.

Off to the right, a line of greenhouses radiated a resplendent shade of purple from grow lights. Through the corrugated plastic walls, she could make out pots of colorful flowers. Most likely pansies welcoming the warmer spring weather. Beyond the greenhouses, acres of fertile fields caressed multiple varieties of perennials.

The moment Gwen stepped from her car, raindrops splashed her head. She snagged her purse and a bakery box, opened her umbrella, and sprinted to the deep protection of Hal's covered porch. Leaning her wet umbrella against the weathered clapboards, she knocked on the frame of the screen door. "Hal, it's Gwen."

"Be right there," he called. A second later, he hurried from the rear kitchen along the narrow hallway, wiping his hands on a towel tucked into his belt.

Distant thunder boomed. Raindrops pinged off the porch's tin roof.

When he opened the door, Gwen smiled. "I love a good storm."

"Me, too. Glad you made it, Gwen. Dinner's almost ready. Come on back."

His grin warm and inviting, he was once again her easy-going

Hal. No hint of his lunchtime possessiveness. Plus, he'd already apologized. *Ease up, Gwen.*

She followed him to the old-fashioned kitchen with its archaic appliances and worn linoleum floor. The dated wallpaper had witnessed generations of Jenkins family memories.

"Glass of wine?"

At her nod, Hal selected two stemmed glasses from a side cabinet, filled them both half-way from a bottle of local cranberry wine, and held one out to her.

Hanging her purse on a caned chair back and placing the bakery box on the huge farm table, Gwen reached for the glass.

When Hal eyed the Sugar 'n Spice logo, Gwen felt heat clamber up her neck. "Sorry, I didn't have time to make dessert from scratch. I edged through the bakery door as they were about to lock up. Convinced the clerk to sell me the last pastry."

When he lifted the box lid, his blue eyes crinkled. "Hmmm. I'm not complaining. Boston Cream Pie: my favorite."

Closing the lid, he clinked his glass to hers. "Here's to spring storms and cooking dinner for my favorite lady."

His favorite lady? Wasn't she his only lady?

Hal stepped to the stove, donned thick mitts, removed a cast iron pot from the oven, and placed it on trivets. With a flourish, he lifted the lid, releasing the homey smell of chicken stew.

"What, no meatloaf?" Gwen teased, leaning over to inhale the savory steam.

"I knew it," Hal snorted. "I knew you loved my meatloaf. Are you disappointed?"

She tossed him an impish grin. "Not at all. Old family recipe?"

"Not quite. I used one of those spice packets. Added potatoes, onions, and carrots."

Sitting on opposite sides of the farm table, they spooned and chewed, all the while exchanging small talk. Hal eyed her empty bowl. "More?"

Conscious of her plan to control portion size, Gwen held up her hand. "No thanks. Your chicken stew was delicious, but I'm stuffed. How about I feed you tomorrow night?"

Hal's smile broadened. "I accept."

After they cleaned up the kitchen together, he refilled their wine glasses. They retreated to the front parlor, a cozy concoction of antique furniture.

"This house hasn't changed since I was a kid," Hal reflected. "When I inherited the property, I was too busy with the planting to make updates."

"No need to apologize, Hal. Vintage is back in style."

He placed his wine glass on the mantel. "Give me a sec to light this fire." He bent down and struck a match to the crinkled newsprint and kindling peeking out from beneath split logs.

As the storm raged outside, Gwen sunk into the softness of the floral couch cushions, curling one leg beneath her, watching the flames lick the wood in a wild dance.

Hal settled in an overstuffed chair near the fireplace, his expression serious. "You never said why you were eating lunch with that detective today."

She'd been waiting for him to bring up the awkward encounter. Gwen took a delaying sip of her cranberry wine. "By the time Detective Snowcrest and I headed back to my place from Liz's bookstore, it was almost noon. He offered to buy lunch and make up for me feeding him breakfast."

"Wait, wait." Hal's eyes flashed. "You fed him breakfast?"

She was taken aback by Hal's alarm. "I didn't want to be rude. The detective stopped by just as Tess and I were about to eat."

Hal lowered his head, peering at her beneath bushy eyebrows. "Just how long have you known this detective?"

"Detective Brown introduced us at the police station yesterday." Gwen's passing acquaintance with Snowcrest as the bicycle lady years before seemed immaterial. After all, she hadn't

113

seen the officer for years. Meeting him again yesterday made him nearly a new acquaintance. "He wanted to question me about my connection to Farley Cooper."

Hal wagged his head. "Back up a little. How did you and this Snowcrest end up at the bookstore together?"

Ignoring her vague regret that Hal had not released his jealousy, Gwen answered his question with the truth. "After I told him what little I know about Farley Cooper, he mentioned questioning Liz. I wasn't about to let Liz deal with a detective by herself. Since Tess and I had already planned to walk down to the bookstore, we invited Snowcrest to join us."

Hal waved her to continue.

"Detective Snowcrest talked Liz through the past few days and wrote down every detail. Very professional." A bit unnerved by Hal's unrelenting stare, Gwen shifted on the couch and tried a bit of misdirection. "Did you know there's a connecting door between her bookstore and Farley's?"

"No, I didn't, but you're changing the subject." He drained his glass. "I hope you're not getting involved in another police investigation. I couldn't bear a repeat of last September. I nearly lost you before our friendship even began."

So that's why Hal was so curious. Gwen debated whether to tell him about chasing down Shirley and Annabelle's photographs, but she quickly decided to keep that bit of sleuthing to herself. After all, she and Tess had been in no danger. No need to worry Hal any more than necessary.

"Detective Snowcrest was adamant he'll do the investigating."

"I'm glad to hear it." Hal moved from the chair to the couch.

For the next few minutes, they both stared into the flames without speaking. Gwen heard herself whisper, "What *is* it about a fire that's so entrancing?"

"Can't say, but we rushed out of the restaurant to watch Farley's fire, didn't we?"

"Only because of the alarm – not to be spectators," she reminded him. Besides, Gwen mused, it was a very different type of fire. As she let her eyes travel from the flames, a familiar item on the mantel caught her eye. Farley Cooper's box of cigars. Gwen ached to rewind the clock to the time before that man arrived in Harbor Falls to complicate their lives.

Why hadn't Hal gotten rid of those damn stogies? Or, knowing she detested cigars and was expected for dinner, at least hidden them from sight?

"What are you planning to do with those?" She pointed at the offending box with her wine glass.

Hal followed her line of sight. "I haven't decided. With Farley in a coma and the cigar bar closed, I can't take them back. Maybe I'll give them to Oscar."

Hal got to his feet and slipped another log onto the fire, speaking sideways. "You may not want to hear this, but I liked Farley. The day I met him, he was cracking jokes with his customers."

Gwen shifted to relieve the tingling in her leg. "I'm trying very hard to understand your fascination with that man. He doesn't care about his smoke ruining Liz's inventory. He implied you're not a man unless you smoke his filthy cigars. He even gave you a box you didn't have to pay for until you gave in and lit up. Farley's a bully. You must see that."

Hal returned to his seat next to her on the couch and placed his weathered hand atop hers. "Why do you hate cigars with such intensity?"

Gwen wished she felt a little less uncomfortable beneath Hal's touch. She was probably overreacting. Should she tell him about Uncle Gus? If she did, would Hal respect her aversion to cigar smoke? Or would he think of her as damaged goods? Now was the time to find out before their relationship went any further.

She slid her hand out from under his and moved off the couch, shaking her tingling leg to restore the circulation. "All right, Hal, I'll tell you. When I was a pre-teen, my cigar-smoking great uncle visited my family one summer. I'll just say he molested me. When I smell cigar smoke, Uncle Gus comes roaring back with all his depravity."

Seeing the shocked expression on Hal's face, Gwen lowered her gaze, embarrassed to admit she was related to such a vile man.

With lightning quickness, Hal erupted to his feet and moved to stand beside her. "Did your family have him arrested?"

She shook her head. "I never told anyone."

In a flash, Hal wrapped his arms around her, his grip gentle but firm. He drew her close. "Now I know why you hate cigar smoke."

"I'm horrified to see you with Farley's cigars. You don't have to stink like a stogie to prove your manhood."

Hal's lips glided along her cheek before finding her mouth, his intent to go further quite obvious.

Gwen wrenched herself from his grasp. "What are you doing?"

He leaned away, his expression startled. "I thought I was comforting you. You shared your childhood trauma. My feelings for you are even deeper now."

"A hug would have been enough. I'm not ready for more than your friendship."

"But I care for you, Gwen. You didn't object when I kissed you at The Wharf the other night. Don't you find me attractive?"

"You're a very handsome man."

"And you're a desirable woman. So, what's holding you back? Your husband's been gone for nearly three years. You must have physical urges like I do."

She'd long ago transferred her crush on actor Hal Holbrook to Hal Jenkins, but she wasn't about to admit her weakness. "If we get physical and it doesn't work out, we couldn't be just friends."

"But we're totally compatible, Gwen. Don't you think it's time?"

She took a few steps back. "I'm just not ready."

Debating the pros and cons would not budge her resolve. Gwen hoped Hal knew her well enough to understand that. She'd already figured out the reason behind her resistance to Hal's charms. For months, she'd tried to summon Parker's ghost without success. She'd signed up for the séance on Friday evening with high hopes that he'd materialize during the proceedings.

If she fell into Hal's arms this evening – not to mention the potential of falling into his bed – and Parker showed up tomorrow night, Gwen would feel like she'd cheated on her husband. The fact that Parker was no longer a living, breathing man didn't make an iota of difference to her way of thinking.

"I should go home before things get out of hand." Gwen pivoted toward the kitchen where she'd hung her purse and jacket.

Hal followed her. "You can't leave now, Gwen. Let's talk about this. I'll put on the brakes if that's what you want."

"The truth is, Hal, I don't know what I want," she lied. "But right now I need to go home and check on Tess. Thanks for the stew and the wine. I'll call tomorrow about dinner at my place."

Chapter Nineteen ... early morning, Friday

After a restless night of little sleep, Gwen slid out of bed at first light and tip-toed down to the kitchen. Amber glared from her feeding station beneath the island overhang.

"Well, that's a fine greeting," Gwen whispered, not wanting to wake Tess.

Gwen filled Amber's empty bowls, not surprised when her pet took only a few bites, cast a scathing look over her shoulder – as only a cat can – and strutted off to parts unknown.

As Gwen set the coffee maker to brew and began to prepare breakfast, last evening's disquieting scene with Hal replayed over and over. She struggled with the notion that they might not be able to salvage their friendship after bruising his feelings, along with his male pride.

Tess wandered down the staircase. "Something smells good. What're you cooking?"

"One of your favorites."

Grabbing a plate from the island counter, Tess held it out while Gwen transferred two banana pancakes from the ceramic pan. Tess topped them with genuine maple syrup and dug in. "How was your dinner with Hal last night?"

"Delicious. Chicken stew." Gwen didn't mention their disagreement about Farley's cigars, her confiding in Hal about Uncle Gus – about which Tess was clueless – or fending off Hal's romantic advances. "How about you and Liz? Have fun?"

"We did." Tess spoke between forkfuls. "Liz agreed to split an incredible fried seafood platter. We moved into the bar and listened to a small jazz band for an hour or so. By the time I walked in the door, you'd already gone to bed, so I watched an old black and white movie. They don't make 'em like that anymore."

Tess swallowed her last bite of pancake. "Were you able to connect with Detective Snowcrest about Annabelle's photos?"

"Yep. He'll be here around ten this morning. He thinks we're premature to assume the fire was connected to Farley's attack, but he's still curious to see who was in the crowd."

Gwen picked up both dirty plates and slipped them into the dishwasher. "Before I forget, I offered to feed Hal tonight. You're welcome to join us."

"I accept, but it'll have to be early. Shirley and Annabelle are due around six-thirty. Liz with Madame Eudora before seven."

Gwen gasped. "I can't believe I forgot the séance."

"Spending time with Hal Jenkins could make a girl forget just about anything." Tess wiggled her eyebrows.

"You don't know the half of it." Gwen leaned against the edge of the sink, recalling Hal's strong arms and what would have happened if she'd succumbed to his impassioned kiss.

Tess walked over and hugged Gwen. "I'm glad you've found Hal to share your life."

Gwen's arms encircled Tess, well aware of how much her sister was missing Nathan.

***

"Hal, I'm so sorry." Gwen clutched the handset of her house phone. "I have to cancel dinner tonight. I forgot I'm hosting Liz's séance. Rain check?"

"No problem. Let me know when you're available."

Even through the phone, she couldn't miss his flippant tone and sense his wariness. His next words were the exact opposite of her expectation.

"Are we okay, Gwen?"

Relief flooded her that he hadn't given up on their friendship.

119

"We're fine, Hal. I'll get back to you before the weekend's over to pick another night."

Gwen hit the red button and noticed Tess gazing off into the distance. "Penny for your thoughts, Sis."

Tess's head jerked up. "What? Oh, I was thinking about the old movie I watched last night. It was about a stalker who followed his victim from one town to the next. Maybe Farley's attacker isn't a new enemy but an old one. Are there any other strangers recently arrived in Harbor Falls?"

Gwen raised one finger. "Jeremy Wakefield."

"Oh. He's the one you and Liz recognized in the crowd shot?"

"The same. He told us he's living with a cousin but never mentioned the cousin's name."

"Does Harbor Falls have an organization for newcomers?"

"Not sure, but if it's active, it'll be listed on the town website. Let me get my laptop and we'll check."

***

"May I speak with Dorothy Nugent?" Gwen held the cordless receiver to her left ear as she doodled around the edges of her legal pad.

"This is Dorothy," the woman answered, her voice evenly modulated. "Who's calling?"

"My name is Gwen Andrews. I found your group listed on the Harbor Falls website. Are you still in charge of Newcomers & Neighbors?"

"I am. Would you like to register?"

"No, no, Mrs. Nugent. I've lived in Harbor Falls more than half my life."

"That's fine, Mrs. Andrews. We depend on our established residents to participate in our programs and familiarize new arrivals with the charms of our quaint college town."

"Oh, I had no idea. Now that I'm retired, I'll consider joining."

Regretting her semi-promise, Gwen forged ahead. "I'm calling because I met a newcomer on Tuesday."

"Go on." Dorothy's tone offered encouragement.

With Tess's input, Gwen had rehearsed her words to come across as a benevolent citizen rather than a Nosey Rosie. "This young man and I had a delightful conversation about hiking. I have some information for him about our local trails, but we were interrupted before he had a chance to tell me where he's staying. He mentioned a cousin. I'm hoping he registered with you."

"Hmmm," Dorothy murmured. "As a rule, we prefer our newcomers to make new friends as they see fit during our social events. But since he's already reached out to you, I see no harm. Let me have a look at my records. What's his name?"

"Jeremy Wakefield." Gwen flipped to a new page in her legal pad, anxious to add more details beneath Jeremy's name.

Dorothy spoke again. "Let me check my logbook."

Gwen gave a thumbs-up to Tess, who was busy watering the house plants.

Dorothy came back on the line. "Ah, here we go."

"You found him?" Gwen couldn't believe her stroke of luck.

"Yes, but he's not the person who contacted me. This must be the cousin he mentioned to you. Her name is Rachel Cooper."

Gwen nearly fell off her stool. Rachel Cooper, a good friend from Gwen's professor days at Baylies College, had provided crucial details and helped solve last fall's uninvited guest mystery. Was Rachel related to Farley? Gwen hadn't connected the last names until now.

Gwen jotted Rachel's name behind Jeremy's, "Thank you, Mrs. Nugent." She disconnected before Dorothy could apply pressure to attend their next function.

Tess must have noticed Gwen's shocked expression because she rushed over, watering can in hand. "What is it, Gwen?"

"You won't believe what Dorothy told me."

Gwen explained Jeremy's connection to Rachel

"Oh, my gosh," Tess uttered. "Farley and Rachel both being Coopers is too much of a coincidence to ignore."

"I agree. Back to our stranger, we can't assume Jeremy's a criminal simply because he's new to town. I'd hate to think Rachel's cousin was involved in Farley's attack. We need more details before we make that leap."

Tess drummed her fingers on the countertop. "If we confirm the family connection and find out why Jeremy appeared within weeks of Farley's arrival, we can either strike him off our list, or pass his name along to Snowcrest."

"We're thinking along the same line, Tess."

"I have a suggestion. I'd love to see Rachel's house again."

"Good excuse. I'll call her at the college offices."

***

"Gwen? Is that you?"

"Yes, it's me, Rachel. Sorry I've been out of touch. How're things at Baylies?"

"Oh, terrific. Did you know I was promoted to office manager?"

"I didn't, but it's about time someone recognized your talents. Congratulations."

"Thanks. I hope you're calling to get together."

"Actually, Tess is here and asked if we could revisit your adorable cottage."

Rachel laughed. "Not so adorable at the moment. My cousin dropped in unannounced. He's not the neatest guy, but his untidiness doesn't have to stop us from getting together. Let's see… what day is it? Oh, it's Friday. How about I fix us lunch tomorrow? Does that work for you?"

"Perfect. We'll bring wine."

After another few minutes of small talk, Rachel signed off.

Gwen disconnected. "Rachel mentioned her cousin and opened the door about Jeremy."

"That's progress." Tess leaned closer to Gwen's laptop. "Any idea if Farley has a website?"

"Haven't checked." Gwen opened a new tab and typed in 'Farley Cooper's Cigar Bar and Smoking Lounge.' Up popped an attractive website with a photo of the initialed entrance door as the header. A scrolling banner announced the hours. Photographs of the renovated space edged the right side of the page.

Gwen leaned closer. "Aha."

"You find something?" Tess's nose hovered only inches away.

Gwen zoomed in on a picture of the display counter and pointed. "See the marble ashtray? It's the same one the police found hidden in Liz's bookstore. This picture will prove to Chief Upton that I wasn't fibbing that the ashtray belonged to Farley. But I know what he'll say."

"What's that?"

"Ownership doesn't mean Liz didn't use it. Let's print this photo and hand it over to Detective Snowcrest. My printer is in the corner of your room."

Gwen hurried upstairs, retrieved the cropped image of the ashtray, and added it to the folder protecting Annabelle's photographs.

***

"You didn't say who took these pictures," Snowcrest commented as he flipped through them.

"A reporter from the Gazette."

"What made you think to check with the newspaper?"

Unsure if the detective was simply collecting details or questioning her source, Gwen fidgeted. "I remembered flashes going off while Hal and I were watching the commotion at the fire. I thought a reporter might have been there."

"And you concluded someone at the fire attacked Farley?"

With Tess looking on, Gwen slid off the island stool, leaned backwards against the kitchen sink, and glared at him. "I haven't concluded anything, Detective Snowcrest." Using his titled name would underscore she wasn't happy with his tone. "Whether these pictures of our citizens watching the fire are relevant is your job, not mine."

Snowcrest tapped the photos into a neat stack. "I didn't mean to criticize you, Mrs. Andrews. Your belief in Liz Phillips' innocence is admirable. I know you're only trying to help."

He glanced at Tess. "Do you think your sister's right?"

"Of course I do. When she remembered the flashes, we agreed pictures of the crowd could be important. Checking with the local newspaper was a logical next step."

He slid the pile toward Gwen. "Hold onto these for now. I'll let you know if or when I need them. Is there anything else before I go?" He half rose to his feet.

Gwen reached for the manila folder and tucked the photos inside. "Actually, there is."

His right eyebrow lifted as he resettled on the stool. "Tell me."

"Better to show you." She removed the printed page and held it out. "This is from Farley's website. The marble ashtray the officers found under Liz's counter belonged to Farley."

Snowcrest accepted the printout, inspecting it closely. "I'll keep this one, if you don't mind."

Before Gwen could say he was welcome to it, the detective's cell phone buzzed. He glanced at the caller ID and strode into the dining room, his urgent responses unintelligible.

Tess leaned toward Gwen. "Should we tell him about Jeremy Wakefield?"

"Let's wait until we spend some time at Rachel's."

The detective rejoined them, his mouth in a pout. "Farley Cooper has died."

Gwen's hand flew to her heart. "Did he wake up and identify his attacker before passing?"

Snowcrest shook his white-haired head. "Afraid not. Chief Upton will be even more determined to make an arrest. We need to find the real culprit sooner rather than later."

Gwen's radar flew to high alert. "Do you mean *we* as in you and us?" Gwen indicated Tess.

"No, I don't. I mean *we* as in me and the other detectives who will be assigned to this case. With the assault upgraded to murder, I won't be working alone."

He tossed both sisters a hard look. "I can't stop you from talking to your friends, but we can't have regular citizens acting like detectives when they don't have the proper training or defensive equipment. You could very easily back yourselves into a corner with no way out. If you think there's someone or something to be investigated, let me know and I'll handle it."

Chapter Twenty ... early evening, Friday

After a light supper of salad and pasta primavera, Gwen and Tess pushed all thoughts of Farley Cooper aside while they prepared for the séance. They added two extensions to the dining room table and hauled down extra chairs from the third-floor loft.

Tess pointed to three pairs of candlesticks on the hutch: sterling silver, crystal, and carved wood. "Which ones do you think this Madame Eudora will prefer?"

Gwen studied the collection. "I'm not even sure she lights candles, but I read an online article suggesting candlelight lends to the ambiance."

At quarter to seven, Shirley rang the front doorbell, her arms wrestling with clumsy tripods. "Sorry we're a bit late, Gwen. Annabelle took longer than we planned to pick up the equipment."

Behind Shirley, Annabelle carried two bulky camera cases.

"Not a problem." Gwen waved them into the dining room as she closed the door. "Liz and Madame Eudora haven't even arrived yet."

As if the world beyond had been listening, the doorbell rang before Gwen had let go of the handle.

A statuesque woman posed on the top step, her jewel-set black velvet turban topping raven hair that cascaded past her broad shoulders. In one hand, she carried an oversized tote.

Noticing Gwen, the woman's face brightened. She extended her free hand as she spoke in a voice deep and husky. "Good evening, my dear. I'm Madame Eudora. You must be Gwen. Thank you for hosting our gathering this evening."

"It was the least I could do for Liz while the damage to her

126

bookstore's being repaired." Gwen peeked around the medium. "Is she with you?"

Madame Eudora flipped her hand. "The dear girl is bringing two more bags."

Sweeping inside, the medium glanced up the split staircase. "What a delightful home. Liz mentioned your architect husband designed the conversion of the abandoned library. Charming. Simply charming." The medium laid a light hand on Gwen's arm. "I was sorry to learn of his passing. Perhaps we can encourage his spirit to visit us during our evening proceedings."

Expecting an offer such as this, Gwen had earlier gathered all photos of Parker scattered throughout the downstairs spaces. If Madame Eudora was the genuine article, she'd need no assistance to describe him.

Parker's ethereal self hadn't responded to Gwen's calls over the past six months. She was willing to give the medium this one chance to entice Parker to appear, but she held little hope. Given her doubts, Gwen simply murmured, "That would be nice."

Madame Eudora scanned the open floor plan. "Where are we assembling?"

Gwen waved toward the dining room. "At my great-great-grandmother's table."

Shirley came up behind them. "If you can tell us where you'll be sitting, Madame Eudora, Annabelle and I will determine the best location for the cameras."

The medium's focus inspected the long expanse of maple. "The far end will do nicely, facing this way. I'd prefer a slightly elevated angle to encompass all participants if possible."

"The staircase landing might work." Gwen pointed to the halfway point where the steps split both right and left.

Annabelle climbed the stairs to study the view into the dining room. "This will work." She lugged her equipment up the steps and began to connect the various devices.

Tess approached the medium and extended her hand. "I'm Tess, Gwen's sister."

Madame Eudora enclosed Tess's hand with her own. "Thank you for filling the ninth chair. Multiples of three improve our communication with our loved ones."

Liz came through the front door with a large fabric bag in each hand. "Where do you want these, Madame Eudora?"

"Thank you, Liz dear." The medium took one tote from Liz and hefted the one she'd carried in herself. "Follow me." At the other end of the table, they placed all three totes on the polished surface.

Zipping open the first, Madame Eudora removed two glass bottles, then a dozen miniature ceramic saucers. Into six, she poured a few drops from one bottle. Into the other six, a few drops from the second, alternating them on the surrounding surfaces. The air filled with a heady scent.

Gwen sniffed the nearest one. "What are these oils, Madame Eudora?"

"One is frankincense, the other myrrh." The medium offered no further explanation as she reached into her tote. "Gwen, dear, I see you have several pair of candlesticks. Would you insert these white candles in each and place them down the center of the table? I'll light them as we begin."

Gwen and Tess did as requested while Madame Eudora draped colored scarves on each chair back. She tucked long swaths of fabric onto the drapery rods and tossed a transparent purple cloth artfully atop the chandelier, bathing the room in an eerie glow.

At the stroke of seven, six women paraded through Gwen's front door. One of them announced to no one in particular, "I'm so sorry, but Verna has backed out. She's afraid her mother-in-law might come through and cause trouble."

"Oh, dear." Madame Eudora, her smile tight-lipped, focused on Shirley.

Shirley's hands shot into the air, palms up. "No, no, don't look at me. I'll be helping Annabelle with the video and still shots."

Madame Eudora's gaze found Liz. "I know you hadn't planned to participate, Liz darling, but our evening's efforts will garner much better results if we preserve the multiples of three." One elegant eyebrow lifted in a hopeful gesture.

Tossing Gwen the look of a cornered animal, Liz acquiesced. "Of course. Anything I can do to make the evening a success."

"Good, good," Madame Eudora murmured. "If you ladies will please silence your cell phones and take a seat, we'll begin."

As the women settled into the chairs, the medium again reached into her tote and extracted a bundle of grass. She struck a wooden match, lit the end, and blew out the flames. Circling the table, she waved the smoldering herb above their heads. "This sage will deter the negative spirits among us."

Retrieving a second braid of herbs, she repeated the cycle. "Sweet grass welcomes the positive spirits and angels." She snuffed out both bundles in a bowl filled with sand, then struck a third extra-long match.

As she lit each of the six candles, Madame Eudora repeated these words three times: "May the light and energy of these candles remove all fear, negativity, and doubt. May these candles attract positive energy to the women gathered here this evening. For the highest good of all and for the good of the universe, so be it, so be it, so be it."

Returning to the head of the table, Madame Eudora stretched each bejeweled hand to her right and left, her fingers wiggling to invite the woman on either side to take hold. "Now, everyone please join hands as we attempt to make contact with our dearly departed."

She moved in a gentle sway, murmuring unintelligible words, then jolted and dropped into her chair with a whoosh.

During the next hour, Madame Eudora interpreted the spirits

129

who came through, though none of them materialized. She described her sense of their appearance, their tone of voice, their body language, their history, the person they were seeking. Many souls retreated unclaimed until one of the participants recognized her estranged sister.

For the next few minutes, the departed sister sent verbal messages using Madame Eudora's voice. The phrases used and the events recollected elicited a tearful reunion and their long overdue reconciliation.

A second matron nearly lost control when she identified her boy child who had died young. Learning her child was safely in the arms of his grandfather provided a great deal of peace.

During each of these events, Annabelle's camera shutter clicked ever so softly. The video machine whirred quietly.

Her voice dropping to an even huskier tone, Madame Eudora announced, "A man is working his way to the front of the group. He wants to speak to you, Gwen. Do you know a Parker?"

From her place at the opposite end of the table, Gwen stiffened. Was Parker actually coming through, or had Madame Eudora searched the Harbor Falls Gazette and found Shirley's article from three years ago?

Before Gwen could make up her mind, a shimmer appeared at the draped window behind the medium. Parker's outline began to take shape. When Gwen found his eyes, he winked at her. A quick glance around the table confirmed the other women were unaware of him.

"Tell me, my dear, can you see this Parker?" The medium contemplated Gwen across the expanse of antique maple.

When Parker moved past Madame Eudora, her eyes followed him as he made his way along the table, her gaze pausing the instant he stopped beside Gwen. To all appearances, the medium seemed fully cognizant of his presence.

Gwen so wanted to reach out to him, but didn't dare let go of

Liz's hand on her left or Tess's on her right, fearing the disconnect might break the spell and Parker would disappear.

Unsure whether to admit she could see this pale version of her deceased husband, it dawned on Gwen that every woman sitting at her table was here for the sole purpose of making a connection. Well, maybe not Tess. But the others would be glad for Gwen, wouldn't they? Or would they assume that as the hostess, Gwen was in collusion with Madame Eudora?

Truth won out. This séance would most likely be Gwen's only chance to expose her knowledge of Parker's ghost without skepticism. She snuck a glance at Tess in the next chair and found her sister gazing back, a look of confusion on her face as she mouthed, "Parker?"

Forging ahead, Gwen answered the medium's question. "Yes, I can see him." Gwen's well-guarded secret was no longer a secret.

"This is indeed a glorious connection." Madame Eudora's dark eyes glistened.

Gasps erupted around the table. Questions overlapped as the group's excitement mounted.

"Can you see him?"

"Where is he standing?"

"What is his expression?"

Madame Eudora rose to her feet in slow motion, releasing and rejoining the hands of the two attendees on either side. She softly clapped her hands and waited for the women to pay attention. Placing one tapered finger to her lips, her other hand splayed in a calming motion. "Ladies, please lower your voices, and do not put any pressure on our visitor."

Toggling her focus from Gwen to Parker, Madame Eudora whispered, "Gwen, would you share what you're experiencing?"

Gwen's gaze moved from one expectant face to the next. "Parker is standing next to me." She raised her eyes to catch him winking at her again. She grinned.

131

"You seem amused, my dear."

Gwen could not hold back her laughter. "He winked at me."

The assembled group tittered with delight.

"Is he willing to make his presence known to the rest of us?"

Caught up in the thrill of Parker's proximity, Gwen couldn't fathom what he could physically do to prove he was standing beside her. She was aware he was unable to do any heavy lifting. Last fall, she'd had to slide open the shower door so he could step inside and write her a note on the soapy glass surface. She'd taken photographs of his words to preserve the incident.

Realizing they were all staring at her, Gwen stammered, "I'm not sure what he's able to do."

Parker laid one gossamer hand on her shoulder, its weight negligible. He leaned down and whispered in her ear. "I think I can make the scarf on the chandelier flutter."

Hearing his voice again – albeit the ghostly version – nearly made Gwen swoon, but she maintained control. "He offered to make that scarf flutter." She nodded upward.

"He's speaking to you, my dear?"

As every pair of eyes searched the area around her, Gwen stammered, "Yes, he is."

One of the women who had not made a connection sat forward, her eyes slitted. "Tell him to move the damn scarf."

Parker laughed and stepped between the chairs. He reached toward the chandelier and waved his see-through hand. The purple fabric swayed back and forth. As he brought his hand down, he waved it near that same woman's hair, making it flutter.

The woman shrieked and reached up a hand to pat her hair, gasping, "He's here."

Silent to this point, Tess spoke. "Has Parker touched you?"

As Parker resumed his position next to Gwen, she nodded. "His hand is resting on my shoulder. His touch is very light, like a butterfly's wings."

Swallowing audibly, Tess glanced around the table. "Parker, I can't see you or hear you, but I desperately need to know you're here. Could you place your hand on my shoulder?"

The tension in the room was palpable. No one spoke as they waited and watched.

Parker moved to stand behind Tess, saying to Gwen, "Tell her I don't think my touch will harm her."

"Okay." Gwen repeated his message, not moving her gaze from Tess.

One millisecond later, Tess's eyes flew open. She jerked upright, sliding like a ragdoll from her chair to the floor.

Chapter Twenty-One ... late evening, Friday

With Shirley's help, Gwen carried the half-dazed Tess to the living room sofa. "Liz, could you fetch a damp facecloth from the powder room?"

"Sure thing. Be right back."

Madame Eudora's voice floated from the dining room. "Our connection has been broken. No more spirits will visit us tonight. I hope you were pleased with this evening's gathering."

The women murmured their satisfaction, several slipping a tip into the medium's hand before making their way toward the foyer. A few finger-waved in Gwen's direction, mouthing, "Thank you," before disappearing out the front door.

Madame Eudora sashayed into the living room and splayed her fingers across Tess's shoulder before training her penetrating gaze on Gwen. "Don't worry about your sister, dear. Her reaction is not unusual. She witnessed the presence of a departed family member for the first time. She may block her reaction for a while. When she does remember, she'll have you to soften the experience."

Gwen hadn't missed the medium's unspoken message. Because Gwen *hadn't* fainted when Parker appeared, she'd revealed that this evening wasn't her first exposure to the hereafter. If anyone would believe Parker's triple visit last September, it would be Madame Eudora. Perhaps Gwen could arrange a private session and learn more about ghostly communications.

Madame Eudora slipped a few business cards from her pocket and handed one to Shirley. "If you would please burn a CD of your pictures plus a DVD of the video and mail them to this address with an invoice, I will send a check without delay."

"Of course." Shirley accepted the card. "I'll email the digital photographs tomorrow. The video copy will take a little longer." The medium nodded her understanding and handed a second card to Gwen. "If you need to talk about your experience, don't hesitate to call." As the elegant woman disappeared into the night, Gwen placed the card on the coffee table.

Liz handed a cool cloth to Gwen. "Sorry, but I need to drive Madame Eudora to the bookstore where her car is parked. I'll come back after I see her off."

Shirley waved her hand. "No need, Liz. I'll stay."

Gwen looked up at Shirley, standing beside the couch. "But Annabelle has packed up her equipment. Don't you need to catch up with her before she drives off?"

"We drove separately. Annabelle is heading back to the office to download her photos and return the special cameras to the ghost hunters."

"In that case, thanks, Shirley." Liz retrieved her purse. "Call if you need me, Gwen. And thanks again for hosting. Will I see you and Tess tomorrow at the bookstore?"

"Most likely."

When the front door closed, Shirley turned wide eyes to Gwen. "Did you really see your husband?"

"Yes, I did. I heard him. I felt his touch. And you saw how he moved the scarves and fluttered that woman's hair. Only Tess can tell you if she sensed his hand on her shoulder."

Tess stirred and opened her eyes, rising to one elbow. "What am I doing on your sofa?"

Gwen spoke in a soothing voice. "I'll explain after you drink the cup of tea I'm going to go the kitchen to make right now." With a gentle push, she forced Tess to the cushions and covered her with an afghan. "You stay right there. I'll be back in a minute."

Shirley followed Gwen. "I never expected my first séance to be so dramatic."

135

"You and me both, Shirley." Not wanting to give the sharp reporter a chance to notice Gwen hadn't fainted when Parker materialized, she busied herself brewing a single mug of tea. "Thanks for your help, Shirley, but now that Tess is awake, I can handle things from here."

"Then I'll get out of your hair. I'll let you know what Annabelle's ghost-hunting friends have to say about the photos and video recording. Their findings would be proof positive that tonight's spiritual connections were real."

When the microwave dinged, Gwen removed the mug of tea, carrying it by the handle as she escorted Shirley to the front door.

"I'll call if I have any questions for my article."

After Shirley slipped into the shadows, Gwen sauntered into the living room and handed the steaming mug to Tess. "Be careful. It's hot."

Tess braved a tiny sip. "What happened, Gwen? I can't seem to recall."

As Madame Eudora had predicted, Tess might be blocking the final moments of the séance. Removing the mug from Tess's hands, Gwen placed it on the coffee table, then flung the afghan aside and helped her sister to her feet. "I don't think you need the tea. Let me put you to bed for a good night's sleep. By morning, you might remember something. If you don't, I promise to fill-in the blanks."

Gwen supported Tess up the staircase to the guest room and waited for Tess to change into her pajamas. Tucking the covers tight, she leaned down and planted a kiss on her sister's forehead. Gwen was overcome by the sense of switching roles. The younger sibling caring for the older one.

Tess glanced up. "Thanks."

By the time Gwen flipped off the light switch, a soft snore filled the guest room.

***

Descending the staircase to lock up for the night, Gwen realized she wasn't the least bit tired. Her thoughts hadn't strayed far from Parker's appearance. He'd taken advantage of the séance to break through from the great beyond, disappearing when Tess fainted. *Where is Parker now?*

She retreated to the kitchen and brewed a second cup of tea. Wrapping her hands around the warm mug, she stood at the French door and peered into the back yard. The barren flower beds were lit by automated landscape lights. The flag suspended from a pole on the rear trellis hung limply. Not a breath of air stirred.

Blowing on her steaming brew, Gwen's eyes caught a motion. If there was no wind, why was the arbor swing swaying? She inched her face closer, jerking when her forehead bumped against the glass.

Suddenly brave, Gwen unlocked the French door and stepped onto the rear deck. Although the evening air had cooled, she barely noticed her goose bumps. The glow of a quarter moon eliminated the necessity of flipping on the back light. Crossing the lower deck, she moved through the trellis onto the lawn, her eyes never straying from the shadowed swing as she made her way along the stepping stones.

When she reached the arbor platform, she paused. Under the contrasting shadow of the rainproof canopy, the swing continued its steady back and forth movement.

A voice whispered, "Hello, Gwen."

"Parker, is that you?" Though she knew the answer, she asked anyway.

His ghostly laugh tinkled. "It's me. I wasn't sure you'd notice the swing."

"If it'd been a windy night, I wouldn't have."

Parker became more visible when she ducked into the same shadow, eliminating the moon light.

He patted the cushion. "Come and sit by me. How's Tess?"

As before, his timbre was light and airy, not at all the deep bass of his human voice.

"She's sleeping. I don't expect she'll wake until morning."

Gwen angled sideways for a direct view into his pale hazel eyes. "I've called you a few times since your last visit, but I guess you haven't heard me. What made you appear tonight?"

As if weighing his words, Parker's pale lips didn't move right away. "I can't explain it. I was drawn back."

"Hmmm," Gwen murmured. "Guess the credit goes to Madame Eudora. Apparently, she's a genuine medium. I noticed her eyes following you as you walked to my end of the table, so I think she could see you. Don't know if she could hear you, but she never let on either way to the other women. She let me be the genuine witness." Gwen tilted her head to take in his translucent self. "I'm so glad you're here."

"Good to know. I have no sense of time passing. How long has it been?"

"Just over six months, since last September." She leaned against the swing cushion, vaguely aware his intangible body barely made a dent in the padded surface next to her.

Parker floated to his feet. "Walk with me, Sweetheart, and tell me how you're doing. Are you dating that Hal fellow?" He reached for her hand.

As before, she imagined Parker's touch, but felt no flesh, as there was none. A lump formed in her throat. "I wouldn't call it dating. We meet for dinner, take nature walks, that sort of thing."

"That's it?" Parker's soft voice bordered on incredulity.

"What do you mean?"

"Well, it sounds like you haven't gotten physical with the man. No chemistry?"

Gwen froze. There was plenty of chemistry. She only had to send Hal an encouraging signal for the fireworks to begin.

138

Parker spoke into her silence. "The rest of your life should be filled with joy, with someone to love you, body and soul. If Hal's the man who can make you happy, don't hold back. You certainly can't count on me." His pale hand indicated his sheer body.

Parker's encouragement startled Gwen. "Wouldn't it break your heart if I slept with another man?"

His lips curved. "You need to live a full, rich life, Gwen."

At that moment, Gwen came to realize that in death – as in life – Parker remained a gentle and generous soul. She fixed her gaze on his pale, but still handsome face. "If I can't have you, Parker, then maybe Hal's the next best thing."

The back yard security light zoomed across the rear gardens. Tess's voice carried across the distance. "Are you out there, Gwen?" Without waiting for a response, Tess moved across the lower deck.

Gwen jumped up and waved. "On the arbor, Tess." She spoke sideways. "Tess is coming, Parker. What should we do?"

When he didn't answer, she tilted her head in his direction. The place he'd occupied seconds ago was empty. Gwen snorted. "Why am I surprised? He's disappeared before."

Gwen wondered if she'd be successful in bringing Parker back again on her own or if she'd have to enlist the aid of Madame Eudora. With the possibility in mind, Gwen strode across the lawn and met Tess halfway. "What are you doing out of bed? I figured you'd sleep until morning."

Tess shrugged. "Don't know. I woke up and wandered to your room. You weren't there, so I started looking for you."

"Sorry. I was too wired to go to bed, but the swinging has made me sleepy. Have you remembered anything?"

"No. I'm feeling exceedingly dumb."

Concerned about Tess's reaction to Parker's touch, Gwen rested her arm around her sister's waist. "Not dumb at all. You're still in shock. Let's go inside."

"Can I sleep with you tonight, Gwen? I don't want to be alone."

"Of course. We'll pretend we're kids again, as long as you don't kick me."

Tess licked her forefinger and crossed her heart. "I'll do my best. Scouts honor."

Chapter Twenty-Two ... late morning, Saturday

Throughout the next morning, Gwen waited for Tess to ask questions about the séance. As they prepared and ate breakfast. As they cleaned up the kitchen. As they vacuumed and dusted the old library. The hours rolled around the kitchen clock. The only topics either sister broached were childhood memories in the Berkshires and speculation about Rachel's luncheon.

At eleven-thirty, they settled into Gwen's white Sonata and drove south.

Tess spoke from the passenger seat. "I feel sneaky checking up on Rachel's cousin without telling her what we're doing."

"So do I. But we could just as easily decide Jeremy wasn't involved in Farley's attack and Rachel will be none the wiser."

"That somewhat justifies our snooping. When will we tell Detective Snowcrest about Jeremy?"

"Not until we decide Jeremy appears suspicious."

Tess slanted her head in Gwen's direction. "Can I ask you about last night?"

Relieved Tess wanted to discuss the séance, Gwen said, "Sure."

Squirming, Tess forged ahead. "You may think me a bit addlebrained, but I still can't recall how the evening ended."

"Addlebrained is not a word I'd use to describe you. What *do* you remember?"

Tess's forehead wrinkled as she drummed her fingers on her knee. "Let me see. The woman to my right recognized her estranged sister. Not sure I believe it was her sister. Or that they reconciled. Then the matronly woman at an angle across from me

141

who nearly fell off her chair thinking her boy child sat on his grandfather's knee. Again, I don't know if that was wishful thinking on her part. After that, nothing."

So Tess had blocked Parker's manifestation. Gwen risked a quick look at her sister. "I promised to tell you what happened, but you need to keep an open mind."

"I will. Just help me fill in the blanks."

After Gwen retold of Parker's appearance, Tess stared at her hands, now shoved between her knees. Nearly a minute passed before she spoke again. "I don't want to insult you, but do you really believe you saw Parker?"

Gwen swerved to avoid a delivery truck taking more than his half of Coast Road.

Tess didn't seem to notice, because she kept talking. "What are the chances you were hallucinating? Maybe there was something in Madame Eudora's oils. Or that sweet grass. Or maybe the sage. One of them could have messed with your head."

"I only know what I saw, Tess." Gwen hoped her personal witness was enough.

And then Tess's words circled back around like a pesky gnat. Could Tess be right? Had Parker's arrival been the result of Madame Eudora's soothing voice combined with Gwen's deep need to see him again? And yes, perhaps some hypnotic effect from the smoldering herbs?

The combination of those three influences could possibly account for Gwen's sighting of Parker during the séance, but they didn't explain his re-appearance on the arbor swing after everyone had left. Unless the influence of the séance had lingered. Had Gwen conjured Parker a second time during the same evening for the sole purpose of giving herself permission to deepen her relationship with Hal? Had the words she'd credited to Parker been her own advice to herself?

Gwen had difficulty believing she could have strayed so far

from reality. Granted, her initial sightings of Parker last fall came at a time when her unbroken grief for his untimely death remained all-consuming. But to imagine his spirit? No, no. Too absurd to even begin to believe. *No*, Gwen vowed in silence. *I know Parker's spirit returned to me. I cannot tolerate any other interpretation.*

Tess pivoted in her seat. "You're a million miles away. What are you thinking?"

"Hmmm?" Gwen forced her befuddled brain to her driving as the tires chattered over a rumble strip. "Oh, just miscellaneous thoughts tumbling around in my head. Nothing concrete."

"Can I ask you another question about the séance?"

"Of course."

"You said I asked Parker to touch my shoulder?"

Distracted by Tess's suggestion of hallucinations, Gwen noticed the speedometer needle and lifted her foot off the gas pedal.

Again, Tess forged ahead without waiting for an answer. "And when he did, I fainted?"

"That's what happened."

Tess shook her head. "I'm sorry, but I'm having a hard time swallowing this."

"Me, too, Tess." Not a lie. Though Tess was referring to last night's séance, Gwen was sweeping all five of his appearances into one bucket. She completely empathized with Tess's struggle to believe in life after death, no matter what form it took.

Tess's mind clamping shut like a lobster claw convinced Gwen now was not the time to confide that the séance was not the first time she'd seen Parker's ghost.

"Do you think Madame Eudora would mind if Shirley gave us a copy of the photographs and recording?" Tess's need for answers never faltered.

"It won't hurt to ask. If there's anything to see or hear, it'll ease both our minds."

The sisters rode in silence until they reached Rachel's Cape Cod-style house. Within seconds of Gwen parking on the dirt shoulder out front, Rachel flew off the front porch and moved her generously proportioned body down the sidewalk at a surprisingly quick pace. "Thanks for coming for another visit."

Tess grinned at Rachel. "I was so impressed with your cute little house the first time, I suggested a sequel."

Chuckling, Rachel threw one pudgy arm around each sister and escorted them up the sidewalk. "Let's get you girls inside. I don't like the look of that sky."

Sure enough, dark clouds had moved in from the west and loomed overhead.

"I apologize in advance for my messy home, ladies. Like I told Gwen when she called, my cousin Jeremy dropped in without notice, and he's not the neatest relative. A few hours ago, my Aunt Kate arrived because there's been a death in the family."

Gwen's exploration of Jeremy's potential as Farley's attacker might be preempted by this family crisis. "I'm sorry to hear that, Rachel. Do you want to reschedule?"

Rachel's thatch of wild brown curls swayed as she shook her head. "No way. I've been cooking all morning. You're both staying for lunch."

When they moved through the front door, Tess sniffed the air. "Smells wonderful."

"Thanks. Roast pork with all the fixin's."

Rachel waved them into the blue and white parlor, snatching a t-shirt tossed carelessly on the arm of a chair. "Make yourselves comfortable. I've got some last-minute preparations."

As Gwen and Tess settled on the floral couch, raised voices made their way through a closed door along the adjacent wall. Overhearing the conversation was unavoidable.

A female voice: "Why didn't you tell me, Honey? I would have confronted my brother long ago and put a stop to it."

144

Gwen mouthed to Tess, "Aunt Kate?"

Tess shrugged and shook her head.

A younger man's voice: "I was too embarrassed, Mom. I didn't know what to say. Wasn't sure you'd believe me."

Not quite recalling the sound of his voice, Gwen mouthed to Tess, "Jeremy?"

When Tess shrugged a second time, Gwen realized her sister had not yet arrived when Jeremy was pulled into the bookstore by Aldrich Jones.

"Oh, Sweetie," the woman cooed behind the door. "Of course I would have believed you."

A full minute of silence passed as Gwen imagined an embrace between mother and son.

"So why did you come to Harbor Falls now, Jeremy?"

"It's the last piece of my recovery. My therapist said I need to forgive him for what he did."

Rachel walked in, her smile fading as she stepped to the closed door and rapped three times. "Aunt Kate and Jeremy, lunch is ready. And I've got some friends out here for you to meet."

The door opened in an instant, revealing a slender woman in jeans and sweatshirt, her auburn hair caught in a ponytail. If this was Jeremy's mother, Gwen guessed her age to be late fifties or so. She had aged well. Her expression revealed she knew they'd overheard her conversation with her son.

Kate's hands went to her mouth. "I'm so sorry, Rachel. You should have told us you were having company."

Without responding to the rebuke, Rachel waved toward Gwen. "This is my good friend Gwen Andrews. We worked together at the college until she retired. This is her sister Tess, visiting from the Berkshires."

The aunt extended her hand. "I'm Kate Wakefield, Rachel's aunt on her father's side. And this is my son Jeremy."

Jeremy stuck his hands in his jeans pockets, an odd look on his face as he studied Gwen. "Didn't I meet you in the bookstore the other day?"

Thinking fast, Gwen snapped her fingers. "That's why you look familiar. We talked about the walking trails along the coast. It occurred to me you might like to borrow my maps, but I didn't know how to get in touch with you. What luck to find you here."

In that instant, Gwen validated her excuse to the president of the Newcomer's Club for seeking out Jeremy. Not that Gwen expected Dorothy Nugent to ever follow up.

"Thanks." Jeremy waved off her offer. "But I don't know if I'll be around long enough to take a hike."

Rachel cleared her throat. "Let's move to the table and eat our lunch while everything's hot."

In the dining room, Rachel's table was impeccably set with blue and white china, sparkling crystal glasses, and polished silverware. "Sit anywhere. I'll be back in a jiff."

Still on their feet, Gwen and Tess both called out, "Let me help," and followed Rachel through the swinging doors.

Rachel signaled them to the far corner. "I'm sorry you were subjected to my family issues."

"No need to apologize." Gwen meant every word. "All families have problems. What can I carry to the table?"

Into Gwen's waiting hands, Rachel placed a platter layered with slices of roast pork smothered with a cranberry compote and surrounded by oven-browned potatoes plus steamed broccoli.

Tess accepted a ceramic tureen filled with silky smooth butternut squash.

Rachel picked up a deep bowl of applesauce, plus a gravy boat filled with thickened roasting juices.

There was little talk as the group devoured Rachel's mouth-watering meal. During the silence, Gwen suspected her time was running short to determine if Jeremy warranted a closer look by Detective Snowcrest. She opened her mouth to speak, unsure of

what would come out until she gazed across at Kate Wakefield.
"When Tess and I first arrived, Rachel mentioned a death in your
family. Please accept our condolences."

"That's kind of you." Kate toyed with her silverware. "My
brother only recently moved to Harbor Falls. You probably hadn't
met him."

"What was your brother's name?"

"Farley Cooper."

Though Gwen had only that morning pondered a connection
between Farley Cooper and Rachel, she'd harbored no expectation
of having the coincidence confirmed. Cooper was a common
enough surname in New England. To learn Farley was uncle not
only to Rachel, but to Jeremy as well, was nothing short of
disturbing.

Kate placed her napkin next to her empty plate. "Delicious,
Rachel. I hate to eat and run, but Jeremy and I need to find out how
soon we can claim Farley's body." Kate switched her focus to
Gwen and Tess. "My brother has been estranged from his wife for
the past few months, and she wants nothing to do with him, alive
or dead."

Rachel laid down her fork. "You do what needs to be done,
Aunt Kate. Let me know if there's any way I can help."

Gwen observed that neither Jeremy, nor Kate, nor Rachel
seemed all that upset about Farley's passing. Had he been the
proverbial black sheep of their family?

As Kate and Jeremy closed the front door behind them, Gwen
collected her dirty dishes. "That pork was so tender. Your
reputation as an excellent chef remains intact. Let us help you
clean up."

"Thanks for the compliment. Remind me to give you my
recipe." Rachel wiped her hands on her apron, her voice becoming
shakier as she spoke. "Now that Kate and Jeremy are out of
earshot, I owe you both an explanation. Jeremy has always been

my quiet youngest cousin. Never mean, never angry, but not much of a talker. He's a gentle soul."

As Gwen washed, Tess dried. Rachel placed each dish and glass in its proper spot as she shared her family history. "When Jeremy showed up on my doorstep a few days ago, he confided that Uncle Farley repeatedly abused him as a boy." Rachel's free hand flew to her chest. "I won't go into the details, but I had no idea. And neither did Aunt Kate."

The parallel to Gwen's pre-teen struggles with her great uncle paled by comparison. Like many victims, Jeremy had required years of therapy to deal with the aftermath of his boyhood trauma at the hands of his uncle.

Luckily for Gwen, Uncle Gus's vacation from the mid-west that long-ago summer had been brief. The following spring, he'd been killed in a farming accident, eliminating Gwen's fear that he'd repeat his unwanted advances during a subsequent visit.

Jeremy had not been so fortunate.

The clatter of Rachel storing the clean dishes brought Gwen back to the present, along with her quandary about Jeremy. *How am I going to find out if Jeremy confronted Farley?*

Scrubbing the roasting pan, Gwen used the activity to disguise her racing brain. She could think of no way to find answers without exposing her suspicions of Jeremy as Farley's attacker. If she asked too many questions about his whereabouts on Tuesday evening, Rachel would catch on that Gwen and Tess were gathering evidence against him and quite possibly toss both sisters out the door, damaging their friendship beyond repair.

Gwen argued with herself about whether to report her speculation to Detective Snowcrest and let him pursue Jeremy. Her duplicity with Rachel for the purpose of proving Liz innocent was bothersome. But if Jeremy had been the attacker, he should be held accountable, regardless of his understandable and lamentable motive.

"Oh, Gwen, you don't need to wrestle with that pan." Rachel scurried to the sink. "Just fill it with soapy water and place it on the counter. I'll deal with it later."

After the kitchen was put in order, Gwen and Tess stayed for another hour, chatting with Rachel about everything except what was foremost on the sisters' minds: How likely was it that Jeremy had attacked his Uncle Farley?

Chapter Twenty-Three ... mid-day, Saturday

From the passenger seat, Tess asked, "Should we tell Detective Snowcrest about Jeremy and his family history?"

"I'm thinking yes." Gwen drove along the country road.

"It's such a shame. After enduring his uncle's abuse and then years of therapy, Jeremy ends up a potential suspect in that same uncle's murder."

Gwen drummed her fingers on the steering wheel. "Bear with me for a minute. I've been working on a possible timeline. On Tuesday, Aldrich Jones found Jeremy hanging around outside Fiction 'n Fables and brought him into the bookstore to introduce him to Liz and me. If Jeremy had been gathering enough nerve to enter his uncle's cigar bar, maybe he had to rebuild his courage, because he stayed in the harbor area for the rest of the day."

"That's right. You spotted him in Annabelle's photograph with the book still in hand. What else do you think happened?"

"Most likely, Jeremy waited until the firemen and police drove away, and then followed his Uncle Farley inside."

"Weren't Liz and Farley told not to go into their stores until the building inspector cleared any safety issues?"

"They were, but, from everything I gathered during my brief encounter with Farley, he didn't seem to think the rules applied to him. And don't forget, that's where the building inspector found him the next morning, so Farley had to have gone inside."

"Good point." Tess picked at a loose thread on her slacks. "Let me take a stab at your sequence of events. Farley wasn't thrilled to see his nephew and told him to get out. Jeremy's long-buried anger and resentment boiled to the surface. When Farley turned his back,

Jeremy grabbed that heavy marble ashtray and struck his uncle. Panicking, Jeremy stumbled into the connecting door and it popped open. He took advantage of the unexpected opportunity to hide the bloody ashtray under Liz's counter. Maybe he expected no one would find it. But now that it's been discovered, he's hoping no one figures out he's the guy."

"Not bad, Tess. All those years of reading mysteries is paying off."

"Yeah, but we could be way off base. Even if Jeremy was not the assailant, I think the attack was a last-minute decision – a crime of opportunity, if you will. From what you've told me about this Farley Cooper, he probably rubbed lots of people the wrong way."

Neither sister spoke for several more miles.

Tess broke the silence. "Do we have time to stop at Liz's? I'm curious if the volcanic rock is removing the smoke from her books."

"Sure. Besides, she asked me last night if she'd see us today." Gwen flipped on her blinker, put her foot on the brake, and drove due east for a few miles until she intersected with Coast Road.

"Should we tell Liz about our Jeremy assumptions?"

"I'm not sure, Tess. I'd hate to get her hopes up if Detective Snowcrest finds that Jeremy has an airtight alibi."

When heavy raindrops suddenly splattered the windshield, Gwen banged the heel of her hand on the steering wheel. "Damn. I left my umbrella on Hal's porch the other night. Do you mind if we stop at his garden center first?"

"Not at all."

"Great. I need pansies for my window boxes anyway. And it's opening day." Although Gwen was worried about seeing Hal after she fended off his advances, she'd promised him dinner, so she had three reasons for stopping at the garden shop. Nothing to do but push aside her trepidation and see what happened when they came face to face.

***

By the time Gwen steered her car up the packed-dirt lane of Jenkins Nursery and Garden Shop, the rain had stopped. Despite the frenetic activity in the parking area, she snagged a spot after an SUV backed out.

She waved Tess to the outdoor plant tables and ducked beneath the awning. "Hi, Maggie."

The face of the gray-haired woman lit up. "How are you doing, Gwen? Who's this?"

"My sister Tess."

"Glad to meet you." Maggie nodded toward Tess before refocusing on Gwen. "Are you shopping for anything in particular?"

"I am." Gwen waved toward the multiple hues of smiling pansies. "We'll browse around for a little while."

With Tess's input, the sisters filled a plastic tray with a dozen six-packs of happy color. Yellow, purple, burgundy, and white.

A few minutes later, Gwen carried the tray to Maggie. "Could you hold these for me? I'll pay for them after I grab my umbrella from Hal's porch."

"Sure." Maggie tucked the tray on a shelf without asking the obvious question.

"Is he around?" Gwen craned her neck this way and that but didn't spot him.

"He's bringing more stock from the greenhouses. You'll probably bump into him out back."

"Tess, do you want to come with me?"

Tess looked up from scanning the tables "If you don't mind, Gwen, I want to wander around out here. All of these flowers are gorgeous and I love the scent." She inhaled an exaggerated breath.

"That's fine. I won't be long. When I get back, we'll take a look at the house plants inside." Gwen indicated the enclosed red building behind the outdoor displays.

"Tell Hal I said hello," Tess called over her shoulder.

Gwen walked the curving dirt lane around the back of the red building and grabbed her umbrella from Hal's front porch. The anticipation of bumping into him made her belly tickle. With Parker's encouragement, she'd likely pursue physical intimacy with Hal. She only hoped it wasn't too late.

When a burst of male laughter exploded nearby, Gwen veered toward the row of greenhouses. At the first one, she opened the door to see tables half-filled with pansies, but no men. The second was crowded with budding perennials. No one inside. When Gwen heard the chuckles again, she closed the door and peeked around the corner to the area between the greenhouses.

Standing not ten yards away, Hal blew a smoke ring into the air. At his feet sat Farley's box of *Robustos*, the lid open. Cigar wrappers littered the ground. When Hal murmured something, Oscar Haze erupted in a snicker.

So much for Hal's promise that he wouldn't smoke Farley's cigars. *How could he betray me like this?* The other night, she'd revealed her deepest, darkest secret about being molested by Uncle Gus. And now Hal was puffing on a cigar like he couldn't care less about her angst.

And why had Hal been laughing with Oscar? Was he making fun of her abuse? If she'd been the brunt of his humor, she'd badly misjudged Hal's character.

Gwen's bruised heart battled with her anger. So much for getting physical with the man. With the cigar stench clinging to Hal's clothes, his hair, his body, she couldn't imagine kissing his lips or snuggling his neck, let alone making love to him.

The smoke drifted across the distance between them and reached Gwen's nostrils. Images of Uncle Gus's lewd advances flashed past. His stained fingers. His rancid breath.

When a sneeze jolted Gwen, her foot bumped a tin bucket, knocking it onto its side with a clatter.

Hal's head snapped toward the noise, his eyes widening when he spotted her. He dropped the arm holding the cigar and slid it behind his back. "Gwen? What are you doing here?"

When she sneezed again, Gwen whirled around and zigzagged through the greenhouses toward the garden shop, umbrella in hand. Rounding the corner, she spotted her sister on the far side of the displays. "Tess, we're leaving. Meet me at the car."

Moving more quickly than most sixty-something women, Gwen ripped her keys from the side pocket of her shoulder bag and jabbed the fob toward her white Sonata.

Tess caught up, her breath labored. "Gwen, where are you going? You forgot your pansies. And you mentioned browsing the house plants."

Gwen glanced over her sister's shoulder to see Maggie's hand waving in the air. At the same time, Hal burst around the corner of the garden shop and sprinted in Gwen's direction.

Swinging the driver's door open, Gwen dropped inside and inserted her key. "Get in, Tess."

As soon as the passenger door slammed shut, Gwen shoved the gearshift into reverse.

Reaching the Sonata, Hal banged on the window. "Don't leave, Gwen. I can explain."

Ignoring his command, Gwen pressed her foot to the gas pedal, the tires kicking up stones and dirt as she barreled down the lane. In the rearview mirror, Hal disappeared in the roiling dust.

Tess shouted above the noise of tires on gravel. "What in the world is going on?"

Gwen's misery smoldered just beneath the surface. She tried to find a way to explain her anguish at the sight of Hal smoking a cigar. Tears clouded Gwen's vision, forcing her to steer the car to the side of the back road and slide the gearshift into park.

Tess squeezed Gwen's arm. "Tell me what happened."

Gwen could barely speak. "I can't talk about it right now."

"Sure, all right. Tell me when you're ready." Tess opened her door. "But you're in no shape to drive. Let's switch places."

Following her sister's logic, Gwen exchanged seats, ignoring Tess's sideways glances. The landscape whizzed by as they approached Harbor Falls.

Chapter Twenty-Four … mid-afternoon, Saturday

Tess steered the Sonata into Liz's parking lot. "Are you ready to tell me what happened back there?"

"Not yet."

Talking suspended, the sisters got out of the car and rounded the corner to the front entrance. A sign on the door announced *'Re-Opening Soon'*.

Inside, Liz was talking to a workman near the de-smoking barrels and didn't notice the sisters' arrival. When Tess headed in that direction, Gwen settled at a harbor-side table with a distracting view of sailboats tacking toward the docks. The dark line of rain clouds had moved far out into the bay, no doubt about to drench Provincetown. Gwen wouldn't need her damn umbrella now.

Liz sat down and wrapped Gwen's hands in her own. "Um, Tess told me about your race from the nursery. I don't know what happened between you and Hal, but you're welcome to cry on my shoulder."

"Or mine." Tess settled in the chair on Gwen's other side. "After all, I'm your favorite sister."

Their decades-old joke drew a half-smile. "You're my *only* sister, Tess."

Gwen worried that Tess and Liz would think her narrow-minded where Hal's cigar-smoking was concerned. She considered her dislike fully justified, but how could they possibly understand when she'd told neither of them about Uncle Gus?

Beyond that, she wasn't sure she could forgive Hal for breaking his promise, not to mention her trust. His disrespect signaled a sad ending to their cherished friendship.

When Gwen's cell phone vibrated, she glanced at the caller ID and punched the ignore button. Twice more, she didn't answer. Despite the questioning looks from Liz and Tess, Gwen didn't reveal Hal as the caller. She wasn't ready to talk to or about him. Her anger flared afresh. *Why did he have to ruin everything?* Even if she hadn't caught him smoking red-handed, her sensitive nose would have detected the cigar residue clinging to his clothes and his hair and his skin.

Deciding a change of topic would provide distraction, Gwen finally spoke. "Any progress on your repairs, Liz?

After a moment of confusion, Liz pointed to the common wall near the entrance. "The dry wall and plaster work are finished. A painter's coming first thing Monday."

"How are the de-smoking barrels working out?" Tess asked.

"Fantastic." Liz beamed. "Come smell the books I removed a little while ago."

"Come with us, Gwen." Tess offered her hand to help Gwen up from the chair. The three women strolled over and sniffed the volumes. Not a hint of cigar smoke remained.

Liz's cell phone buzzed. "I'm at my bookstore." She paused as the caller responded. "That's fine. See you soon." She disconnected and answered their unspoken question. "Detective Snowcrest is on his way."

Gwen suddenly came back to life. "What's your gut instinct about his investigation?"

Liz didn't respond right away, as if collecting her opinion. "He seems fair-minded. Chasing facts and collecting evidence. The complete opposite of Chief Upton, who's blamed me for Farley's attack just because I yelled at the man after Tuesday's fire."

"Not that I'm defending the chief, but they did find that bloody ashtray beneath your register."

Liz's eyes flashed. "I'm not stupid enough to hide an obvious weapon in my own store."

"I know, Liz. I'm just trying to justify the reasoning behind the chief's suspicion."

"There *is* no reasoning," Liz shot back. "Either Chief Upton has lost his mind or Farley had thoroughly brainwashed the chief against me."

Tess held up both hands. "If I could be the peacekeeper for a second, Liz, my sister's only playing devil's advocate."

Further friction was halted when Snowcrest strode into the shop. "Good afternoon."

He focused on Gwen. "Actually, Mrs. Andrews, I'm glad to see you're here." He waved them to a window table, choosing a chair with a view of the harbor. Again, he peered at Gwen. "Are you getting a cold? Your eyes are red."

His reminder of her recoil at Hal's cigar-smoking threw Gwen for a second, but she recovered quickly. "Not a cold. Maybe I'm developing an allergy."

He shrugged off her explanation. "Let's keep this discussion sequential. You first, Mrs. Phillips. You've explained your multiple conversations with Mr. Cooper about the filtering system. Now, tell me everything that happened before and after each one. Don't leave anything out. The smallest observation could be important."

For the next few minutes, Liz recited the sudden disappearance of Penelope's children's clothing store, the construction noise next door for several weeks before the cigar bar opened; The blue haze creeping through her ceiling tiles; Her failure to convince Farley to split the cost of a filtering system; Requesting Gwen give it a try; Chief Upton's warning not to pester Farley; The fire on Tuesday evening; The inspection the next morning; The inspector's discovery of the unconscious Farley; and their recognition of Farley on the stretcher because of his red ponytail.

The detective wrote furiously. "Now you, Mrs. Andrews."

Watching the sailboats tie up in their slip, Gwen mentioned the bartender's surly attitude; Farley's argument with an older man and a younger companion, who turned out to be Wade Grainger and Billy; the black marble ashtray on Farley's check-out counter; the shadowed men behind the smoked glass of the back room; the drinkers at the bar who witnessed Farley's combative reaction to Gwen's request to improve his ventilation. There was no need to repeat Liz's retelling of the chief's warning, the fire, or the inspector's find where they had both been present.

Liz splayed her hands palm up. "Were these details helpful?"

Snowcrest wagged his head. "Too soon to know. The more I dig into this case, the more I find people who Farley Cooper rubbed the wrong way."

Liz's mood brightened. "Like that bartender? Or even Wade? Or Billy? That's good news for me."

All thoughts of Hal's betrayal swept from Gwen's mind. "Who are the others, Detective?"

Snowcrest's intense gray eyes found hers. "Forget I mentioned them, Mrs. Andrews. Like I told you the other day, just let me handle this investigation."

With a shake of her head, Gwen sent a silent message to Tess that the detective would not be happy about their visit with Rachel. Or did Snowcrest already know about Cousin Jeremy?

Liz leaned on her forearms. "Has the lab identified the fingerprints on that ashtray?"

Behind them, a voice boomed, "Snowcrest! I thought that was your unmarked car parked out front."

The group whirled around to see Chief Upton standing not three feet away. The fact they hadn't heard his heavy steps was nothing short of miraculous.

"Didn't I assign you to track down Cooper's wife?" Chief Upton's strident voice echoed off the bookstore walls.

The detective scrambled to his feet, his notebook clattering to the floor. "Yes, sir. I did. Got back a few minutes ago."

"Then you should be at the station filing your report. Sounds like you were about to share confidential police evidence with my main suspect."

"No, sir. Mrs. Phillips asked about the fingerprints, but I wasn't going to answer."

"Humph," the chief murmured, his intense stare finding Liz. "Then you're here to arrest her?"

Snowcrest appeared flustered for a few seconds before setting his shoulders. "Is that why *you're* here, Sir?"

"Don't be impudent, Detective. I'm not so stupid that I've missed the fact that you disagree with my assessment of this woman's guilt." Chief Upton waved at Liz. "But trust me, as soon as the state lab gets off its collective butt and connects her to that bloody ashtray, *you'll* realize I was right all along, and *she'll* find herself in a jail cell for assault with intent to kill."

Gwen's concerns about the chief's recent behavior resurfaced. Did he realize he'd just answered Liz's question about the fingerprints?

Charles Upton had always been the epitome of intelligence, striving to uphold the law in a fair and equitable manner. Clinging to Liz as a suspect without evidence and dressing down Snowcrest for harboring doubts befuddled Gwen's admiration of the chief's usual integrity.

And why was he spouting his frustration with the detective in front of three civilians when he should be expressing his dissatisfaction in private?

What had caused such a drastic change? Was Chief Upton having marital problems? Health issues? There had to be a logical explanation for his mystifying conduct.

The drama continued as he paced back and forth. "In fact, Snowcrest, you've been working against me for some time now. I'm putting you on suspension for insubordination and assigning this investigation to a detective who will follow my orders."

Snowcrest's white eyebrows shot upwards, wrinkling his forehead. "Sir, you used to respect my gut instincts when it came to criminals. For the past few months, you've brushed off my opinions like I'm a rookie."

"I don't need your input to run my department." Chief Upton stretched out his hand. "Give me your badge and gun. I'll consider re-instating you after this case is closed."

Detective Snowcrest got to his feet in slow motion, retrieved his badge from an inside pocket, unclipped his weapon and holster, and slapped both into the chief's palm.

"Don't lose any sleep over reinstating me, Chief. Did you forget I submitted my retirement paperwork to the county last month? Consider this my last day."

His face beet red, Chief Upton hitched his thumb toward the street. "In that case, drive your department car to the station and leave the keys with the desk sergeant. If there's any paperwork to be handled, we'll deal with it later. Go now."

The chief stormed out. The three women and Snowcrest all stared after him in silence.

Chapter Twenty-Five ... late afternoon, Saturday

Gwen turned her attention to Snowcrest. "Did you mean to take it that far?"

His lips pursed, the detective closed his eyes and shook his head. "That's not the way I planned to leave the department. But I'm maxing out with more than thirty-five years on the force, and I'm a few years past the fifty-five-age minimum for full benefits. I guess it's time."

"What will you do now?" Gwen was genuinely concerned for his welfare.

Snowcrest gave her a shrug. "I'm not ready to sit around and vegetate. Maybe I'll apply for my P.I. license. Put my experience to good use."

Liz surged to her feet. "Detective Snowcrest?" Her hand flew to her mouth. "Oh, I'm sorry. What should I call you now? Mr. Snowcrest?"

"Ben will do."

Liz's demeanor switched to serious. "What happens now with the investigation?"

"Chief Upton will assign another detective."

"And will the new detective blindly follow the chief's assumption that I'm the one who bashed in Farley's head and hid the weapon beneath my own register?"

"Hard to say." Ben ambled toward the bookstore exit without his usual urgency. "I've gotta go. See you around." And he was gone.

When the door closed, Liz grabbed Gwen's arm. "What am I going to do now? Snowcrest seemed to believe I'm innocent."

Tess came up beside them. "Why don't we sit and talk?"

The three retreated to the first window table – their de facto meeting spot – and sat glumly, each lost in her own thoughts.

"Liz?" Gwen whispered, taking her friend's hand.

Liz's head flew up, her expression sullen. "What?"

"You know I'll do whatever I can to help you out of this jam."

Tess scooted her chair closer. "Me, too."

Liz offered a hand to each sister. "Thanks, but what can you possibly do that will help?"

"Have you forgotten?" Tess waved at Gwen. "My sister proved herself a fine detective last fall."

"I remember." Liz glanced at each of them in turn.

Gwen picked up the thread. "How about Tess and I do the same for you?"

Liz didn't skip a beat. "Oh, I wouldn't impose on you. Besides, it could be dangerous."

"Not if we stick together." Tess thumped the table. "All we have to do is follow the clues and see where they take us."

***

When a car with a reverberating muffler parked outside the bookstore, all three women hurried to the street-side window, their curiosity aroused.

A sleek red Corvette with dual exhaust pipes cut its engine. The driver's door swung open and Ben Snowcrest unfolded his long body from the snug seat.

Liz let out a chuckle. "Well, this is a side of the detective we haven't seen."

The newly-retired police detective entered the bookstore a different man. Dressed in jeans, a collarless shirt, and a leather jacket, his shoulders appeared relaxed, his half-smile amiable.

"Didn't expect to see you again so soon." Liz looked him up and down. "Did you leave something behind?"

"Nope." He remained just inside the entrance door.

"I see you've got new wheels." Gwen waved out the front window toward his sports car.

"Yep. Left the boring detective car at the station as instructed."

With her alter ego of amateur detective resurrected, Gwen needed to slide into the comfort zone of asking questions. "Did you bump into anyone while you were there?"

"Most were out working cases. Mike Brown was buried in paperwork. I told him what happened between me and the chief."

Perhaps Snowcrest was simply looking for an audience after terminating his connection with the other officers. If Gwen kept him talking, maybe he'd drop a detail that she'd deem worthy of pursuit. "Did you tell him you're planning to apply for your P.I. license?"

Gwen didn't care if she sounded nosey. Although Snowcrest applying for his P.I. license was unrelated to Liz's situation, his future plans were as good a place to start as any.

He dipped his head. "I mentioned it. Mike thought it was a good idea not to waste my training, but some of the other detectives might not be so open-minded."

"I think I know what you mean."

Liz and Tess stood by, their curious glances observing Gwen.

"I usually read mysteries, detective, but once in a while I dive into a thriller. A recent story included a passage about policemen resenting detectives who switch to the private sector. I think they called it 'crossing over'."

"Yep, that's the term."

"Will you lose some of your cop friends?"

Snowcrest gave her an amused expression. "Possibly."

Liz jumped into the conversation. "What will you say to the guys who give you grief about being a private investigator?"

"I'll just tell them I'm still chasing criminals, but on behalf of my clients."

164

Concerned about Snowcrest's welfare, Gwen forged ahead. "How long will it take to obtain your license?"

"You're kind to worry about me, Mrs. Andrews."

"No more worried than you were when you found me in a ditch after tumbling off my bicycle years ago. And, please, call me Gwen."

Snowcrest laughed deep and long. "All right, Gwen. I'd forgotten about your bicycle incident until you reminded me the other day."

Gwen liked this more relaxed version of Ben Snowcrest.

"You asked how long to get my P.I. license?" He favored her with a quirky smile that would charm information from just about anyone. He'd be an effective private eye. "Probably a few months. In the meantime, I'll join the state association and learn the down and dirty differences between police detectives and private investigators."

Liz shifted her weight. "You never did say why you're here."

"No, I didn't. Do you have a few minutes?"

"Of course." Liz led him to their table and retook her seat.

Although itching to hear what he had to say, Gwen wasn't rude enough to horn-in. She walked to the table to retrieve her jacket and shoulder bag from the back of the chair. "Tess and I will take off so you two can talk."

Ben glanced at the sisters. "I'm sorry, I meant all of you. Can you stay a while, Gwen? Tess? I'm no longer officially involved in the Farley Cooper case, but I wanted to warn you three ladies about someone who might show up in Harbor Falls."

Gwen and Tess sat down.

Liz waved him to continue. "Who's the person?"

"Did any of you hear Chief Upton ask me if I'd located Farley's wife?"

Gwen and Tess answered at the same time. "I did."

"Well, her name's Violet, but shrinking she is not. Tracked her down on the North Shore this morning. She made me stand outside while I informed her of her husband's death. Violet claims Farley cleaned out their joint account and she has no intention of burying the bastard. Her words, not mine."

"How did you find her?" Gwen wanted to learn his methods.

From one pocket, Ben removed a used notebook and pushed it aside. "Earlier this morning, I inspected Farley's apartment above the cigar bar. The place is bare bones. No sign of a female. No women's clothing. Found a bank statement with his wife's name." From his other pocket, Ben withdrew a new notebook.

The fact that Ben had two journals drew Gwen's attention. "Is the used notebook the official one?"

Ben snorted. "No. Had to leave that one in the case file for the next detective. I always make a duplicate for my personal records. I'm starting this second one as a private citizen."

To Gwen's ears, his statement meant he intended to continue working the case, even as a retired detective. That could only mean a better outcome for Liz.

Ben dragged the dog-eared journal closer and flipped through the pages. "Let's get back to Violet. She refused to give me an alibi for Tuesday night. Before she slammed the door in my face, she told me to contact Farley's sister to handle his burial ..." he paused as his finger moved down the page, "... Kate Wakefield."

Gwen shot Tess a look and shook her head, satisfied when Tess nodded her understanding not to share they'd met Kate at lunch.

Instead, Tess asked a question. "Why are you concerned about Violet coming to town?"

Ben cleared his throat. "I can picture her attacking Farley, so I want you to be watchful. She might show up in Harbor Falls to claim his property. Let me give you a description."

Dangling his hand above his head, Ben described Violet as close to six feet, weighing at least two hundred pounds, large head, scraggly blonde hair, and a mean scowl.

166

Gwen nearly choked. "She sounds like a female wrestler."

"If she was, she's let herself go. If you see anyone who looks like her, stay clear and let me know. He reached into a pocket and brought out three Harbor Falls Police Department business cards. He flipped each one over and wrote a phone number. "That's my personal cell phone if you need to get in touch."

The legs of his chair scraped the floorboards. "That's what I came to tell you. Be watchful until Farley's attacker is caught."

As Ben strolled out the door, the three women remained glued to their seats, regarding each other with flabbergasted expressions.

Liz broke the silence. "Wow. I didn't expect the detective to show so much interest. I think he truly believes I'm innocent."

Gwen picked up her jacket and shoulder bag. "And that's why Tess and I will be checking out a few things around town."

Liz's hand flew to Gwen's arm. "You might be tempting fate to think you can solve another mystery without consequences. I'm not sure your luck will hold a second time."

"You let me and Tess worry about that. You concentrate on repairing your bookstore so you can re-open. I just thought of someone who might provide us with new details."

Liz's face took on a hopeful expression. "Who's that?"

"Penelope Grainger."

Tess looked sideways at her sister. "She's the lady who used to own the children's clothing store next door? You think she might know something relevant?"

"Her husband Wade and son Billy were the targets of Farley's outburst on Tuesday morning. Chances are Wade told Penelope about it over dinner. Not that I think Wade attacked Farley, but you know how one clue leads to another."

"That's for sure." Tess gave Gwen a thumbs up. "When are you thinking to meet with her?"

"Let's invite her to join us for the Sunday morning brunch at The Wharf."

Liz got to her feet. "Great idea. You can say you feel awful about her losing her store and thought a breakfast with the girls might cheer her up."

"I'll also invite her friend Beatrice. Remember she complained about her husband's bossiness after spending time at Farley's place? No telling what we'll learn. If they accept my invitation, do you want to join us, Liz?"

"Probably not. I'd love to, but I've got to stay on top of this de-smoking project. The sooner my books don't smell like cigars, the sooner I can re-open."

Tess raised her hand. "Liz, do you want me to stay and change out another batch?"

"That would be a great help, Tess. When we're done, I'll treat you to dinner at the Bayside Café. Want to join us, Gwen?"

"Thanks, but I need to get home and feed Amber. I'll see you later, Tess."

Liz walked Gwen to the bookstore door. "I'll drop her off before I head home."

In fact, Gwen welcomed some alone time to mull over Hal's betrayal. With her ignoring his phone calls, he was bound to show up on her doorstep at some point in the near future.

What would she say when he caught up with her?

Chapter Twenty-Six ... early evening, Saturday

When Gwen came through her front door, she nearly stepped on Amber. Sliding her purse off her shoulder, Gwen dropped it to the foyer tiles and picked up her pet.

"Amber, sweetie. I'm so sorry I've been ignoring you the past few days." Gwen nuzzled the top of the tabby's head.

Not one for overly-long cuddling, Amber wiggled her chubby self, her signal to be released.

Gwen lowered the cat to the floor. "All right, all right. Let's get you fed and watered."

The converted library seemed overly dark, so Gwen took a detour into the living room and switched on a few lamps. The warm glow instantly provided a sense of home-coming.

A white card sitting on the coffee table beckoned her. Madame Eudora's business card: a reminder that both sisters wanted to see the images recorded by Annabelle's video and still camera.

Tess merely wanted proof that Parker's spirit had joined them – or not – during the séance.

Gwen harbored the same doubt. Had his spirit manifested at Madame Eudora's beckoning? Had he re-appeared on the backyard swing later that same evening without the medium's assistance?

Tess's suspicion of hallucinations simmered just below the surface. If Parker's essence had registered on Annabelle's recordings, Gwen could relax that her sanity remained intact.

When a loud meow interrupted Gwen's ponderings, she slipped the card into her pants pocket and circled through the music studio. In the kitchen, she filled the impatient cat's bowls. While Amber ate, Gwen descended the basement steps and cleaned the litter box.

169

Her catly duties done, Gwen pulled out Madame Eudora's card and settled on an island stool to dial.

When an answering machine clicked on, the medium's breathy voice spoke into Gwen's ear:

'*You have reached an answering machine. Madame Eudora is out in the world communing with the loved ones of others. Please leave a message explaining your desires. She will contact you as soon as is earthly possible.*'

Thrown for a second, Gwen collected her thoughts and requested a call back.

Retrieving her shoulder bag from the foyer, Gwen removed her pad of lined paper and prepared to call Penelope. Not knowing the woman's home phone number, Gwen glided her laptop from great-great grandma's sideboard and opened the phone search website. Up popped the listing for Wade Grainger, Penelope Grainger, and William Danforth. Odd. Why did Billy have a different last name? Wasn't he their son? Shaking her head at the inconsistency, Gwen jotted the Grainers' phone number at the top of a new page and dialed the landline.

After three rings, a shaky female voice answered, "Hello."

"Penelope? This is Gwen Andrews. How are you today?"

"Oh, I'm okay, I guess. What can I do for you, Gwen?"

"Actually, I'm hoping I can do something for you."

"You are?" Penelope's voice gained a little spark.

"I was shocked when I heard you'd lost your clothing store to Farley Cooper."

Penelope growled under her breath. "That's one way to describe what happened."

Gwen forged ahead. "How about breakfast out with the girls?"

"How sweet of you. When and where are you planning this breakfast?"

"The Wharf offers a wonderful Sunday Brunch. Are you free tomorrow morning?"

"I'll make myself free. Wade and I attend the early church service, so I could meet you there around ten."

"Perfect. My sister Tess is visiting and will be joining us. Would your friend Beatrice like to come, too? Do you think she'll accept my invitation?"

"Oh, I'm quite sure Bea would enjoy some time away from her husband." Penelope lowered her voice as if someone was close enough to listen-in. "She's been so unhappy lately. But I don't want to gossip over the phone."

"No need to air her dirty laundry. Do you have her number?"

"Why don't I extend your invitation myself? She won't refuse me. I'll even pick her up. We'll see you there. And thanks, Gwen."

Despite Gwen's ulterior motives for the invitation, she nonetheless felt she was doing a good deed by providing both Penelope and Beatrice with a respite from the recent challenges in their lives. Digging for dirt about Farley Cooper and his possible enemies over breakfast without giving away she was on a snooping mission would require all of Gwen's subtlety.

Her belly growled from all the talk about food. Remembering Tess would be eating dinner with Liz, Gwen opened the freezer door and stood there, debating which frozen leftovers she favored. Living by herself, Gwen found it practical to cook large batches of a recipe and freeze most of the food for easy future meals.

A few minutes later, she carried re-heated beef stew into the living room and placed it on the lift-top table facing the flat screen mounted above the fireplace. How many times had she and Parker eaten in this very spot while they watched a TV drama or an old movie? She missed the little things the most.

Scrolling through the shows deemed worthy of recording, Gwen chose an episode of *Murder, She Wrote*, a favorite series from the mid-eighties into the late-nineties. Perhaps some of

Jessica Fletcher's techniques – dreamt up by the script writers – would come in handy to solve the Farley Cooper case.

At seven-thirty, in the middle of Jessica's sleuthing, Gwen's house phone rang. She paused the recording and hurried to the kitchen.

"Hello?" Her voice was more breathy from her sprint than she cared to admit.

"Gwen, darling, this is Madame Eudora."

"Oh. Hello. Thanks for returning my call. Were you hosting another séance?"

The medium's titter echoed through the phone line. "Not this time. A private session with a widower a few towns over. He was so distraught until his beloved wife communicated with him through me. She did not manifest, but the words she spoke through me heartened him."

"Must be satisfying for you." Gwen was suddenly envious that the medium had connected with Parker when Gwen had failed for months.

"My gift is rewarding now, Gwen, but it took me a while to ease into my skill. At first, communicating with those who had passed-on scared me. When I realized how much comfort I could provide to the earth-bound, I relaxed and allowed the dearly departed souls to come through."

"Well, you were quite impressive last night."

"Thank you for saying so. Is the séance the reason you called?"

"Yes, it is,"

"Tell me what's on your mind."

Gwen pictured Madame Eudora lounging as they spoke, a glass of wine in her manicured hand. "My sister and I wondered if you'd allow us to view the still shots and video Annabelle recorded during the séance."

Madame Eudora's voice softened. "Has Tess fully recovered from your husband's touch?"

172

Gwen was moved by the medium's concern. "She's fine, but questioning the events of the séance."

"That's not unusual. Give her some space to accept the truth." Madame Eudora paused. "Concerning your request for the photos and video, let me explain my arrangement with the paper. When I contacted the *Harbor Falls Gazette* to record the séance, Shirley made me an offer. She would provide gratis copies of the photos and video in exchange for my permission to publish an article about our private event. Her story will be published in this week's edition of the paper, I believe. So to answer your question, the video and photographs belong to *The Gazette*. You'll have to ask Shirley if you can have a look."

Gwen sat back, absorbing these tidbits. Could the medium sense when a spirit would manifest or did she record all of her séances? Wouldn't it be fascinating to view other videos?

Realizing Madame Eudora was waiting for a response, Gwen stumbled over her words. "Oh, I had no idea. In that case, I'll contact Shirley."

"I doubt she'll deny you." Madame Eudora hesitated. "If you don't mind me getting personal, Gwen, you and I spoke of your sister's reaction, but not yours."

Gwen wished she had an old-fashioned phone cord to stretch and relieve the tension. Her portable house phone provided no such release. "I firmly believe you connected with my husband, and I thank you for that, Madame Eudora."

"May I be bold for a moment?"

Somehow, Gwen was not surprised. "Of course."

"Our séance was not your first exposure to the beyond, was it?"

Here was further proof of Madame Eudora's gift. As Parker had moved toward Gwen, the medium's eyes followed his every step. There was finally no doubt in Gwen's mind that Parker's appearances had been genuine. No more thinking she'd gone over the edge. Viewing the video and still shots would only serve to support Gwen's certainty. "Um," she stumbled. Rather than answer directly, she asked a follow-up question. "How did you know?"

Madame Eudora's sultry voice soothed Gwen's heart. "You weren't in the least disturbed by his appearance. In fact, the excitement in your eyes convinced me you were overjoyed to see his spirit again. How many other times has he manifested to you?"

If Gwen couldn't discuss Parker's multiple visits with Madame Eudora, who *could* she talk to? "Three and a half."

The medium chuckled. "My dear, you must explain."

"Last September, Parker came to me three times. The half is when he stood at the edge of our woods and waved because I wasn't by myself. That was the last time until your séance."

"Ah, then I am pleased. When your Parker disappeared after Tess fainted, I could see you were disappointed. Would you like to schedule a private session to connect with him again? There are no guarantees, but I'm certainly willing to give it my best effort."

Madame Eudora had no way of knowing Parker appeared on the back swing after the attendees left and Tess was tucked in bed. Although it was possible he'd never left after the séance.

Before Gwen had a chance to decline the medium's offer, Madame Eudora continued. "Give me a minute to find my calendar. I'll check if I have any events near Harbor Falls."

Gwen imagined the woman gliding through her home in search of her Day-Timer.

Seconds later, Madame Eudora came back on the line. "Hmmm." Pages swished in the background. "I have sessions in New Hampshire and western Massachusetts, but nothing scheduled in your South Shore area."

Gwen dropped onto a kitchen stool. She wasn't ready for a private session with the medium. She wanted to try calling Parker on her own at least once before seeking assistance. "You're sweet to offer, but I need time to absorb everything."

"Understandable, my dear. You have my card. Call if you need me. Perhaps we can come together on a future day."

Gwen disconnected and wandered back to the living room, once again settling on the loveseat facing the TV and fireplace. Although the evening had chilled, it was too late to start a fire. Gwen stared into the shadows of the darkened firebox as she half-listened to Jessica Fletcher solve another case.

Confused thoughts of Parker's ghost jumbled around in Gwen's mind. And then there was Hal. *What am I going to do about Hal?*

Whatever decision she made would impact her life in a big way. At least her blood pressure had resettled to somewhat normal levels since she'd caught him smoking the damn cigar, but her indecision remained.

***

Gwen jolted awake at the sound of pounding. She bolted upright on the loveseat, where she'd obviously dozed off.

The noise was the rattle of glass in her French door. She stumbled to her feet and moved around the far end of the fireplace wall. In the unlit music studio, she picked up a statue of Beethoven and tip-toed to the back door. When she flipped on the security light, a familiar, but not altogether welcome face, stared at her.

Her heart racing, Gwen twisted the lock and opened the door.

175

Chapter Twenty-Seven ... mid evening, Saturday

"Why are you here?" Gwen demanded.

Hal's face took on a defiant expression. "Why did you run off this afternoon?"

How can the man be so clueless? "You can't seriously be asking me that question."

"Would I call your cell phone three times if I wasn't serious? Why didn't you pick up?"

"I would think my anger was obvious after I caught you smoking Farley's damn cigars."

Gwen's emotions surged to the surface. She struggled not to cry like a teenager who'd had her heart broken for the first time. Is that what Hal had done? Broken her heart? During the months of claiming she wanted no more than his friendship, had she secretly wished for more?

Hal raised both hands in a defensive posture. "I gave them to Oscar, just like I said I would."

"You also promised you weren't going to smoke them."

Hal looked sheepish for only a moment. "Oscar offered me one, and I didn't want to be rude."

"You didn't want to offend Oscar, but you had no problem breaking your promise to me?"

"It was only one cigar, Gwen. If you hadn't caught me, you would've never known."

When he stepped toward her, she backed away. As she'd expected, the tobacco residue clung to his clothes and hair and breath. A disturbing odor she couldn't abide.

"Of course I would know, Hal. You reek." Through a strange

176

trick of her brain, Uncle Gus's sneering face superimposed itself onto Hal's.

When Hal made a move toward the kitchen stools, she blocked his way, thankful his own face was back in place.

His voice grew louder. "Would you please listen to reason?"

"No. You need to go." She matched his volume as if that alone would force his departure.

Before Hal could object, the front door slammed. Tess hustled around the staircase in their direction. "What's going on? I could hear your voices from the front walkway."

Gwen stepped around Hal and opened the French door. "Hal was just leaving."

"We're not finished, Gwen."

"We *are* finished."

Even with her short stature, Gwen found the strength to push him through the opening and onto the rear deck. She slammed the door and twisted the lock.

Through the glass, he stared at both sisters before stomping away. His footsteps trudged along the boards, down the end steps, and onto the driveway until they faded into the night.

What disturbed Gwen more than anything was that Hal didn't seem sorry for his actions.

"Okay, Gwen. Time to fess up."

Knowing she had no choice but to reveal the sordid details about Great Uncle Gus, Gwen's resistance dissolved.

***

Tess paced around the kitchen island. "Why didn't you tell me? Did Mom know?"

Shaking her head, Gwen dropped onto a stool and rested her forehead in her palms. "It would have been his word against mine. No one would have believed good ole Gus had molested his pre-teen great niece. You remember how everyone loved him."

"But you didn't."

"I tried to stay out of his way, Tess. Honest, I did. But he always managed to find me when no one was around."

Tess moved closer and draped an arm across Gwen's shoulder. "You don't have to tell me, but what did he do?"

Gwen took a deep breath, somewhat relieved to share this trauma with her sister. "Groping, kissing. He was much stronger than me, so I never managed to break loose from his grip. He's the reason I can't abide cigar smoke."

Tess closed her eyes. "I forgot about him smoking cigars, but it never bothered me as much as you. Now I know why."

"He snuck into my bedroom one night."

Tess gasped. "Where was I? We always shared a bedroom."

"You were spending the night with one of your girlfriends."

"He didn't rape you, did he?"

"No, no. He stopped short of rape. I told him to get out or I'd tell everyone what he'd been doing. I guess he believed me, because he didn't bother me again for the rest of his visit."

Tess wrapped both arms around Gwen. The kitchen clock ticked away the minutes. "I'm sorry you went through his abuse alone." Tess pushed Gwen to arm's length. "I wish you had told me."

"In hindsight, I wish I had, too. But he left a few days later, and then he was killed in a tractor accident the following spring. All I wanted to do was forget about him."

"I don't understand what this has to do with Hal."

Gwen explained how she caught Hal smoking a cigar with Oscar between the greenhouses, reneging on his promise.

"No wonder you rushed out of there. Do you think you two have a future? I've been hoping you'd become a real couple."

Gwen shook her head. "I just don't know, Tess. I need some alone time to think. Do you mind?"

"Of course not. I'll go upstairs and read for a while. Stick your head in and say goodnight."

***

Knowing the evening air held the chill of April, Gwen carried a fleece throw to the rear arbor and settled on the swing. For a long time, she rocked back and forth, back and forth, uncertain how to proceed if she ejected Hal from her life.

Would talking to Parker's spirit provide any solace? Gwen stopped swinging and called his name. Nothing.

A second attempt, a little louder. Still nothing.

Her voice trembling, she yelled one last time.

A hollow laugh reached her ears. She'd succeeded: Parker was in the vicinity. Gwen swiveled left and right, trying to spot him. When a movement caught her eye, she whirled to see his ghost taking shape near the oversized field rock at the edge of the woods. She jumped up and ran toward him, stopping only inches away.

Parker's gossamer hand touched her cheek, the sensation on her skin still reminiscent of butterfly wings. She could think of no other comparison.

His soft voice whispered, "I think I've figured this out. When you're upset, I can hear the anxiety in your voice. What's bothering you, sweetheart?"

Horrified to learn that Parker's awareness of her summons depended on her distress, Gwen sobered.

Belatedly hearing Parker's question, Gwen was suddenly overwhelmed by her disappointment in Hal. She began to weep, stuttering through her tears. "It's all so complicated, Parker."

"What are you talking about?"

She swiped angrily at her cheek. "Hal Jenkins."

"What about him?"

"It's all gone to hell."

He led her to the swing, easing his see-through self onto the adjoining cushion. "Sorry, I'm not following you."

Gwen explained catching Hal smoking a cigar.

Parker chuckled, the sound hollow compared to his deep guffaws when he was alive. "Oh, cigar smoke. I remember how you avoided people who lit up. You don't think you can get past it and forgive the man?"

Gwen inhaled a deep breath and let it out in a loud huff. She'd never told Parker about Great Uncle Gus.

Time to share...again.

***

Parker's shadowed face exploded in anger. "What a bastard!" He reached over and stroked her hair, his touch only minimally felt. "You're fully justified to eliminate Hal from your life. Don't worry, sweetheart, he's not the only man in town. Someone equally fascinating will come along to share dinners and take walks with you. You're still a good-looking woman, Gwen. Any man in Harbor Falls would be pleased to keep you company."

Gwen sniffed, relieved that Parker understood. About someone else walking into her life to replace Hal, she wasn't so sure.

Could I ever give my entire self to another man? Will I cling to my visits with Parker's spirit and keep all other men at arm's length? How could I possibly juggle a living man on this side and Parker on the other?

Life – and death – that's what was so complicated.

Chapter Twenty-Eight ... mid-morning, Sunday

The brisk mid-morning walk down Harbor Hill to The Wharf provided Gwen and Tess their daily exercise. The sisters entered the restaurant at ten o'clock sharp. The mixed aroma of bacon, French toast, and home fries filled the air.

Following a brief chat with the hostess, they were led to a booth near the two-sided brunch buffet. At one end, an omelet chef sautéed mushrooms and spinach for a waiting customer.

Relieved they weren't seated at the window table where Hal had kissed her on Tuesday evening before revealing Farley's box of cigars, Gwen slid onto the bench seat.

Tess settled across from her. "Do you think they'll show up?"

Before Gwen could comment, Penelope and Beatrice approached the booth.

"What a wonderful idea, Gwen." Penelope sat next to Tess. "Sunday morning breakfast with the ladies is definitely a treat."

Beatrice took the empty seat beside Gwen. "Thanks for including me. Frank hasn't brought me here since this restaurant opened last year." Her eyes roamed the décor, her melancholy evident.

Gwen's stomach growled. "I'm starving. Shall we eat?"

After placing their drink orders with the waitress, the four women joined the line for the buffet, each filling their plates.

As they all savored the first few bites, no one spoke. Holding her fork aloft, Gwen tossed out her ice-breaker. "Penelope, I came upon something odd when I searched online for your number."

Penelope wiped a crumb from the corner of her mouth with a dainty pat. "What was that?"

181

"Well, you and Wade are listed with the last name of Grainger. But Billy's registered as William Danforth."

A wistful expression shadowed Penelope's face. "Billy's story is a sad one. When he was about to graduate high school, his parents, who were our best friends in the world, were killed in a boating accident. There were no relatives, so Wade and I stepped in as Billy's unofficial foster parents. We never legally adopted Billy. That's why his last name is different."

Gwen recalled Billy's tenderness as he and Wade escorted Penelope from the bookstore the other morning, then fetched sandwiches and drinks for their impromptu picnic in the gazebo at the end of the pier. Their relationship also explained why Billy called her Mrs. G. and not 'Mother' or 'Mom'. And Wade by his first name instead of 'Dad'. "No wonder he's so fond of you."

Penelope blushed. "Billy has grown into a fine young man, though he's not so young anymore. Let me think…" She squinted at the ceiling. "Thirty-three next month."

Gwen had guessed a few years older, but people aged at different rates based on genetics and life's challenges.

Penelope continued Billy's story. "I've never managed to put any weight on that boy's bones. He's just as wiry now as the day he moved into our spare room. His grades weren't good enough to pursue a college education, so Wade hired him for the window and door business. Those two are as thick as thieves. We've never pressured Billy to move out on his own."

Another scene popped into Gwen's mind: Billy's eagerness to retrieve Wade's pricing pad from the truck for Liz's replacement window quote. Their closeness was touching.

Beatrice shared a humorous story from when Billy had first moved in with Penelope and Wade. The women all laughed. Tess lifted her empty plate. "Anyone for seconds besides me?"

Beatrice pushed her dirty plate to the table's edge for pick-up by the wait staff. "I could use another bite. Let's go."

After Tess and Beatrice wandered to the buffet, Gwen poured herself another cup of tea from the pot, refilled Penelope's cup, and ventured another question. "You don't have to answer, but how did Farley Cooper manage to oust you from your store?"

Penelope huffed. "That man's lack of conscience still gives me heartburn, but I don't mind telling you." Despite her brave facade, Penelope dabbled at one eye with her napkin. "When I opened my store back in the seventies, rent was cheap, so Wade and I decided against buying our center section of the building. In the eighties, interest rates sky-rocketed, so we put our plans to own on permanent hold. It never occurred to us that the owner would sell it out from under us."

"So Farley swept in and bought your space?"

"Swooped in like a turkey vulture. He gave me one week to clear out my inventory."

"Which explains why you didn't hold a going-out-of-business sale. Where are the children's clothes now?" She pictured the overflowing racks of colorful garments.

Penelope sniffed, her tone indignant. "They're in storage until I decide whether to look for another storefront. If I don't, I suppose I could sell the new items back to the vendors at a loss and donate the gently-used articles to Goodwill."

"What was Wade's reaction to losing your store?" Gwen recalled Farley's belligerent words to Wade in the cigar bar Tuesday morning, though at the time, she hadn't realized the older man was Wade and the younger one Billy.

Penelope stirred her tea. "Wade's still upset that Farley Cooper ruined my business..." Penelope made the sign of the cross. "May his soul rest in peace, whether he's up or down." She leaned across the table and whispered, "To tell you the truth, Gwen, although I loved my store, and I'm still plenty upset that Farley forced me out, I'm getting a bit long in the tooth to start all over again. I just don't have the energy."

"Does Wade know you might not reopen somewhere else?"

"Not yet. I don't want to say anything until I've made a final decision."

Gwen stopped short of asking if Wade might have taken revenge on Farley, though it was a distinct possibility. Annabelle's impromptu photos during Tuesday evening's fire clearly showed Wade, Penelope, and Billy standing at the edge of the crowd.

If Gwen asked Penelope whether Wade had been home all night, she'd expose her snooping. If Wade's fingerprints were matched to that ashtray, the case would be solved without Gwen upsetting her relationship with Penelope. That is, if Wade's fingerprints were in the system. Gwen had no idea if he had a criminal history or even if he'd served in the military.

Tess and Beatrice resettled in the booth and wasted no time diving into their second helping. Gwen was not concerned about her sister's waistline. Tess had the metabolism of a teenager.

Penelope's eyes opened wide at Beatrice's pile of food, but she made no comment. "Gwen and I have been talking about Farley Cooper, Bea. Didn't you say Frank acted differently after he attended the cigar bar's opening a few weeks ago?"

Beatrice swallowed the food she'd forked into her mouth. "Not only the grand opening. He'd gone back a few more times." She glanced around at their rapt faces. "My husband had always been such a kind man. But when he got home after spending time in that cigar bar, he became someone I didn't recognize. Bossing me around, saying he didn't care if he smelled like cigar smoke, telling me the jokes about keeping wives in line. I've been so hurt by his disrespect."

Gwen covered Bea's hand with her own. "Now that Farley's place is closed, maybe your sweet Frank will come back to you."

"I hope so." Beatrice sniffed and moved her glance from one face to the next. "Do you think there could have been some sort of drug in those cigars?"

Gwen did a double-take. "That's an interesting theory." She flashed on Chief Upton's belligerence toward Liz in the bookstore the other morning. Then Hal's seemingly unrepentant attitude about breaking his promise not to smoke Farley's gift cigars. And now the disrespect of Bea's husband Frank.

Gwen only half-listened to the other women reminiscing about the trouble with husbands. She was too caught up in her own dire ramblings.

Could Farley Cooper have introduced drugs into quiet Harbor Falls? As far as Gwen knew, there had been no evidence of the national epidemic either in the dorms of Baylies College or the town itself. Or were the changes in the men who frequented Farley's place simply the result of acting macho and upping their testosterone levels?

With the cigar bar closed, did it matter? She'd keep Bea's drugged cigar idea in mind. Maybe it was true, but maybe not. Perhaps she'd pass it along to Ben.

Tess's fork and knife clanged onto her plate. "I'm officially stuffed. No lunch for me today."

Penelope maneuvered out of the booth. "I had such a delightful time, Gwen. Thank you for making the suggestion."

Beatrice chimed in. "That goes for me, too. We should do this again."

The four women settled their bill with a generous tip. Echoing the cheerful goodbye from the hostess, they exited to the front porch. Penelope and Beatrice waved goodbye, descended the steps, and headed into the parking lot.

Glancing sideways, Gwen noticed a man with a handlebar mustache sitting in one of the rocking chairs at the far end. *Who is he? Of course, the bartender at Farley's place.* When she'd walked in there on Tuesday morning for her doomed chat with Farley, Mr. Mustache hadn't smiled or joked with the customers. Perhaps an unhappy employee. No telling what information he could share about Farley's dealings. She and Tess should take advantage of this opportunity and have a chat with the bartender.

Gwen grasped Tess's sleeve to prevent her from descending the steps. "See the man at the end of the porch?" Gwen tilted her head in his direction instead of pointing.

Tess looked past Gwen. "The one with the big mustache?"

Gwen nodded. "That's the one. He worked for Farley. Let's go say hello."

As the sisters approached the adjoining rockers, the mustachioed man leapt to his feet and tipped his hat. "Good morning, ladies."

"Don't I know you from somewhere?" Gwen began. Better for him to bring up the topic of the cigar bar.

He squinted, studying her face, then snapped his fingers. "Aren't you the woman who came into Farley's place last week?"

Gwen favored him with a big grin. "That's it. You're the bartender."

"Used to be the bartender."

"Oh, dear, I'm sorry. Will Farley's relatives re-open the business?"

He shrugged and shook his head. "No idea, but I'm not counting on it. Don't know if he had any relatives. Don't recall any coming into the bar. At least no one who claimed to be a relative."

At a loss about how to keep the conversation moving, Gwen defaulted to manners and extended her hand.

"My name's Gwen Andrews, and this is my sister Tess Walker. She's visiting from the Berkshires."

He reached out and squeezed each hand in greeting. "Lance Lynch. Nice to meet you both under more pleasant circumstances." He indicated the restaurant's porch, the boardwalk edging the waterfront, and the harbor itself to underscore his meaning.

Gwen grasped at the opening. "I hope you don't mind me saying so, but you didn't look very happy the other day."

186

Lance indicated they should sit. "Very perceptive, Mrs. Andrews. After your short time with Farley, you must have noticed he's quick to lose his temper."

"We're safe to call that an understatement." Gwen recalled Farley's abrupt about face when she brought up Liz's offer to split the cost of a filtering system.

"That man could be excessively nasty," Lance continued. "But never to his customers. Farley charmed them all."

"He did?"

"Oh, sure. He spoke to his patrons with a honeyed tongue, but he treated me and Quincy like yesterday's garbage." Lance crossed one ankle over his knee, seeming to appreciate an audience for his gripe session. "Farley yelled at me for putting too much liquor in the drinks and at poor Quincy to put more pressure on the vendors for a deeper discount. And then there was the construction crew."

Gwen ran her palm along the arm of her rocker. She didn't want to ask questions too quickly and make Lance suspicious of her intent. Better to comment and encourage Lance to vent his frustrations at his own pace. "I have to say the crew did a fantastic job. I was quite impressed with the results."

Lance stopped rocking. "Well, I'll give Farley that. He had a keen eye for how the place should look. I heard he pestered the construction foreman day and night to get all that work done in an abbreviated amount of time."

From Gwen's other side, Tess leaned forward to be in eyesight of Lance. "The cigar bar was cordoned off with crime scene tape by the time I arrived in Harbor Falls to visit my sister. I've never seen the inside."

Good for you, Tess. Gwen almost shouted her glee but caught herself. Tess had subtly introduced the topic of Farley's attack and death, now the elephant sitting on the porch with them.

Gwen responded to her sister's comment. "The interior was quite beautiful, Tess. Rich paneling and overstuffed chairs."

"And don't forget the mirrored wall and solid mahogany bar." Lance clicked his tongue. "Prettiest slab of wood I've ever seen, and I've tended bar in a lot of places."

Gwen moved forward. "Any idea where Farley purchased it?"

"Custom built by an old guy up north. When he hauled it down here a few weeks ago for installation, he grumbled that the deposit check bounced. Farley told Quincy to write another check for the full amount, promising it wouldn't bounce. On his way out, the old guy snarled that he hoped it didn't because the custom-built bar wasn't saleable to anyone else."

"Oh, dear." Gwen rocked in her chair. "That's not good for a businessman's reputation."

"Sure isn't. The construction company got stiffed as well. Same thing. Bounced check."

Tess pushed up from her chair and moved to the railing. "How did you find out about the second one?"

Lance leaned his forearms on his knees. "I overheard Farley lambasting Quincy about a legal notice demanding payment."

Gwen slid back in her rocker. Farley's office papers should identify the craftsman and the construction foreman. She considered each man's likelihood as the attacker. Why would either of them want Farley dead and ruin any chance of getting the money they were owed?

Lance pushed himself to his feet. "Nice chatting with you, ladies, but I have an interview for a new bartending job up the coast. See you around." He moved along the porch to the steps and disappeared into the parking lot.

Opening her shoulder bag, Gwen removed her legal pad and scribbled the details Lance had revealed.

Chapter Twenty-Nine ... late morning, Sunday

As the sisters began their trek up the slope of Harbor Hill, Gwen turned to Tess. "What do you think of Lance as a suspect?"

Tess shrugged. "I can't imagine him attacking Farley and putting himself out of a job."

"Me, neither, but we should keep him in mind. The same with the craftsman and the construction foreman."

Halfway up the hill, the door of the Bayside Café flew open and Billy bounded out with three cups of coffee balanced precariously in his hands.

"Whoa there, Billy." Gwen came to a dead stop to prevent a collision. "Why are you in such a rush?"

Billy's eyes widened behind his glasses. "Oh, sorry, Mrs. Andrews. Should watch where I'm going. Just getting coffee for me and Wade and Mrs. Phillips."

Gwen glanced across to Liz's bookstore. "Did her replacement window arrive?"

"Sure did." Billy beamed. "We're about to install it. That's why I'm in such a hurry."

Tess reached for one of the coffee-laden paper cups. Gwen took the other. "We'll walk over with you. I'd like to watch how it's done."

"Fine by me. Why're you two down here on a Sunday morning?"

"We invited Penelope and Beatrice to brunch at The Wharf."

"That was nice." Billy's forehead wrinkled. "Strange Mrs. G didn't tell us. But me and Wade were busy loading the window after church. Did she have fun?"

"She seemed relieved to vent about Farley Cooper. So did Beatrice."

Checking for traffic, which was light on a Sunday morning, the three of them walked through the median strip to Liz's side of Harbor Hill.

With his free hand, Billy opened the bookstore door and held it for Gwen and Tess.

Liz was talking. Wade was listening. "… and he retired on the spot. I don't know who's going to take his place. But Gwen and her sister Tess are asking around to see what they can find out."

Gwen gasped to hear Liz sharing information with Wade, a person she'd newly added to her list of potential attackers.

Wade's mouth dropped open. "Wow. You're fortunate to have friends like the sisters. Especially with Chief Upton thinking you did it and all."

Liz accepted the cup of coffee from Gwen. "Hey, thanks. Any news to share?"

Her brain catching up with her mouth, Liz clamped her lips shut. It must have dawned on her that Penelope's husband and son were standing right there, and she'd nearly given away Gwen's secret snooping expedition with Penelope.

Billy stared at Liz. "What do you mean, Mrs. Phillips?"

Gwen's brain kicked into high gear to turn this conversation in another direction. Billy knew the sisters had just come from brunch with his unofficial foster mother. "Oh, I can explain, Billy. I offered to check out The Wharf as a possible venue for Liz's re-opening party."

Liz picked up Gwen's diversion without skipping a beat. "Thanks, Gwen, but after we talked about possible locations, I decided to have it right here in the store. More cost effective. I should have told you not to bother."

"Not a problem, Liz. I like your plan better." Having the party in the bookstore had been the plan all along.

190

Billy sipped his coffee, but asked no more questions.

Tess handed the third cup to Wade, who took a gulp before setting it on the register counter. "Let's haul Mrs. Phillips' window inside and get it installed, Son. I'm sure these ladies want to enjoy the rest of their Sunday."

On his way by, Wade paused near Gwen, "Liz tells me the plywood covering the broken window belongs to your friend Hal Jenkins. Let him know we'll leave it out back so he can pick it up. No sense in wasting a perfectly good piece of lumber."

Gwen balked at speaking with Hal, so she typed a short text on her cell phone: '*Liz's replacement window being installed. Your plywood placed out back for pick-up.*'

Within seconds, his answer dinged in: '*I'll pick it up next time I'm in town. Thanx.*'

Gwen didn't want to give Hal false hope of reconciling, so she resisted a confirming text and clicked out of her messaging app.

Following in Wade's footsteps, Billy also stopped near Gwen. "Sounds like you're tracking down the guy who attacked the cigar man. You be careful, Mrs. Andrews."

"Thank you, Billy. I'm always careful."

Chapter Thirty ... noontime, Sunday

Gwen stood at her French doors, staring at her back gardens.

Tess came up beside her. "What's got you so distracted?"

"I'm just thinking about this mess with Hal."

"Have you decided what you're going to do?"

Gwen's head moved ever so slightly. "I believed him when he promised Farley's cigars were no threat to us."

"Does he know about Uncle Gus?"

"Yes. I told him after dinner at his place on Thursday." Gwen gazed into Tess's face. "When he smoked the cigar yesterday, he made it clear he doesn't respect me."

"What did you say when you caught him?"

"Nothing. I ran for the car. I guess that makes me a coward."

Tess released a jittery laugh. "You've always avoided confrontations."

"You're right. Whenever I react without thinking, I always regret my words."

The sisters stood side by side until Tess spoke. "Why don't we take a walk in your woods?"

"Sure. I need to check for winter damage. Did you bring a pair of boots?"

"They're in my trunk. I'll go get them." Tess opened the French door and walked along the rear deck toward the driveway.

Gwen slipped her feet into her own boots, grabbed a pair of clippers, and made her way across the lower deck, meeting up with Tess at the potting shed. They skirted the large field boulder separating the backyard from the modest woods and stepped onto the winding path.

Tess tossed a small branch off to the side. "Would you like to hear my opinion about Hal?"

Gwen's left eyebrow lifted. "Go ahead."

"You need to talk to him and clear the air, so to speak."

Gwen snickered at her sister's cigar-smoke pun.

"Until you do," Tess persisted, "you won't have enough details to decide whether to move forward or call it quits."

Gwen pulled the clippers from her pocket and snipped at some shrubbery encroaching on the pathway. "That's sensible advice. I'll think about it."

Approaching Parker's first footbridge that spanned an active stream far below, Gwen motioned for Tess to halt, tested the strength of the replacement lumber hammered into place last fall, and pronounced it solid. Every so often, she thought about the previous September and the Henrietta incident. Gwen's reflection drifted, considering how her own life would end.

"Gwen? Gwen?" Tess called, snapping her fingers. "Where were you just now?"

"Oh, just pondering life and death."

Tess tossed a stick as they crossed to the other side of the footbridge. "What we need is a distraction. Do you have any eggs in your fridge?"

Gwen came to a full stop. "I think there are a few left."

"Are they white?"

"I don't recall which color I bought." And then Gwen grasped Tess's hand. "Easter eggs. Yes, that'll do it."

"Great. I know the holiday is still a week or so away, but I may be back home, and I won't bother coloring eggs just for me."

Gwen hesitated at her sister's implied departure. As they'd hunted down clues on Liz's behalf, talked about Hal, and made their way through each day, Gwen hadn't considered that Tess would return to the Berkshires one day.

When Tess drove off, Gwen would resume her private music

lessons with the local youngsters, but that would fill only a portion of her day. Her falling-out with Hal would leave a gaping hole in her evenings. No more meeting for dinner. If Gwen went to the movies, took nature walks, or attended productions at the local theater, she'd be going solo.

Shaking off these depressing speculations of impending solitude, Gwen walked beside Tess as they circled the woodland path, crossing back over the stream on Parker's second footbridge. When they re-entered the back gardens, Gwen touched Tess's arm. "So you're thinking of leaving?"

"Not immediately. But I can't lean on you forever, Sis. I need to get used to living in my home without Nathan, and I can't do that while I'm here in Harbor Falls."

***

Tess whipped open the fridge door and frowned. "You've only got three eggs, and they're brown. Do you know if the convenience store around the corner has white ones?"

"Probably not. We'll have a better chance at the regular grocery store. Do you want me to drive?"

"No need. You find a pot big enough to boil a dozen. Do you have food coloring?"

Gwen walked to the cabinet and pulled out four bottles of drops, holding them up for Tess's inspection.

"Okay. I'll be back in a few minutes with the white eggs."

When the front door closed behind Tess, someone knocked on the glass of the French door. When Gwen saw Hal's granddaughter Jenna grinning and waving, she threw the door wide open and wrapped her former flute student in a long-overdue hug.

Jenna backed away. "Wow, that's not the welcome I expected."

"Why would you expect anything less?"

The girl shuffled her feet. "Granddad took me to dinner and told me about the cigars and that you don't like the smoke."

Gwen's dislike went much deeper, but she wasn't about to burden Jenna with disturbing tales of Great Uncle Gus.

Motioning the girl into the music studio, Gwen settled into one of two tapestry wing chairs that flanked the double-sided fireplace. "Did your grandfather ask you to come and see me today?"

Jenna lowered herself and her backpack to the Steinway's piano bench. "He suggested it, but I've been meaning to stop over for quite a while anyway."

Gwen wasn't thrilled about Hal placing Jenna in the middle of their adult conflict. "Did he tell you he promised not to smoke the cigars Farley Cooper gave him?"

Jenna's blonde head bobbed. "And he's sorry."

"Good to hear. But he hasn't apologized to me."

"He said you're ignoring his phone calls. That's why he stopped over yesterday, but you made him leave."

"That's true."

"He's hoping I can convince you to hear his side of the story."

The bare bones truth was Gwen's best option. "I'm sorry, Jenna, but I'm not ready to have a sit-down with your grandfather. He hurt me deeply, and I need time to think about our future."

Jenna reached over and touched Gwen's sleeve. "Can I tell Granddad what you said?"

"Be my guest. But I'm making no promises." *Will Hal catch my underlying message?*

Jenna slid off the piano bench. "Sorry to leave so soon, but I have an essay due tomorrow."

Rising, Gwen again enfolded the girl with a heart-felt hug. "Your studies are more important than our grown-up difficulties."

Jenna glanced at the shelves tucked between the mullioned windows of the music studio. "Can I borrow a few of your books?"

"Of course. Take whichever ones you need."

As Jenna perused Gwen's collection, the front door opened and Tess yelled, "I'm back."

Jenna's head whipped around. "Is that your sister?"

As Tess entered the kitchen and placed her grocery bag on the island, Gwen called over, "Look who dropped by."

Glancing over to the music studio, Tess said, "Well, I'll be." Her arms wide, she closed the distance within seconds.

Jenna walked into Tess's embrace, her voice bubbly. "It's so great to see you again."

Tess had accompanied Jenna for last fall's music competition. Then the girl sobered. "Granddad told me about Nathan's passing. I'm so sorry. He was a sweet guy. I need your address so I can send a card."

"Thank you, Jenna, but you don't need to." Tess pushed back an errant strand of blonde hair. "Your condolence in person means more to me than Hallmark."

"How long will you be here?"

Tess lifted her shoulders. "Undetermined."

"Darn. I wish I could stay for a while, but I've got to get back to my room and work on a paper."

"You go on. Maybe Gwen and I can treat you to lunch or dinner before I go home. Let us know when you're available. Or hungry. Whichever comes first."

Jenna snickered. "You may be sorry you offered. The kitchen staff at the college cafeteria needs to take some cooking classes." From Gwen's collection, Jenna plucked three books and slid them into her backpack. "I'll call you." Jenna waved goodbye and was gone in a heartbeat.

"Such a sweet kid. If you decide to break it off with Hal, will you and Jenna remain friends?"

"I hope so, Tess."

The disturbing question settled in Gwen's mind.

Chapter Thirty-One ... late afternoon, Sunday

Minutes after Jenna left, the roar of a car engine worked its way indoors. "Sounds like Ben's sports car," Gwen commented as she strode to the front door and swung it open. Sure enough, the red Corvette braked to a stop at the curb.

Ben emerged and bounded up the front sidewalk, climbing the granite slab steps two at a time. "Hope you don't mind me coming around without an invite."

"Not at all." Now that he was no longer an official police detective, his arrival didn't worry Gwen in the least.

He thumbed toward his parked car. "That young lady who walked away as I was driving up gave me an odd look."

"She's Hal Jenkins' granddaughter." Gwen searched for Jenna, spotting the girl's lithe figure half-way around the village green, heading in the direction of Baylies College. "She was probably wondering why the owner of a Corvette would have any business with an old lady."

Ben chuckled. "*Old* is the last word I'd use to describe you."

"That's nice of you to say." Gwen's cheek warmed. "Any particular reason you're here?"

"Mike Brown reminded me that you're tenacious and obstinate."

Gwen smirked. "My husband would have told you I can be quite stubborn."

"Not necessarily a bad quality. After I left you, Tess, and Liz at the bookstore this morning, it occurred to me you might try to prove Liz's innocence on your own."

"Not quite on her own." Tess came up beside Gwen.

197

"Of course. Didn't mean to leave you out, Tess. I advise you against trying to track down Farley's attacker as private citizens."

"Don't you mean amateur sleuths?" Tess corrected.

"An accurate title in a mystery story, but it doesn't alter my advice to let the police handle this investigation. Despite your success last fall, Gwen, you're heading down a potentially dangerous path."

So, I misinterpreted his comment during our delayed lunch on Thursday. Based on his words just now, he hadn't intended to give her permission to snoop. Then again, at that point, he'd still been an official policeman. *Perhaps I can change Ben's mindset now that he's also a private citizen.*

She opened the door wide. "Let's discuss this inside. Tess and I are about to boil some eggs."

***

In the kitchen, Gwen half-filled a large pot with tap water and swished in baking soda. Tess arranged a dozen white eggs in a single layer on the bottom, placed a glass lid on top, then hoisted it to the stove.

Watching from his stool, Ben asked, "Why the baking soda?"

Gwen swiveled to look at him. "Makes the hard-boiled eggs easier to peel. How does your wife do it?"

"Don't have a wife. At least not any more. She got tired of my late hours when I was on a case and divorced me years ago."

Tess flattened the egg carton. "So you're a bachelor?"

"I guess that's the best term."

His lack of a wife explains his appreciation of my home-cooked breakfast the other morning. Gwen turned the burner on high, but didn't move away from the stove. "I disagree with your warning."

He waved her on. "I'm listening."

"If the detective who replaces you follows Chief Upton's orders, the investigation won't probe beyond Liz."

"Unfortunately, that's probably true."

"If Tess and I want to remove Liz from the suspect list, we have to find the guy who bashed-in Farley's head and hid the ashtray in her bookstore."

Ben's forehead wrinkled. "That doesn't alter my concern about private citizens chasing a criminal. If I was still a police detective, I'd consider locking you up for obstructing a police investigation. Since I'm not, I can't stop you from sticking your noses where they don't belong." He rubbed his temples. "Have you at least taken self-defense courses?"

Gwen squared her shoulders. "First of all, we aren't obstructing the investigation. Second, our noses belong wherever they need to be to protect a dear friend. And, to answer your question, I took the series offered by the Harbor Falls police about four years ago."

She and Parker had also taken a fire-fighting course, though she'd never had any reason to use her kitchen extinguisher.

Ben smiled at Gwen's defiant tone. "And you, Tess?"

"Nathan and I signed up for self-defense classes, but we'd only attended one." Tess's voice faded.

Gwen mentally completed the remainder of her sister's unspoken answer. Nathan had died before they took the second class. Her admiration for Tess's strength and control deepened.

Ben's gaze stayed on Tess a moment longer. "One class is better than none."

He switched back to Gwen. "If you insist on pursuing this, at least you're somewhat prepared to defend yourselves." Ben ran his finger along the smooth granite. "I wish I hadn't lost my temper with the chief and retired before solving this case." He sat up straight, a light coming into his eyes. "I have a suggestion."

Tess twirled the empty egg carton. "What is it?"

"How about I work alongside the two of you? I can't do anything on an official level, but I can put my investigative skills to good use and watch your backs at the same time."

Gwen stared at him. "And catching the culprit will satisfy your need to solve the case and prove to Chief Upton your instincts about Liz were valid."

"Exactly." Ben reached into his pocket for his new notebook, flipped to a new page and noted the date of their partnership.

"I can't speak for my sister, Ben, but I welcome your expertise, official or otherwise." Gwen lifted one eyebrow at Tess. "What do you think?"

"Can't hurt."

Gwen considered their new partnership. "I was planning to stay in touch with Detective Brown, assuming he's been assigned to Farley's case."

"Mike didn't confirm it, but I suspect he will be."

"If he is, will he tell you what he's thinking and doing?"

Ben eyed each sister. "Hard to predict. Mike might not share anything if the chief's hovering over his shoulder."

Gwen peeked through the glass pot lid to see bubbles forming. "Did Mike give you the impression he disagrees with Chief Upton about Liz attacking Farley?"

"Not in so many words, but Mike's a good man. He'll go where the evidence takes him, and I firmly believe it will not lead to Liz."

Tess continued to play with the carton. "So it's up to us to pass along the name of anyone we suspect might have been involved?"

"That's what it boils down to."

Grinning at Ben's timing and unintended pun, Gwen heard the eggs bounce. She slid the pot off the burner and set the timer for twenty minutes. "At the bookstore, you mentioned Farley's sister, Kate Wakefield."

"That's right. But I quit before I had a chance to find her."

Gwen hesitated for only a second. Now that the three of them had formed a task force, Ben should know everything the sisters had found out. "Tess and I met Kate at lunch yesterday."

200

His jaw dropped. "How'd you manage that?"

Gwen and Tess spoke in alternate spurts, summarizing all they'd learned about Jeremy Wakefield, especially his claim that his Uncle Farley had abused him.

Ben's facial muscles twitched. "Mike Brown's right about you, Gwen. You have a knack for finding relevant details."

"Oh, I don't know about that. It's more like details find me."

"Maybe, but you made the effort to track down a stranger. Most people wouldn't bother."

A second blush worked its way up Gwen's neck. "It was Tess's suggestion. She watched an old movie the other night."

"Doesn't matter where the idea came from. Sounds like your Jeremy had a valid motive to attack his uncle. I'll pass him along to Mike." Ben flipped to a new page and scribbled Jeremy's name.

Gwen hissed-in a breath. "I don't want my friend Rachel to know I was checking up on her cousin."

"I won't tell Mike where I got the name, just Jeremy's connection to Farley Cooper."

Gwen knew she had no choice but to trust Ben to protect her friendship with Rachel. She had let the proverbial cat out of the bag. *What's the old saying? You can't un-ring a bell?*

"Will you get into trouble for protecting your sources?" Tess slid her hand along the granite. "You're not a private eye until you have the license in your pocket."

"I don't think it'll cause me any problems, but I'll be careful. If Mike doesn't ask who suggested Jeremy, I won't have to refuse."

Ben stopped writing, his pen poised. "I have to say, you've made some interesting inquiries in a short amount of time. If you have any other ideas, I can do some of the legwork."

Gwen appreciated his offer and thought it very likely that Ben could be lonely. Without a wife, he had no one to share the daily tasks of living. Without a job, he had nothing to keep his brain active and his body moving.

She finally decided that it didn't matter. With Ben's help, the odds of finding Farley's attacker could only improve.

Chapter Thirty-Two ... mid-afternoon, Sunday

Gwen retrieved her legal pad and flipped a few pages. "We've got two more suspects, plus a theory."

Ben eyed her notes. "You should get a P.I. license, Gwen." His boyish grin reminded her of the much-younger police officer who'd offered her a hand up from the ditch after her bike-riding spill all those years ago.

Gwen waved him off. "No, no. Not for me. I'm enjoying retirement. I don't want anyone making demands of my time."

He tipped his head to acknowledge her attitude. "So tell me about those two suspects and the theory you've developed."

"Actually, the theory comes first, and it isn't mine. Tess and I had brunch this morning with Penelope and Beatrice. We were scouting for anything relevant about Farley Cooper."

"Isn't Penelope the lady who used to own the store next to Liz's?"

"The same, plus her best friend Beatrice. We assumed they'd be more talkative if they had each other for support."

"Did either of them say anything useful?"

Gwen nodded as she ran her finger down the page. "For one thing, Beatrice thinks Farley's cigars might have been tainted with some kind of drug that altered her husband's personality."

"Hmmm." Ben stroked his clean-shaven chin. "That's the first I've heard that one."

"Beatrice could be all wrong," Gwen conceded, "but Tess and I figured it was worth a mention. If it's true, it might explain the chief's recent testiness." Gwen balked at bringing Hal into this conversation.

Ben raised an eyebrow. "Anything else of interest?"

"This next bit may have nothing to do with Farley's attack, but I asked Penelope why her son Billy is listed with the last name Danforth, since her surname is Grainger. She explained Billy came to live with them after his parents were killed in a summer boating accident fifteen years ago. Because he was eighteen at the time, they never officially adopted him."

"I remember that accident." Ben tapped his pen on the notebook page. "That spring, the Danforths had spearheaded a fundraising event to erect a memorial at the police station for fallen officers. After the two of them were killed, we passed a hat for Billy, but I lost track of him. He never got into any trouble."

"Well, Billy seems to be doing okay," Gwen offered. "He joined Wade's window and door business. In fact, they're the ones who installed the bookstore replacement window just this morning. Tess and I stuck around to watch."

"Okay, you told me about Bea's drug theory and Billy's history. Who are the two suspects?"

"The bartender, although Tess and I don't think he would have bludgeoned Farley and put himself out of a job. His name is Lance Lynch."

"Don't tell me. You had a conversation with the man."

"We bumped into him on the porch of The Wharf after brunch this morning."

"You two are something else with all you're managing to dig up without a shovel." Shaking his head, Ben added Lance's name to his notebook. "I'm registered on websites to run background checks. I'll see what comes up on my home computer. And the other one?"

"Actually, there are two more possibilities, but I don't know either name. One's the man who fabricated the mahogany bar. Farley's deposit check bounced. The other's the construction foreman that Farley pushed to finish the job ahead of schedule, also stiffed on the deposit."

The twenty minute timer went off. Gwen lifted the pot into the sink, drained the hot water, and covered the eggs with cold water.

Ben scribbled more notes before glancing at his watch. "Unless you have some additional ideas, I'll head back to my apartment and log onto the internet. I'll let you know if anything pops up." He got to his feet, tucking his notebook and pen into his jeans pocket. I'll call Liz to arrange another look at her connecting door."

"Why?" The sisters asked in unison.

"When she showed us that door, I didn't check for scratch marks. I put a note in the case file to have the lab tech come back and lift fingerprints, swab for DNA, and take photographs. I have no idea if Peter Quinn made it back there yet, but I want to take a closer look." Ben winked at Gwen. "See ya."

Both Gwen and Tess walked him to the front door and waved goodbye. The Corvette engine roared to life, the noise disappearing as Ben circled the village green.

***

"This is the prettiest one yet," Tess pronounced. She lifted a multi-striped egg from the dye bath with a wire loop and eased it onto the upside-down egg carton to dry.

Gwen tilted her head to view the collection. "Oh, I don't know. I think they're all gorgeous."

"Did I see Ben wink at you as he was leaving?" Tess teased.

Gwen gave Tess a questioning look. "Wink at me? If he did, it was involuntary."

"Oh, I don't know, Sis. I think his attentions go much deeper than solving this case."

"You're daydreaming, Tess. Are you reading romance novels now?"

Tess snickered. "Not yet. I wouldn't be surprised if Ben shows up here every day though."

"Well, of course, he will. Especially if he has anything to share." Gwen shoved Tess in a playful manner as her glance traveled over the colored eggs. "I just love these hues. Yellow, pink, purple, blue, green. They're all so cheerful."

"Should we pretend we're kids again and hide them in your gardens? Pretend it's Easter?"

"Why not?" Gwen agreed. "No sense in going to all this trouble if we don't look for them where the Easter Bunny might have hidden them. We should take a few to Liz before she locks up for the day."

"Good idea. They'll give her a much-needed chuckle."

"You know, Tess, I've been thinking about Farley snatching the savings out from under Violet. That's probably the capital he used to buy Penelope's space plus the old video store on her other side."

"We should ask Liz if she was approached by a real estate agent."

"Good question. If she was, I'd bet the agent was working on Farley's behalf. If he had his sights set on owning the entire building, he wouldn't care if his smoke was oozing into her bookstore. When the aggravation forced her to give up and close her doors permanently, he could snatch up her third and own the whole thing."

"Do you think Farley was that shrewd," Tess asked.

Gwen lifted one shoulder. "I only met him one time, but I'd say he was a man who liked to play games. Now we have two reasons for paying Liz a visit."

Chapter Thirty-Three ... late afternoon, Sunday

Gwen and Tess once again walked through the village green and down Harbor Hill. As they passed Farley's closed-up shop, Gwen pointed. "Look, Tess."

On the corner of the unbroken right-side window, a small label credited the construction company for the conversion into Farley's Cigar Bar and Smoking Lounge.

From her shoulder bag, Gwen pulled her legal pad and jotted the name, address, and phone number.

"Planning some renovations?"

"No, no. This is for Ben. Just in case he wasn't able to identify the company on the internet." Gwen finished her note-taking and tucked the legal pad away.

"How soon do you think he'll get back to us?"

"No specific day or time. I guess he'll ring my doorbell after he finds something relevant."

Continuing along the sidewalk, the sisters entered Fiction 'n Fables Bookstop. The fan previously sitting inside the door was nowhere in sight. The smoke-eating candles were nearly burned down to the wick tabs. The air smelled fresh with no lingering cigar odor.

At one of the de-smoking barrels, a woman leaned half-way inside, her upper body lost to view, identification impossible. A few seconds later, Liz emerged and caught sight of the sisters. Her hand flew to her heart. "I didn't hear you come in. What are you two doing inside on such a beautiful day?"

Tess held out the pink and green wicker basket they'd chosen from Gwen's stash. "We come bearing gifts."

"What's this?" Liz lifted the striped towel shielding the contents. "Oh, my. Easter eggs. When did you color these?"

Gwen peeked in to admire the hues. "After Ben left."

"Ben was at your house again?"

Gwen smiled. "He stopped by to warn Tess and me against searching for Farley's attacker on our own. Then he decided we'd be safer if he joined us."

"He did? That can't be a bad thing."

Tess laid a conspiratorial hand on Liz's sleeve. "If you ask me, he's more interested in my sister. Chasing this case gives him a good excuse to hang around."

Liz lifted one eyebrow. "Hmmm. An interesting theory. Guess we won't know the good detective's real intentions until the three of you prove me innocent."

Gwen play-smacked Tess's shoulder. "Don't listen to her, Liz. Ben is right. We'll have a better chance of identifying Farley's attacker if we work together. And he wants to prove that his instincts were on-target about your innocence."

"Prove to Chief Upton, you mean?"

Gwen nodded. "Exactly."

"Whatever Ben's reason, I'm glad he's back on our team." Liz held up the basket. "I need to put these eggs in my mini-fridge. I'm already drooling about an egg salad sandwich."

When Liz rejoined them, Tess introduced a new topic. "Were you been approached to sell your third of this building?"

Liz's eyes widened. "How did you know?"

"Gwen and I were theorizing earlier. What did you say to the real estate agent?"

"Told the pushy woman no way. I don't know why I even kept her card. This bookstore is my life. Has been for decades. And I won't let anyone force me to sell. What's your theory?"

Gwen stood quietly, letting Tess handle the conversation. "That Farley wanted to own the entire building."

"Makes sense. And that sure would explain why he refused to split the cost of a filtering system." Liz wilted. "If his relatives re-open the cigar bar, the smoke issue will begin all over again."

Tess craned her neck toward the aisles of books. "Making any headway with the de-smoking barrels?"

"Moving at a fast enough pace that I'm re-opening on Tuesday." Liz held up two thumbs.

Gwen gave her a high five. "That terrific news!"

"I've already registered an announcement in the Wicked Local online newspaper for Harbor Falls and the surrounding towns. I've printed posters plus ordered a banner and balloons. They should be here first thing tomorrow morning. And, finally, I sent a blast email to customers who've been avoiding my store since the cigar bar opened."

"You've been busy. Before Tess and I leave, give us a handful of your flyers. We'll find places to tack them."

"Thanks." Liz sobered. "You know, in the spirit of searching for Farley's attacker, I've been thinking about Aldrich Jones and how quickly he ran out of here when I mentioned Farley's quick trip through the licensing offices."

"Why do you think the permits matter?" Gwen asked.

"Think about it. What if Aldrich helped Farley grease a palm or two at town hall and was worried he'd be found out?"

"You think Aldrich attacked Farley?"

"Oh, I don't know." Liz threw her hands up. "I guess I'm grasping at straws."

Gwen crossed her arms, her mind reeling. "Who did you speak to last week at the Downtown Association office to have Aldrich stop by here on his way back from lunch?"

"Joanie, the secretary."

"I'd bet Joanie knows everything that happens in the Association office, including whether Aldrich applied any pressure to the town officials on Farley's behalf."

"Why don't we invite her to lunch?" Tess suggested.

Gwen made a face. "That might throw up a red flag."

Liz brightened, "Joanie hasn't come in to buy books for quite a while, so I'm not sure she was included in my email blast. Let's invite her to my re-opening. I'm serving snacks and wine. That'll loosen her tongue so you can wheedle info from her."

On a fresh sheet of Gwen's legal pad, she wrote Joanie's name. "How about Tess and I visit the association office tomorrow and extend your invitation in person? Where are your flyers? We can give one to Joanie, and tack another one on their bulletin board."

"They're in my office."

The sisters followed Liz and grabbed a handful of flyers. Gwen slid them between the pages of her legal pad for safe keeping.

From the top of her file cabinet, Liz lifted the wicker basket and held it out to Tess. "Thanks again for the colored eggs. They made me smile."

Tess grasped the handle. "If you need me, I can stay and switch out more books. I've become quite adept."

Liz laughed. "You sure have. I can't tell you how much I appreciate your help."

"Then it's settled. I guess I'll see you later, Gwen."

Gwen reached over and took possession of the basket, waved her hand in the air, and headed for the door.

Chapter Thirty-Four ... late afternoon, Sunday

Swinging the wicker basket as she walked, Gwen trekked up
Harbor Hill until the rumble of an engine came near.

When Ben's red Corvette stopped at the curb, he rolled down
the passenger window. "You sure do a lot of walking, Gwen."

She peered inside. "I like to walk. Besides, it's a cheap form of
exercise and easier than trying to find a parking spot. Were you
down at the harbor?"

"Yep. Fishing for spring flounder off the pier, but I didn't get a
single bite."

Gwen grinned. "Apparently the fish in these parts are smart.
Do you eat the ones you catch?"

Ben shrugged and shook his head at the same time. "Never.
I'm strictly a catch and release kind of guy. Besides, cooking fish
stinks up my apartment for three days. Want a lift home?"

She'd always wanted to ride in a sports car, but had never
known anybody who owned one until now. She couldn't deny the
thrill of anticipation. "Best offer I've had all day, Ben."

After observing Gwen's attempts to maneuver into the low-
slung passenger seat, Ben chuckled. "Sit down backwards, then
swing your legs inside."

Following his instruction, she slid into the seat like an old pro.
"This car is not far off the ground."

"You're right. I've gotten used to it, but my passengers usually
have trouble the first time."

How many of those passengers were women? Gwen mentally
slapped herself. None of her business who Ben had spent time with
since his divorce. Securely inside, she placed the wicker basket at

211

her feet before glancing his way. "This is my first time in a Corvette."

Ben gave her a friendly smirk. "I kinda guessed." He braked at the North Street traffic light. "Would you like to take a spin before I drop you off?"

A devil-may-care feeling came over Gwen. "Sure. Why not?"

"Then fasten your seatbelt. I know a perfect destination. It's not far."

Leaving the town limits, Ben guided the Corvette onto a side road, steering through the curves with the confidence of a racecar driver.

Surprised at the barely discernible swaying as the Corvette moved smoothly around corners, she glanced at Ben's profile. "Want to tell me where we're going or keep it a mystery?"

"Have you visited the Myles Standish State Reservation?"

"The one in Plymouth?"

"No, that's the state forest. The names confuse a lot of people. There's a monument at the South Duxbury park. It's usually open on Sunday. The view from the top is magnificent."

Duxbury? Whenever Gwen and Parker had found themselves near this part of the coastline, they'd usually strolled across Powder Point Bridge and wandered Duxbury Beach. In fact, that was the backdrop of Parker's photo on her foyer table.

But South Duxbury was a section Gwen didn't know at all, so this drive with Ben would provide a modicum of local education.

When a black Corvette passed from the other direction, Ben lifted his fingers from the wheel.

"Do you know him from a car club or something?"

Ben laughed. "No. Corvette owners acknowledge each other as a sign of brotherhood."

They zoomed along the country roads in companionable silence for another ten minutes. Ben angled the car into a lane at the bottom of a forested hill. He struck the steering wheel with his palm, pointing to a barrier slung between two stone pillars across the roadway ahead. "Damn. I forgot they don't open on Sundays until summer. Sorry, Gwen."

"Can we walk to the monument?"

"It's a steep climb. Are you up for it?"

"Well, we're here. It would be a shame to waste the chance to explore."

Before Gwen could untangle her feet from the wicker basket, Ben had hopped out and come around to her side. He opened the door and extended his hand. Reversing his original instruction, she swung both feet to the ground before attempting to stand up. "Thank you, Ben."

"My pleasure."

The hike up the entrance road wasn't overly exhausting, but Gwen needed to catch her breath by the time they reached the upper section. Continuing through the parking lot of a dozen or so spaces, she paused at the steps leading up to the monument base, debating whether to make the extra effort.

Ben came up beside her. "With the park closed, the tower's locked as well, so we can't climb to the viewing area." He waved at the top of the tower. "I *can* tell you that Myles Standish is pointing toward Provincetown. From up there, you can see Duxbury Beach and Plymouth Harbor to the south."

With the sun behind her, Gwen didn't have to shade her eyes. Behind the statue, the blue sky was streaked with white clouds. "We might as well go as far as we can."

Without waiting for Ben's agreement, Gwen started up the first smooth incline then ascended twenty steps to the next one until she stood before the monument door. No doorknobs, only a pair of locks greeted her. Leaning her head back to check the lentil stones, she spotted the initials of the six New England states. Ben pointed a third of the way up the tower. "On seven of the eight sides, the fourteen Massachusetts counties are spelled out." He led her halfway around the base of the monument, reading the county names out loud.

On the backside of the monument, Gwen pointed to a group of upright pillars at the end of a grassy knoll. "What are those?"

"I don't know. Let's walk down there and have a look."

Ben followed her until they reached what appeared to be an arbor. Rusty bolts stood atop each concrete pillar, an indication that a roof of sorts may have once been attached. There were no signs to explain the purpose of the structure.

"Well, that's disappointing," she said.

They retraced their steps to the rear of the monument and finished reading the other half of the county names as they circled to the front.

"Ready to go, Gwen?"

"I guess so. We've done and seen all we can do and see."

The return walk down the curving lane to the Corvette was not as strenuous.

Ben opened the door and helped Gwen into the passenger seat.

As she swung her legs inside, Ben said, "I plan a return visit in the summer when the tower's unlocked. Maybe you can come with me. I'd hate you to miss the view."

Gwen stiffened. *Is Tess right about Ben? Is he seeking more than friendship?* From Gwen's perspective, he hadn't made any romantic overtures – verbally or physically. This ride in his Corvette had seemed harmless enough. He's simply looking for a buddy to share adventures… isn't he? Gwen purposely kept her answer light and non-committal. "Let me know. If I'm not busy, I might come with you."

When Ben only nodded, Gwen relaxed. As they whizzed along the backroads toward Harbor Falls, she brought up the Farley Cooper case. "Any luck with your background checks?"

"Some. I'll show you what I found when we get back to your house. My files are in the back."

When Ben pressed the gas pedal, the power surge forced Gwen against the cushioned seat.

***

Sitting at the kitchen island, Gwen closed the folder containing Lance Lynch's internet history. "The man has certainly led an interesting life, but I see nothing here that makes me think he would have attacked Farley."

"That was my impression. His criminal record is sparse, and most of those incidents occurred when he was in his late teens and twenties. I'm chalking them up to raging testosterone, not an indication of adult belligerence."

Gwen tapped the folder. "Don't customers pour out their souls while he's pouring them a drink?"

"That's the rumor. I think Lance is worth a personal interview. He might know if Farley provoked any of his customers."

Gwen pushed the folder across the granite countertop. "What reason will you give to talk to him?"

"Haven't decided yet. I'll come up with something believable."

"Wait a minute." Gwen's timbre increased a few notches. "Lance mentioned the other man who worked in the cigar bar." She tapped her lip trying to remember the name. "Quincy. His name is Quincy. He was a combination purchasing agent and shelf stocker. Lance didn't mention the last name, but he said Farley yelled at Quincy all the time."

"Locating this Quincy is a perfect excuse to talk to Lance."

Ben jotted down Quincy's name before pushing another folder toward Gwen. "Here's what little information I could find about the mahogany bar craftsman. He's from New Hampshire, and has taken several of his customers to court for non-payment, but there's no record of violence."

She flipped open the file and browsed the scant two pages. "Doesn't sound like he would have driven all the way down to

215

Harbor Falls to bludgeon Farley."

"I think you're right. Besides, he'd never get his money unless Farley was alive to earn it, so what would be the point?"

Gwen nodded her agreement and accepted Ben's third file. "And this is for…"

"The construction company," Ben filled in the blank.

Gwen reached into her shoulder bag, removed her legal pad, flipped several pages, and pointed at the same name and number.

Ben gave her a wide-eyed look. "How'd you find this?"

"There's a small sticker on the right window of the cigar bar. I planned to mention it next time I saw you. You beat me to it."

"And that, my dear lady, is what makes me the professional." Ben tossed her a half-grin.

Gwen didn't acknowledge his subtle flirtation. Instead, she moved to the safe haven of another suspect. "Did you research Jeremy Wakefield, or are you leaving him for Mike Brown to investigate?"

"Haven't had any success there." Ben opened a fourth folder, revealing a single sheet printout with little more than Jeremy's name in the search bar. "His juvenile record is sealed. No criminal history that I could find. Mike will have a better chance at uncovering Jeremy's background."

Ben tucked the four folders into an accordion file. "That's all I've got for now. Can I take you to dinner?"

Again, Gwen debated if Tess was right about Ben. Was he trying to start a romance or simply hungry and didn't want to eat all by himself?

She answered without questioning his reason. "Thanks for the invite, Ben, but I've got to rustle up some supper. Tess'll be back from Liz's bookstore any minute. You're welcome to join us."

"I have a better idea. Instead of you cooking, how about I go to the butcher shop around the corner and buy three steaks? We can barbeque them on your grill."

"I haven't used my grill for ages. I'm not sure how much propane is left in the tank. Although I think there's a backup in the shed. Don't you think it's a bit chilly to cook outside?"

"Not at all. I grill at least once a week on my balcony."

"In that case, while you go out and buy the steaks, I'll throw together a salad."

Within a quarter of an hour, Ben walked through the door with a packet wrapped in brown butcher paper.

Gwen seasoned the steaks with garlic salt while he carried the extra propane tank from the shed to the upper deck.

He cleaned the grill with a wire brush and oiled the surfaces. After a few tries, he succeeded in lighting the flames and slapped the three steaks on the cooking grid.

A man's voice called out, "Well, isn't this cozy?"

Gwen whirled to see Hal climbing the deck steps.

Chapter Thiry-Five ... early evening, Sunday

"What are you doing here, Hal?" Gwen was positive she'd said nothing to Jenna that he could misconstrue as an invitation.

He pushed past Gwen. "Didn't take you long, did it, buddy? Snowcrest, isn't it?" Hal's speech was somewhat slurred.

"I don't know what you're implying, Mr. Jenkins."

"Oh, don't play dumb with me. I caught you Thursday having lunch with Gwen, and here you are grilling steaks on Sunday night. You move mighty fast."

Gwen tugged Hal to face her, only then smelling the scotch on his breath. She didn't want to rile him any further, so spoke in a soothing voice. "You need to calm down. Ben and I have been discussing the Farley Cooper case. He offered to provide supper for me and Tess. There's nothing more to his being here."

A haze of acrid smoke blew in their direction. Gwen whirled to see the steaks smoldering on the grill, flames shooting up from the metal tubes below the grate. As Ben flipped the knobs to cut off the propane supply, Gwen rushed into the kitchen, returning with her fire extinguisher.

Standing a few feet from the grill, she removed the pin, pressed the trigger, and shot the stream of powder toward the flames. The fire flared and died in a cloud of white smoke.

When Hal rushed toward Gwen, she aimed the nozzle at him. "Don't come any closer."

His hands flew into the air. "All right, all right, I'm leaving."

"Mr. Jenkins, you're in no condition to drive. Let me take you home."

"Get away from me, you scoundrel. I'm perfectly fine." Hal gripped the railing as he moved slowly along the deck. Before he descended the steps to the driveway, Hal slurred over his shoulder. "Call me when you're finished fooling around, Gwen. And I'm not sorry your dinner is ruined."

She cringed, risking a glance at Ben. "I'm so sorry."

"An impressive show of control."

"Defusing Hal's anger or handling the fire extinguisher?"

"Both, I guess. I'm afraid grilling a perfect steak will have to wait for another day."

Waving off his unnecessary apology, Gwen moved toward the French door. "I'll check what I've got in the freezer. Tess will be starving, so we need to get moving."

Finding a batch of frozen meatballs and sauce, Gwen proceeded to defrost and reheat.

Ben filled a deep pot with water, then added olive oil and placed it on the stove. "Where's the pasta?"

"In the cabinet above your head. Can I get you a drink? I have water and wine."

He pretended a debate. "Wine, thanks."

Stemware in hand, the two of them stood silently side by side at the stove. While it's difficult to burn water, Gwen wanted to ensure nothing else went wrong with their dinner.

The front door slammed and Tess whirled into the kitchen. "Hey, what's going on here? You hire a chef, Gwen?"

Ben answered. "Not a chef. A guy who burned the steaks."

"What steaks?"

"The ones I was grilling for your dinner."

"Sounds delicious. Where are they? I could go for a juicy steak right about now."

Gwen lifted three oversized bowls from the cabinet. "Hal made a surprise appearance and we ignored the steaks sizzling on the grill so we moved to Plan B."

Without commenting, Ben dumped the angel hair pasta into a strainer at the sink.

"Oh." Tess elongated the letters. "Up in smoke, eh?"

"You could say that," Gwen smirked as she retrieved a chunk of parmesan from the fridge, plus a grater from the drawer, and handed both to Tess. "And, where there's smoke, there's trouble. Right now, let's eat. I'm famished."

***

A half hour later, Gwen laid a fire and knelt to strike a match to the waded newspaper, not retreating until the kindling caught. A comforting heat radiated into the living room, chasing away the chill of the April evening.

Ben sat in Parker's old recliner, observing her movements.

Tess was busy in the kitchen.

Gwen was reminded of the blaze in Hal's fireplace on Thursday night when he'd kissed her with such passion. If only he hadn't smoked that damn cigar with Oscar on Saturday, Hal would be here tonight instead of Ben.

When Tess carried in three mugs, Gwen closed the grate and stood up. "Ben, why don't you show Tess the results of your internet research?"

Ben set his hot chocolate on a table. "Sure. I'll get my files."

***

Tess closed the fourth folder. "It sounds like none of those leads panned out."

"I'll have a chat with the bartender," Ben advised, "but I don't expect much to come of it."

Gwen scooted back on her leather couch until her back touched the buttery-soft cushions, her mug balanced in one hand. "Liz reminded us about Farley's quick trip through the town bureaucracy. Tess and I are planning to visit the Downtown Association tomorrow. We'll invite the secretary Joanie to Liz's re-opening on Tuesday."

Ben sat up straight. "When did she decide to re-open?"

Tess answered him. "This afternoon when she realized how close she is to de-smoking the last of her books. That's what I was doing this afternoon."

Nodding his approval, Ben toyed with a shoelace. "Let's get back to this Joanie. What are you expecting to learn?"

Gwen shifted on the couch. "For one thing, if Aldrich helped Farley bribe town officials. The fire chief, the building inspector, the board of health. Anyone who issues permits."

"And you're thinking if any of them took a bribe from Farley, he or she might be worried Farley would brag about it and cause a scandal."

"Not only that," Tess added, "but a scandal might force the official to resign. Getting rid of Farley would keep any secret arrangement under wraps."

Ben flipped to a page in his notebook. "The more I listen to your analysis, the more possible that sounds."

"Do you know any of those officials, Ben?"

Gwen sat in silence to give Ben a chance to answer.

"I do. How about this? Tomorrow, I'll visit each of them. Tell them I've retired. Let them tease me that I must be bored. I'll say my only regret is not solving the Farley Cooper case. Their body language will tell me if they're hiding anything."

Ben expanded his strategy. "I don't know if Mike has thought to go in this direction. I'm meeting him Tuesday afternoon for a beer. If we learn anything relevant between now and then, I'll pass it along."

Gwen downed the last of her hot chocolate. "I'm glad you and Mike are still on speaking terms."

"You and me both." Ben got to his feet. "Listen, I should go. Thanks for dinner. I owe you both a grilled steak. Let me know what you learn from Joanie tomorrow. I'll do the same about the town officials. I'll let myself out. Night."

Chapter Thirty-Six ... early morning, Monday

"May I speak to Shirley Knapp, please?"

"Please hold."

Five seconds later. "This is Shirley."

"Shirley, hi. This is Gwen Andrews. Do you have a minute?"

"For you, Gwen, I'll make time. I've almost finished my article about the séance. It'll be in this week's edition. And don't worry: I didn't include your address."

"Thanks for that." Gwen hadn't considered the possibility of being hounded by curiosity seekers. "Actually, I'm calling about the séance. Madame Eudora explained that the *Harbor Falls Gazette* owns Annabelle's video and photographs."

"That's true. We provided media services in exchange for permission to write an article about a private event."

"Is there any way I can get copies?"

"Copies, no. But I'll let you view them. Listen, I hate to cut you off, but I'm heading out on another assignment. I'll be back after lunch. Why don't you stop by the paper around two?"

After Gwen disconnected, Tess rested her chin in her palms. "Well, what did Shirley say? I only heard your side of the conversation. Did she see Parker?"

"She didn't say. She can't give us copies, but she said to stop by the office around two and she'll let us view everything."

Tess stood up and stretched. "After we drop in on Joanie?"

"Exactly."

***

As the hour hand approached twelve, Gwen opened the door to the Downtown Association office and waved Tess inside.

A youthful woman looked up from her computer keyboard. "Can I help you?"

Gwen moved toward her. "Are you Joanie?"

"Yes." Joanie stared at the sisters. "I'm sorry, but I don't recognize you."

Gwen smiled. "That's okay. We've never met. My name is Gwen Andrews, and this is my sister Tess Walker."

Joanie extended her hand across the desk. "Nice to meet you. Are you planning to open a business in Harbor Falls?"

"Oh, no. I retired a few years ago. I'm...," Gwen glanced at Tess, "...*we're* good friends of Liz Phillips at Fiction 'n Fables near the harbor."

Joanie's chubby face fell. "I hate to admit it, but after the cigar bar opened next door, I stopped going into that shop. And it's always been one of my favorite places to browse. The cigar smell was just too awful. Our president Aldrich Jones felt awful that he couldn't help. He was so upset after meeting with Mrs. Phillips that he closed himself in his office and made phone calls most of the afternoon. I'm sure he was trying to find a solution."

Or had he been notifying his cronies that Farley was causing problems? Encouraged by Joanie's eager attitude, Gwen stayed on topic. "Dealing with that smoke has been a challenge for Liz, but it's under control now that the cigar bar is closed."

"Such a shame about Mr. Cooper. There he was, moving into a new town, starting up a new business, and a few weeks later, BAM!, someone conks him on the head. Not that I cared for the man all that much. Still..." Joanie's voice trailed off.

Gwen grasped the opening. "So you met Farley Cooper?"

"Several times."

Before Gwen had a chance to ask a follow-up question, the outer door opened and Aldrich strolled in. Because he was reading a pamphlet, he didn't notice Gwen until he nearly bumped into her. "Oh, I didn't see you there, Mrs. Andrews."

223

Is that fear in his eyes? Or am I overanxious to blame someone – anyone other than Liz – for Farley's attack? She pushed her imaginings aside. "We're here to extend an invitation."

"We?" Aldrich's eyes darted to her left and right.

Gwen waved Tess forward. "I don't believe you've met my sister, Tess Walker."

Aldrich pasted on a half-smile and nodded in Tess's direction. Joanie's bubbly voice interrupted the introductions. "What's the invitation?"

"Liz is re-opening her bookstore tomorrow, and would love you both to be there. She asked us to invite you personally."

"Oh, that's great news. I just knew she'd find a way to bounce back."

Tess handed flyers to both Joanie and Aldrich. "I've been helping Liz de-smoke her books. She'll be serving wine and appetizers."

Not wanting to ask Joanie too many questions in front of Aldrich, Gwen shifted her shoulder bag to the other side. "Can we tell Liz you're coming?"

Joanie's grin widened. "I never refuse free food and wine."

Gwen felt a surge of hope. After a few glasses tomorrow, who knew what Joanie might divulge? She turned to Aldrich. "How about you? Can you join us for Liz's celebration?"

Shaking his head, he grasped the knob of his office door. "Afraid not. I've got a lot to do tomorrow." He disappeared inside.

After another minute of social chitchat with Joanie, Gwen and Tess headed for the car.

Tess belted herself into the passenger seat. "If Aldrich helped Farley jump the line for licenses and permits, I'm not sure Joanie's aware of it. But she might have access to his phone records."

"Good point, Tess."

***

The sisters stepped into the newspaper's reception area scant seconds before two o'clock. Except for a fresh bouquet of daffodils poised on the seating area table, it looked the same as it had a few days ago when they'd retrieved copies of Annabelle's fire photos. Gwen strolled up to the sliding glass window and asked if Shirley was on the premises.

"Are you Gwen Andrews?"

"I am."

The receptionist beamed. "Shirley left instructions to send you into the newsroom the moment you arrived. Please go through those double doors. I'll let her know you're here."

An intercom announced, "Shirley, your visitors are on their way in."

Pausing to allow her sister to catch up, Gwen entered the inner sanctum with Tess by her side. Printing presses heaved in the background. Reporters and editors scurried from one area to another, yelling to each other and waving proof sheets.

Shirley gestured from the other side of the cavernous newsroom and headed toward them. "Good to see you both again. Follow me. I've set up the video in our conference room so you'll have some privacy." Shirley didn't offer her opinion of the content.

After settling Gwen and Tess into comfortable chairs, and switching on the machine, Shirley left them to view the séance recording from beginning to end.

First, Madame Eudora's opening rituals with the burning herbs, the lighting of the candles, and the blessing for the attendees.

For quite a while, the medium described spirits on the other side that none of the women recognized.

The first connection was with the woman on Gwen's left, speaking back and forth to her sister, using Madame Eudora's voice, but no manifestation.

More souls without resolution.

225

Then the lady who cried about her grandchild in the arms of her deceased husband. Again, there had been no materialization, only Madame Eudora's voice to help them communicate. Finally, Gwen's segment with Parker came into view. The flickering candle light plus the lingering pale smoke from the burning sage and sweet grass created hazy images of Parker's essence as he strolled toward Gwen.

She was disappointed the video hadn't captured his spirit more clearly. She'd looked into his eyes. He'd winked at her. *I couldn't have possibly imagined our connection. Could I?*

The video recorded Gwen tilting her head sideways and laughing. Her conversation with Madame Eudora and the excited questions of the women sitting around the table. Tess's shy request to have Parker touch her shoulders. Tess falling from her chair. The last few frames were unfocused on the ceiling and floor. Annabelle must have bumped the equipment. And then nothing.

Tess did not comment on the video. Unable to decipher her sister's reaction, Gwen walked from the conference room and called Shirley's name.

Shirley's head popped up on the other side of the newsroom. She rushed in and shut off the machine. "Did you see what you were looking for?"

Tess found her voice. "I can't say I did."

Gwen resisted the urge to quibble, waiting for Shirley's response.

"That was my reaction, Tess," Shirley offered. "Annabelle explained that videos taken during a ghost-hunting session are not usually crisp enough to be conclusive."

Tess shrugged. "Are the photographs clearer?"

"I think so, but that's why I wanted you to watch the video footage first. Come with me."

Arriving at Annabelle's desk, Shirley tapped the younger woman on the shoulder. "You have those séance photographs?"

When Annabelle jumped, the pictures scattered across the floor. "Sorry. Sorry. I'm such a klutz. But these are time-stamped, so it'll be easy to put them in order."

All four women squatted and picked up the pictures, concentrating on the time in the corner instead of the images themselves. They called out numbers from their handful, re-sorting the individual shots into sequence until they had a neat stack.

Annabelle carried the photos to the adjoining empty desktop without dropping a one. "When Mrs. Andrews' husband appeared on Friday evening, I switched the infrared camera to automatically take a picture every few seconds so we wouldn't miss anything." She pushed the first few photos aside, and laid out the next dozen side by side. "The still camera captures images more distinctly than the video camera. Take a look."

Gwen and Tess leaned close to concentrate on the pictures.

"Look at this shadow, Tess." Gwen touched each picture, placing her finger on Parker's likeness as he'd progressed from Madame Eudora to Gwen. She'd seen Parker's ethereal self much more clearly than these snapshots had captured. But she'd read somewhere that ghosts appear to humans in exactly the way they are expected. So Tess had been partially correct. Gwen had seen what she wanted to see. But at least the video and these photos proved there had indeed been something *to* see.

"I don't know, Sis," Tess protested. "These are not proving much. Let's keep going," Tess pushed aside the first group, as well as those of Parker moving the scarf. The next ones showed Gwen and Tess speaking to each other.

"That's when you asked Parker to touch your shoulder."

The shadow moved behind Gwen. The next picture showed a sliver of smoke reaching out toward Tess. The last clear photo had caught Tess falling from her chair.

Annabelle fluttered her hands. "When you fainted, I knocked against the camera. Sorry. The rest of the pictures are blurry."

Gwen touched Shirley's sleeve. "I know you can't give me copies, but can I take reference shots with my cell phone?"

Shirley glanced around the newsroom. "No one seems to be paying any attention to us. Put your flash in the off position and have at it."

After Gwen snapped a picture of each photo, Tess tidied them into a pile. "I have to admit I do see something here, but I'm not sure it's Parker's spirit."

Gwen harbored no such doubts. Even if the infrared camera had captured nothing more than these indistinct shadows, Gwen had seen Parker very clearly. Madame Eudora's awareness of his presence combined with these photos convinced Gwen she should cease questioning her sanity. Parker had truly broken through from the great beyond.

Chapter Thirty-Seven … mid-afternoon, Monday

After leaving the parking lot of the *Harbor Falls Gazette*, Gwen drove in silence until Tess spoke. "I know you don't want to hear this, but I think that smoke at the séance made you hallucinate."

Arguing with Tess would be fruitless. Her sister wasn't ready to believe Gwen's experience. Tess hadn't taken the next step that if Parker had come back to Gwen, Nathan might come back to her. Gwen would let Tess come to that conclusion in her own time.

Instead of taking a right onto Library Lane, Gwen turned left down Harbor Hill. "I want Liz to have a look at these photos."

"Good idea. I'd like to hear her opinion. After all, she was at the séance, too."

Is Tess hoping Liz will harbor the same doubts?

When the sisters walked into the bookstore, a man wearing paint-splattered overalls was tapping the lids onto paint cans near the common wall. The scent of turpentine and fresh latex permeated the air, the comforting smell of fresh and new. Gwen knew from painting with Parker during the library conversion that the fumes would soon dissipate.

Liz glanced over from arranging books. "Hi, you two. The clean-up company is picking up these de-smoking barrels within the hour. I'll be so glad to have my store back." She glanced from Tess to Gwen. "Hey, what's wrong? You're never this quiet."

"Tess and I just came from viewing the séance video and pictures. Shirley let me take quick snaps for reference."

"Let me see." Liz slipped the last book into place.

Gwen opened her photo gallery and held her cell phone at an angle, pointing to the sequence of shadows.

"Oh, my goodness. And you say this shading was Parker?"

Again, Gwen regretted the camera had not registered his presence as clearly as she'd seen him.

"Gwen says yes," Tess volunteered, "but I'm not sure. There was a lot of smoke to explain these shadows."

"But, Tess, you fainted when he touched you." Liz looked back and forth between the sisters.

"I know. I know. But I could have convinced myself that someone touched me."

Liz's mind seemed open to the possibility. Gwen held tight to her belief that Parker appeared at Madame Eudora's bidding, regardless of what these photos did or did not confirm to Tess.

"Gwen, are you concerned about the article Shirley's writing for the paper?"

"Not at all. She's *not* including my address."

"Good. If I'd been able to hold the séance here in the bookstore, I'd welcome any extra traffic, gawkers or not, but people swarming your home would drive you nuts." Liz walked to the new release kiosk and straightened the books. "Anything new with Hal?"

Gwen launched into Ben's burned steaks because of Hal's unexpected interruption. She purposely left out the afternoon drive in Ben's Corvette and their climb to the monument. No sense in providing Tess with fodder for her romantic imaginings.

"Do you think you're being too hard on Hal?" Liz challenged.

"I've been thinking the same thing, Sis, but I didn't want to say it. I totally get it that you hate cigar smoke. No one's perfect. Even Parker, who was a terrific guy, had his faults. Do you think you can get past Hal smoking one cigar and forgive him?"

Gwen was relieved that Tess hadn't mentioned Uncle Gus. If she had to tell one more person about her pervert uncle, Gwen knew she'd burst.

A voice called from the bookstore entrance. "Hello?"

A tall rangy man ducked below the door jamb. "I'm here with your banner. If you'll tell me where to hang it, I'll get started."

Liz hurried toward him. "Thanks for putting a rush on this. Let me show you where to hang it."

Joining Liz and the man from the print shop on the sidewalk, Gwen and Tess watched the proceedings. When Liz offered to hold the other end, the man retrieved a stepladder from his delivery truck and helped her to the upper rung.

Liz called from her lofty position. "Is this hanging straight, Gwen? Tess?"

Gwen tilted her head. "About an inch higher on your end, Liz."

"Yep, that'll do it," Tess confirmed.

A blue sedan parked in front of the print shop truck. Fannie got out and joined the group, glancing up at the banner. "I received your email, Liz. You must be thrilled that you're re-opening tomorrow. And I have more good news for you."

Liz climbed down the ladder. "What is it?"

"Your insurance company is going after Farley's insurance company to pay for your repairs."

"Oh, such a relief." Liz pressed her hand to her heart. "I've been calculating how many books I'd have to sell to reach my deductible."

"Well, now you don't have to worry about it. Listen, I have some errands, but I'll be back tomorrow to help you celebrate."

Gwen stepped closer. "Hold on a sec, Fannie. Tess and I found some photos taken during the fire last Tuesday. Do you think they would help with the claim?"

"Sure would. How soon can you get copies for my file?"

"Right now if Liz will let us use her copy machine. The file's in my back seat. I'll go get it."

After Fannie drove off with the color copies, Liz turned her attention back to the sisters. "Did you have any success at the Downtown Association?"

"Yes and no. Joanie met Farley several times, but before Tess or I had a chance to chase the details, Aldrich walked in."

"What impressions did you get from him?"

"He didn't seem happy to see us and he refused our invitation to attend your re-opening party tomorrow."

"Hmmm," Liz murmured. "That sounds suspicious."

"But Joanie's coming. She can probably access Aldrich's phone records and find can out who he called after your meeting."

Tess snickered. "We'll keep Joanie's wine glass filled."

Liz snapped her fingers. "Thanks for reminding me. I need to double-check with the caterer and make sure they're on schedule."

"Before you do, one other tidbit: Ben is visiting town officials today for anything they might divulge about Farley."

Liz inhaled and let the air out in a huff. "I just wish Ben had convinced Chief Upton that I wasn't the guilty person before he lost his cool and retired. Then the entire police department would be out looking for Farley's real attacker."

"That's true. I'm just glad Ben decided to stick with the investigation, even with his unofficial status. He did some background checks on Jeremy Wakefield, the NH craftsman, the bartender, and the construction company."

"Did he find anything promising?"

Gwen recited Ben's findings. "He wants a second conversation with the bartender but doesn't expect much."

"Do you have any other ideas, Gwen?"

Gwen opened her file folder, removed Tuesday night's crowd photo, and placed it on the counter between them. "Let's take another look at the people who were watching the fire. It would have been easy enough to hang back and sneak into the cigar bar later to confront Farley."

"Give me the list we created the other day." Liz's focus moved to a spot past Gwen's shoulder. "Oh, Billy. I didn't hear you come in. Did you leave something behind yesterday?"

232

"No, ma'am, but Wade forgot to give you back your key."

Liz extended her open palm. "Didn't I give him two?"

When Billy scuffed his feet and dropped his head, his glasses slid down his nose. "I only have this one. I'll ask Wade."

"I'm sure it's just an oversight. I'm closing up in a little while. Why don't you bring the second key tomorrow and help me celebrate my re-opening?"

"Sure." Billy craned his neck sideways to look at Gwen's photograph. "Isn't that the picture you showed me the other day, Mrs. Andrews?"

"It is, Billy."

With one hand, he reached around her and picked it up. With the other, he pushed his ever-sliding glasses where they belonged. He pointed to himself. "There I am. I heard you talking about Farley Cooper's attacker again. Do the police know you're looking for him?"

"In a round-about way," Liz answered. "Gwen and Tess are working with the detective who resigned. They're chasing connections Chief Upton doesn't consider relevant."

Gwen wished Liz wasn't so eager to share information.

"Like this photograph?" Billy grinned and dropped the picture onto the counter. "You're clever, Mrs. Andrews."

"I'll take it one step further." Liz reached for the list Gwen had also removed from the file. "If Gwen and the detective hadn't pointed out the lack of hard evidence, Chief Upton would have tossed me in jail by now."

Chapter Thirty-Eight ... early morning, Tuesday

Gwen swallowed the last of her morning coffee and added her mug to the dishwasher.

"Sis?" Tess's faint voice called from an island stool. "Do you mind if I walk by myself this morning?"

Whirling around, Gwen noted the downward tilt of Tess's eyelids, the hint of sadness. She opted not to press her sister about wanting alone time. "Of course I don't mind. You don't have to spend every waking minute with me. Have you picked a destination?"

"The boardwalk along the shoreline." Tess twisted her wedding band on her finger. "Don't worry, I'm still planning to help you set-up Liz's bookstore for her re-opening party. I'll meet you there in an hour or so." Tess tucked her cell phone into the pocket of her green jacket, grabbed her purse, and headed out.

Tess missing Nathan came as no surprise. "See you later."

Gwen added a soap pack to the dishwasher and pressed the start button. When someone knocked on the French door, she leaned sideways to see Ben and waved him in.

"Good morning, Gwen." He placed his accordion file on the island. "Is this a good time to compare notes? Is Tess here?"

"You just missed her. She's taking a walk along the harbor. You have something to share?"

"Yep. Caught up with Lance Lynch last night. He snagged a bartending job at The Lucky Lobster up the coast. Evening shift. I ordered a drink, explained who I am, and asked him a few questions about Farley."

234

"What was your impression?"

"I agree with your instincts. Lance doesn't have the temperament for violence. He's just a guy trying to earn a living. But he told me something about Farley's other employee..." Ben flipped a few pages in his notebook. "...Quincy."

"And what was that?"

"One afternoon when Farley was yelling at Quincy, Lance overheard words like 'jail time' and 'parole.' He couldn't swear Farley threatened Quincy, but Lance heard enough to steer clear."

"You're thinking Quincy might be the attacker?"

"A distinct possibility. Where's your photo of the crowd at Tuesday's fire? Lance gave me a description of Quincy."

Retrieving her file, Gwen placed the photo in front of Ben.

He referred to his notes for the description and peered at the gawking faces.

Gwen racked her brain to recall an image of Quincy. Farley had chased him out of the humidor so fast on Tuesday morning, she'd barely had time to look at the man, and mostly from behind as he stood on the ladder. "Is he there?"

Ben shook his head. "Can't be sure."

"Did Lance know Quincy's last name or where he lives?"

"A dead end. I'll pass along what we've uncovered. Mike can dig deeper using his law enforcement connections."

Gwen glanced at the kitchen clock. "Hate to chase you away, Ben, but I've got to get to the bookstore and help Liz set-up for today's re-opening."

"Then I'll get out of your hair. I want to see what else I can find out about Quincy before I meet with Mike this afternoon."

***

Because the bookstore door was locked, Gwen knocked on the frame. A tall woman with gray hair captured in pigtails grinned as she flipped open the lock.

235

"Olivia, you're here!"

The pigtails wiggled. "Yep. I'm thrilled to be back. Liz called me as soon as she realized she could reopen today. She's in her office. Do you want me to get her?"

"No, let her be. What can I do to help with the preparations?"

"You can start with those." Olivia pointed to three cloths stacked on the first reading table. "Use the hurricane globes as anchors in the center of each table." Olivia hurried away.

As Gwen flipped one of cloths open, she jumped when a finger tapped her shoulder.

"Liz, you gave me a fright."

"Sorry, Gwen. Isn't Tess with you?"

"She's meeting me after her walk." Gwen glanced at her watch. "I expected her to be here by now. If she doesn't arrive soon, I'll call her cell phone."

Liz helped Gwen smooth the cloth. "Thanks for your help."

"You're welcome." Gwen shook out the second cloth. "If you have things to do in your office, Olivia and I can handle the preparations out here."

"You're a peach, Gwen. Yell if you need me."

While Olivia strung balloons, Gwen taped streamers along the windows. In the aromatherapy corner, she stirred the bowl of potpourri, a sweet earthy concoction of sandalwood, lavender, and patchouli that would not offend the majority of shoppers.

At quarter to ten, the caterer arrived with finger sandwiches, appetizers, and mini desserts. Gwen arranged plates, cups, napkins, and utensils. Olivia carried a variety of sodas and bottled water from a cooler in Liz's office. Bottles of wine and stemmed plastic glasses perched on an extra table next to the register.

When a hum outside grew louder, Gwen and Olivia peeked out the front windows. A group of chattering women formed a line.

"Oh, my goodness!" Olivia slapped her hands against her cheeks. "I think we're going to have a banner day."

"I hope those women aren't here just to drink the wine and eat the food," Gwen quipped.

"Oh, I doubt it," Olivia commented.

A minute later, Liz joined them. "Tess never showed?"

Rattled that she'd lost track of time, Gwen whipped out her cell phone and punched speed dial for her sister. No answer. "That's not like Tess."

Liz touched Gwen's arm. "Olivia and I can handle the crowd. Why don't you search for Tess? She said she was planning to walk the shoreline?"

"That's what she told me this morning."

***

Gwen scurried across Coast Road and through the parking lot of The Wharf Restaurant. Stepping onto the boardwalk, she looked in both directions, racking her brain to remember what Tess had been wearing when she left for her walk.

But it was no use. Gwen could not recall Tess's outfit. Doing an eeny-meeny-miney-mo, she set off in a southerly direction, striding along the boardwalk, searching the beach to her left and the sand dunes rising on the right. Seagulls flapped overhead, but since Gwen had nothing to offer, they soon flew off to find better prepared humans. No sign of Tess.

When a marshy inlet ended the quarter-mile walking deck, Gwen dialed Tess's cell phone again. No answer. *How can I find Tess if she won't answer her phone?* Maybe Ben could orchestrate a location ping on the cell towers. If it came to that.

She reversed direction and headed back toward the pier, then continued her search along the northern section. Maybe Tess had decided to go somewhere else.

The moment Gwen conjured the variety of calamities that could have waylaid her sister, she spotted a body on the grassy slope above the boardwalk fifty feet ahead. The brown mop of hair matched Tess's color and she recognized her sister's green jacket.

Gwen scooted up the slope, her feet slipping on the blades of grass, willing Tess's chest to move up and down. She reached over and shook her sister as gently as she could.

"Huh? What?" Tess mumbled, her eyes squinting.

Gwen helped Tess to a sitting position. "Are you okay?"

"Yea, I'm okay." Tess struggled to remain upright on the slanted surface. "Why did you track me down?"

"Because you were supposed to meet me at the bookstore an hour ago."

"That can't be right, Gwen. I only sat here a few minutes ago."

"And promptly fell asleep," Gwen admonished, her tone softening. "Were you thinking about Nathan?"

"I was." Tess lowered her chin for only a second before lifting her gaze to Gwen. "Whenever we visited Harbor Falls, Nathan and I always walked the shoreline. With his binoculars slung around his neck, he identified all the birds. I needed to relive those memories."

"I understand, Tess." Gwen helped her sister to her feet, dusting off loose bits of grass.

"I'm sorry I worried you, Gwen. I guess the sunshine and the lapping of the waves lulled me to sleep. I only meant to close my eyes for a second."

"I'm just glad you're all right." Gwen slipped her arm around the taller Tess's waist.

Tess glanced down at Gwen. "Let's get back to the bookstore and see if Joanie has arrived. We've got some snooping to do."

Chapter Thirty-Nine ... late morning, Tuesday

When Gwen and Tess re-entered Fiction 'n Fables, they zigzagged through the throng of shoppers. The line at the register was three-deep as Olivia rang up their purchases, all the while chatting away about the chosen titles.

Liz detached herself from a group and hurried over. "Oh, good, you found Tess. Grab something to eat before it's all gone."

"I'll grab the food, Gwen. You snag the wine."

Gwen wandered to the extra table near the register and poured two glasses of Zinfandel.

"Hello." A female voice spoke from behind. "Gwen, isn't it?"

Trying not to slosh the wine, Gwen pivoted. "Hi, Joanie. I'm glad you could make it."

"Great crowd. I found two books I've been wanting to read." She held up paperbacks, then tucked them under her arm.

Gwen noticed Joanie's empty hand. "Can I pour you a glass of wine?"

"Sure. Red if you have it. I went straight to the shelves to grab these before someone else did."

Setting down the two glasses for her and Tess, Gwen filled a third glass with Lambrusco and handed it to Joanie. "Did Aldrich come with you?"

"No, he didn't. I told him it would be a nice gesture of support, given Liz's difficulties with the cigar bar. But when my boss's mind is made up, there's no changing it."

Gwen grasped at the opening to do a little digging. "We never finished our conversation about Farley Cooper yesterday. You met him a few times?"

"I did." Joanie sipped her wine, easily consuming half the contents. She placed her two books on the table, grabbed a napkin, and patted her mouth. "He came into our office more than a month ago and had a closed-door meeting with Aldrich."

"Let me refill your glass." Gwen lifted it from Joanie's hand, topped it off, and handed it back to the young woman.

"Hmmm, this is good." Joanie swigged another big sip. "I guess I'm thirsty."

Gwen had only tasted her own. "You were telling me about Farley's meeting with Aldrich."

"Oh, yeah. Mr. Cooper left carrying one of those white Tyvec envelopes, but I have no idea what was inside. When I asked Aldrich for details to put in the file, he told me not to bother."

"Here's your food, Sis." Tess held out a filled plate. "Hi, Joanie. Good to see you again."

Gwen brought her sister into the conversation. "We were just talking about Farley Cooper."

"Never met the man myself." Tess bit into a miniature chicken salad sandwich.

Joanie scoffed. "No big loss. He didn't say much to me beyond demanding to see Aldrich. Mr. Cooper gave off very negative vibes. I hate to speak ill of the dead, but I'm not surprised someone did him in." She hiccupped. "Oh, forget I said that. Please!"

"Can I get you some food?" Tess offered.

"No, no, but thanks. I need to cash out and get back to the office. Nice to see you both again." Joanie finished her wine and picked up her books, swaying as she joined the check-out line.

Tess tugged at Gwen's sleeve. "How much wine did she drink?"

"Only two glasses, but some people can't hold their liquor. I've only taken two sips of mine because I'm one of them." Gwen clinked her glass against Tess's. "Let's see how Liz is doing."

They found Liz in the aromatherapy corner. Gwen lowered her

voice. "Tess and I had an interesting conversation with Joanie. I think we were right to suspect Aldrich and Farley were in cahoots. Ben's the best one to follow-up. I'll call his cell phone and ask him to stop by." Gwen checked her watch. "You staying open until seven?"

"Later if customers are still wandering around. Need to rake in all the sales I can while the energy is high." Liz moved away toward a young couple.

When Gwen dialed Ben's number, her call went straight to voice mail, so she left a message. As she pushed the disconnect button, Rachel and her Aunt Kate came through the entrance. Gwen waved. "Rachel!"

If Ben was meeting Mike Brown that afternoon to tell him about Jeremy Wakefield, Rachel wouldn't yet be aware her nephew had been added to the list of Farley's potential attackers. Although Ben had no intention of revealing Gwen as his source, she knew that sometimes these conversations didn't proceed as planned.

Rachel fluttered her hand and met Gwen halfway. "You remember my Aunt Kate?"

"Of course." Gwen offered her hand. "How are you holding up?"

Kate accepted the handshake. "I'm surviving, thanks. Rachel has been a godsend."

"The autopsy's done," Rachel added. "My uncle's body has been released."

Good news to Gwen's ears. At least that stage of the investigation was completed. Beyond the medical examiner's findings, they were still waiting for the state lab techs to confirm the ashtray as the weapon, the blood as Farley's, and the fingerprints that belonged to someone besides Liz.

How long before Liz could resume her life as a bookshop owner without the threat of arrest hanging over her head?

Kate's voice brought Gwen back to the conversation. "Since my brother left no instructions, we decided to cremate. Do you think anyone in Harbor Falls would attend a memorial service?"

Gwen hadn't expected Kate's question. Lance mentioned that Farley's paying customers seemed to love him. But would those customers translate into mourners? "I'm afraid I'm the wrong person to ask, Kate. I only met your brother once." Gwen kept her negative opinion of Farley to herself.

Liz came up beside them as Tess asked, "Is Jeremy with you?"

"No." Rachel's tone was edgy. "When we mentioned cleaning out Farley's apartment above the cigar bar, Jeremy announced he planned to hike the Blue Hills today."

"Sounds like he was inspired by the book he bought here on Tuesday," Liz offered.

"Maybe." Kate slid a split ring with two keys from her pocket. "It's more likely he wants nothing to do with his Uncle Farley."

Gwen seized the opportunity. "Did they have a falling out?"

"Yes. I hope they reconciled. Jeremy hasn't said one way or the other." Kate glanced around at the busy bookstore.

If Gwen probed any further, she'd reveal her involvement in the investigation. She itched to ask what time Jeremy showed up at Rachel's house on Tuesday evening and whether his clothes were spattered with blood. Unsatisfied and stymied, Gwen's only option was to pass these minor details to Ben and let him share with Mike Brown for further investigation.

Liz parlayed her focus from Rachel to Kate. "Why don't you both have a bite to eat before tackling Farley's apartment?"

Rachel shifted her purse to the other shoulder. "Good idea. And congratulations on re-opening your bookstore."

Kate touched Liz's sleeve. "I'm sorry my brother's cigar bar caused you so much trouble."

Chapter Forty ... early afternoon, Tuesday

While Liz greeted new arrivals and worked the crowd, Olivia continued ringing up the non-stop sales. Shirley popped in, bringing with her a tear sheet of the séance article to be published in Thursday's edition.

Retreating to a quiet corner, Shirley, Liz, and Tess peered over Gwen's shoulder while she read the article to them out loud. Gwen finally lifted her head, her eyes bright with excitement. "This is wonderfully written, Shirley. You captured the events of the evening perfectly without being melodramatic. It's quite believable."

Shirley beamed. "Thank you. I'm hoping my article combined with the photographs will provide you with a sense of closure."

Gwen wasn't sure what Shirley was trying to say: That she believed Gwen had witnessed Parker's ghost or that Gwen should stop chasing his spirit.

Grinning, Gwen resolved it didn't matter what anyone else had taken away from the séance. She had acquired a new respect for mediums, especially Madame Eudora. Gwen would live out her days with the knowledge that there is indeed life after death.

Shirley refolded the tear sheet. "Sorry, but I can't stay. Gotta chase down another story on the other side of town. Congrats on re-opening, Liz. I'll phone Annabelle to take photos and we'll do a write-up about you." Shirley hustled from the bookstore.

While Liz schmoozed the dwindling shoppers, Gwen and Tess rejoined Rachel and Kate as they finished their finger sandwiches, salad pinwheels, and brownies.

Kate dried her fingers on a napkin. "Would you like to see my brother's apartment? I hate to admit this, but I'm spooked to go up there, even with Rachel by my side. A few more people might make it easier."

Gwen jumped at the chance. There was no telling what they might come across that the police had overlooked as irrelevant. "I understand spooky. I'll go with you."

"Me, too," Tess added. "Since I never met your brother, seeing where he lived will give me a better sense of him."

Gwen slipped to Liz's side to explain where they were going.

"Rats. Wish I could go with you. I use my second floor for storage. I'm curious how Farley converted his space into an apartment."

Gwen shrugged her shoulders. "We're about to find out. I'll fill you in when we get back."

***

Crime scene tape no longer blocked the entrance to Farley Cooper's Cigar Emporium & Smoking Lounge. Tuesday's fire had left charred wood on the broken window frame nearest the common wall with Liz's bookstore.

Gwen, Tess, and Rachel stood on the sidewalk while Kate slipped the key into the lock and pushed in the fancy carved door. Craning her head past the doorframe, Kate peered to the left and right, but made no move to step inside.

Rachel hustled her generous body up the steps with surprising energy. "I'll go first, Aunt Kate." Inside, she reached her hand to the left and flicked a light switch several times. The interior remained dark. "Hey, there's no power in here."

Gwen stepped inside. "Liz had to have her wiring replaced. The wiring over here is probably toast as well."

Despite the dimness, Gwen could see the finish on the floors had become hazy white from the standing water. Farley's side of the common wall appeared sodden from the fireman's hoses.

"This is such a shame, Kate." Gwen indicated the ruined interior. "Liz started her cleanup the next day, but Farley wasn't here to make arrangements. What are you going to do with it?"

Kate's face fell. "I just don't know. I doubt if Violet has any interest in re-opening the cigar bar. She'll probably tell me to sell it and let the new owner deal with the cleanup."

Rachel glanced around the dark interior. "We can't see much of anything."

"Wait." Tess rummaged in her purse. "I still have Gwen's little flashlight. We can still do a quick check of your brother's apartment upstairs if you want, Kate."

Kate hesitated. "All right. As long as we're here, Rachel and I can get an idea of what we're up against. Where are the steps?"

Assuming the layout was similar to Liz's bookstore, Gwen pointed. "They should be on the other side of that windowed room." She led them past the mahogany bar, the previous shine now muted with a thin layer of dust and gray ashes. The surface of Farley's connecting door had been sanded and refinished to a dark walnut to match the new paneling, making it nearly invisible.

Down a short hallway, she found the stairs exactly where she expected and waved Kate ahead of her. "After you."

Kate shone the flashlight beam on the stairs, taking one step at a time as she ventured up. Rachel followed, with Tess and Gwen bringing up the rear.

The apartment upstairs was even worse than Gwen had imagined. Ben's description of bare bones with no feminine touches had been perfect. The space appeared to have been a good-sized bedroom from the Colonial days, converted into a one-room apartment. Gwen could easily see how Liz used her similar space for storage.

Kate strode to the front windows and freed the shades. Light streamed in, illuminating the dankness.

A small kitchenette ran along the back wall. A door in the far corner probably led to a bathroom. The only furniture was a double bed – unmade – plus a shabby dresser, a small table piled with papers, two folding chairs, and a thread-bare upholstered chair. How depressing to think this was where Farley had lived.

Kate and Rachel wandered about the room, their fingers trailing through dust on every surface. "Gosh, Rachel, I don't see much here worth saving."

"I agree, Aunt Kate. Why don't we come back tomorrow with trash bags?"

"My thoughts exactly."

Rachel knocked something from the kitchen counter, but didn't bother to pick it up. "I can get in touch with the local Salvation Army and offer the furniture. I think they'll haul it away."

"I don't know if they will even want it." Kate huffed a breath through her nose. "But we need to clear out all this stuff before we can put Farley's property on the market."

Gwen drifted toward the table, eyeballing the paperwork for anything interesting. And then she spied it. The edge of a white Tyvec envelope. She signaled Tess to stand beside her before deftly sliding the envelope from the stack until it fell on the floor. It landed upside down, along with some other documents, so she stooped to flip it over. The logo of the *Downtown Association* marked the top left corner.

Barely able to contain her excitement, Gwen lifted her eyebrows at Tess in a silent question: Should she tuck it beneath her jacket before Kate noticed or be more honest about their interest?

"What have you got there?" Kate had snuck up behind them.

Willing herself not to jump at being caught, Gwen regained her composure. "Sorry, Kate, I knocked this paperwork off the table."

"Let me see." Kate sorted through the various flyers and envelopes, tossing the junk mail into a cardboard box sitting next to the upholstered chair. She tucked a few official-looking envelopes under her arm. "I'll take these bills. They need to be paid from Farley's estate."

When Kate came to the Tyvec envelope, she didn't even open it. "No sense in keeping this. Farley's membership won't be renewed." She added it to the other discarded paperwork.

Rachel peeked over her aunt's shoulder. "Are you finding anything legal? You know, the mortgage papers or the deed? Maybe a will?"

"Not yet, Rachel." Kate opened each drawer, rifling through the contents, throwing nothing more into the cardboard box. "When we come back tomorrow, we'll take all these papers back to your place for an in-depth analysis. With Violet's permission, I'll contact his vendors and try to sell back the cigars and liquor."

Gwen said, "A man named Quincy can probably help you with the details. He was Farley's purchasing agent and stockman. Maybe you'll find his name and phone number in the paperwork."

Rachel hugged herself. "So we're finished here for now? This place is creeping me out."

"I think so." Kate closed the final drawer. "Let's go back to the bookstore. Maybe Liz will buy Farley's spaces and expand her business. I'm sure Violet could use the cash after Farley cleaned out their savings."

Gwen and Tess lagged behind. When Kate and Rachel headed for the top of the stairs, Gwen nodded for Tess to grab the white envelope from the cardboard box. Tess tucked it under her green jacket, squeezing her arm to keep it from falling out.

Chapter Forty-One ... late afternoon, Tuesday

Back in the bookshop, Gwen listened as Kate and Liz discussed the availability of Farley's sections of the building.

"Gosh, I don't know, Kate." Liz wasn't usually so indecisive. "I'll have to think about it."

"You do that, Liz. I'll clear my offer with Farley's wife. I'm sticking around until we wrap up my brother's affairs. I'll check with you again before I leave town."

"What are you going to do with his ashes?" Rachel asked.

Kate's shoulders rose and fell. "Not sure. I'll ask Violet if she and Farley owned cemetery plots."

"Good luck." Gwen remembered Ben's words. "The police detective who was handling Farley's case said Violet had no interest in laying her husband to rest."

Kate sneered. "Violet's refusal to handle the final arrangements for her husband is the only reason I drove here. She's a real piece of work, but Farley wasn't much better. They were a good match. When he cleaned out their bank account, Violet washed her hands of him." Kate refocused on Liz. "It was so nice to meet you. I wish it had been under more pleasant circumstances. And again, I apologize for all the trouble my brother caused you."

Liz waved away the apology. "Just because we're related to someone doesn't mean we're responsible for their actions. My bookstore is back in business now, so all is right with the world." Liz hesitated. "If I don't buy the rest of this building, are you going to sell it to someone who might re-open the cigar bar?"

"Oh, heavens, I hope not," Kate exclaimed. "I'm giving you first dibs, Liz. Do you know a real estate agent who can set a fair value and handle the paperwork?"

"As a matter of fact, I do. Let me go find her card."

***

Rachel and Kate waved goodbye, pushy real estate lady's card in hand, promising to visit Liz the next day after they cleaned out Farley's apartment. Wade Grainger, Penelope, and Billy ambled into the bookstore.

Wade held out something to Liz. "Here's your second key. Sorry I forgot to give it to Billy yesterday."

Liz slipped the key into her pocket. "No problem. Thanks."

Penelope wandered over from the new book kiosk. "Looks like your re-opening is a success, Liz. You must be glad the cigar bar's closed. Any idea if it will be resurrected by the relatives?"

"As a matter of fact, Farley Cooper's sister was just here, and offered to sell his two sections of this building. Are you interested in buying your old space, Penelope? Or the smaller space on his other side where the video store used to be?"

Penelope's surprised expression was not quite delight.

Wade gently grasped his wife's shoulders. "What do you think? Do you want to take your inventory out of storage and re-open your store?"

Penelope laid her hand on his sleeve. "Oh, gosh, I don't know. Let me think a moment."

The group stood in silence as Penelope stared at the floor, all the while fidgeting with her purse strap. Within seconds, her eyes traveled from Liz to Wade and back again. "You told me about all the dark paneling. And the whole place will stink of cigar smoke for some time to come. I think it's time to move past that phase of my life. But thank you, Wade, for considering the possibility."

Wade wiggled his head, but said no more.

"What will you do now, Mrs. G?" Billy stood on her other side.

"Oh, I'm not sure, Billy. Get a part-time job at the mall. Do some volunteer work. There are so many options." The three of them wandered off.

A man's voice called from the entrance. "Am I too late?" Hal strolled through the door.

"Too late for food," Liz reported. "But there's still some wine."

"Perfect. I'll pour it." He emptied the last bottle into the one remaining stemmed glass.

Although Gwen had known he'd show up to retrieve his plywood, she felt awkward in his presence, so she set about straightening up and let him banter with Liz, Tess, and Olivia.

"Congratulations on re-opening, Liz." Hal grinned wide. "You must be relieved."

"I sure am. And get this. Farley's sister is giving me first crack at purchasing Farley's sections of this building."

"Are you going to do it?"

"I'm not sure. Tony's due back from his Allagash fishing trip either tonight or tomorrow. We'll take a look at our finances and decide if it's worth the risk. My mind's whirring with ideas."

"I bet." Hal's eyes flitted around the bookstore, pausing briefly on Gwen. He waited until she met his gaze before refocusing on Liz. "I'm here to pick up my plywood. If you can tell me where it is, I'll get out of your hair."

"Wade leaned it against the back of the building. Cut through the stock room and out the back door to the alley. You'll see it."

When Hal disappeared, Gwen nodded to her sister. Tess slid her hand up her jacket, pulling out the white envelope. "This thing has been burning a hole in my side."

"What is it?" Olivia asked.

"Something Joanie mentioned that Kate tossed in the trash." Gwen took the envelope.

"Open it," Liz demanded.

Gwen slid her finger beneath the flap to break the seal and reached inside, roaring when she saw the contents. Window stickers for the Downtown Association. Assorted sizes. Various colors. "Looks like Aldrich cleaned out his stash."

"You're kidding." Tess's tone was unquestioningly disappointed. "This is no help."

Liz dropped into a chair at the first reading table. "We should have known any under-the-table dealings wouldn't be so obvious. Whatever Farley and Aldrich were up to, they probably didn't leave a paper trail."

Tess also sat down. "We're back to square one. I was so sure we'd figured out who harbored the best reason to get rid of Farley."

"This doesn't mean we're wrong." Gwen used her most soothing voice. "It only means we have no proof...yet." She pushed the stickers into the envelope, closed the clasp, and held it out to Liz. "Here you go, though you probably have enough already."

Hal strolled out of the stock room and gave Gwen a cautious look, but didn't speak to her directly. "I found my plywood, Liz. I'll back my truck into your alley and load up. See ya."

After Hal left, Liz focused on Gwen. "Still on the outs with Hal?"

When Gwen only nodded, Liz didn't press. "So, tell me about Farley's apartment."

Gwen made a face. "I hate to be unkind, but it's a rat hole. He must have used up all his cash on the cigar bar renovation because he didn't spend a dime to furnish his apartment."

Tess absently slapped her pockets, pushed aside empty party platters, and dumped the contents of her purse.

Gwen peered over her shoulder. "Lose something?"

"My cell phone. Didn't miss it until just now."

"Maybe it fell from your pocket when you took a nap near the boardwalk."

Tess shrugged. "That's the most logical explanation. I'll go down there and have a look."

251

"If it's not lying in the tall grass, someone might have taken it to the Harbor Master's office near the pier."

"Thanks, Sis. I won't be long. Will you be heading home soon?"

"Not sure. I left several messages for Ben to meet me here. I planned to tell him about Joanie's white envelope, but now we know it's a dead end. I'll try his cell phone again."

"In that case, I'll stop by before I walk up Harbor Hill to check if you're still around."

The last of the shoppers had left with their purchases. Most of the food had been devoured, and all that remained of the wine was empty bottles. Gwen offered to clean up from the party, so Liz sent the exhausted Olivia home.

Chapter Forty-Two ... early evening, Tuesday

"Gwen?" Liz came out from her office grasping an overstuffed envelope. "I don't want to leave all this cash lying around so I'm going to drive to the bank and make a deposit." Liz glanced at her watch. "It's close to my normal closing, so I'm going to lock up."

"But you can't, Liz. Ben's supposed to meet me here."

"Can you meet him somewhere else?"

"I would, but he's not answering his cell phone. Do you mind if I stick around until he shows? Besides, I promised Olivia I'd clean up the party mess."

"Sure. And thanks again for all your help. I'll swing back after my bank run."

***

Clearing the bookstore of the party debris would fill the time while Gwen waited for Ben, but first, she needed a trash bag. After checking beneath the register and in Liz's office, Gwen entered the stock room and flipped on the light, perusing the shelves. Spotting a box of Hefty lawn bags on an upper shelf, she stretched up, but could only touch it with the tips of her fingers.

A split second later, footsteps approached from the back. A hand closed on top of hers, its thinness belying its strength. She whirled around. "Billy? What are you doing here? You nearly gave me a heart attack."

"Let me get that box for you, Mrs. Andrews. You're too short to reach that high."

Gwen drew in a breath to calm her racing heart. "Are you looking for a book that's not out front?"

253

"Looking for a book?" he mimicked in a falsetto voice before pushing up his glasses.

Why is Billy mocking me?

The few times she'd bumped into him during the past week, he'd struck her as timid, even introverted. And why hadn't he left with Wade and Penelope?

"With my eyesight, Mrs. Andrews, I don't read much. Barely graduated high school. But I can reach that box for you."

Gwen feigned nonchalance as she plucked the Hefty box from his hand.

"Thank you." She escaped the suddenly claustrophobic stock room, striding down the nearest aisle of bookshelves before making a beeline for the window tables. Billy's footsteps echoed behind her.

"If you need something from Liz, she'll be back any minute."

"Nope. Just hanging out."

The hairs on Gwen's arms lifted. There was no earthly reason for Billy to be in the stock room. She couldn't just walk out and leave him here. She'd distract him until someone – anyone – walked into the bookstore.

Damn it, how soon will Liz return from the bank? Why hasn't Ben returned my calls? And where's Tess with her found phone?

Gwen's mind wrestled with her limited options. Conversation seemed to be her only choice. *Just keep him talking.* "I guess you found the perfect job with Wade, Billy. You two work well together. I was impressed with that window installation."

Billy picked up a dirty paper plate and handed it to her. "Wade and Mrs. G. are the best. They took me in when my parents died. Treated me like their son. I'd do anything for them."

"You never said why you were hiding back there."

He let loose a nervous giggle. "I been hidin' at least an hour. Almost got caught when a man cut through to the back alley."

The man had been Hal. Gwen shuddered and moved to the

other side of the reading table, making a show of picking up plastic wine glasses. She risked a direct glance at Billy. His gaze wavered behind his thick lenses, not quite focusing. *Is he on drugs? Or do his eyes move like that all the time?* She'd never looked closely at him before now. *Keep him talking.* "Why on earth were you hiding, Billy?"

"I was hoping to get some time alone with you."

Will a joke keep him off balance? "I think I'm a little old for you, Billy."

He didn't laugh. "I been hearing you talk to your sister, and Mrs. Phillips, and the detective fella. You been trying to track down the guy who bashed in the cigar man's head. Didn't know you were such a clever lady. Sounds like you check in places the police don't look. Without you, they'll never find the attacker."

A chill crawled along Gwen's skin. *Does Billy know who attacked Farley?* "I'm flattered, Billy. So you think it was clever to track down a stranger in Harbor Falls?" It didn't matter that the stranger theory had been Tess's suggestion.

Billy's forehead wrinkled. "What stranger?"

Aware she had to throw anything and everything at Billy to keep him off-balance, Gwen saw no harm in sharing what she'd uncovered. "A man named Jeremy. Turns out he was molested by his Uncle Farley when he was young. My money's on him."

Billy's face morphed into outrage. "That son of a bitch Farley. I knew he was rotten. One more reason it's good he's gone."

For a split second, Gwen feared she might have chosen the wrong information to share. Too late now. She could use Farley to side-track Billy until he either revealed his reason for staying behind, or walked out. "He's more than gone, Billy. Farley Cooper's dead."

Billy laughed. "You think I don't know that? Wade and Mrs. G. read the newspaper article out loud at supper a few nights ago. The police chief thinks Mrs. Phillips did it."

255

"He does, but Liz's friends – including me – believe she's innocent. As soon as the state lab completes their comparison of those fingerprints, Liz should be eliminated as a suspect. We're all hoping they find a match to someone registered in the database."

"Don't hold your breath, Mrs. Andrews." Billy's chuckle echoed off the walls. "I've never been in any trouble. With these eyes," he half-pointed to his glasses, "and my bad ear, I never went into the army. My fingerprints aren't in any damn database. They'll never match anything to me."

Chapter Forty-Three ... early evening, Tuesday

Gwen nearly dropped the bag of trash. *Did I hear Billy right? His fingerprints aren't registered in any database and could never be matched? Is he claiming the prints dusted on the black marble ashtray are his?* If Billy was telling the truth, there was only one conclusion... he'd been the one who attacked Farley Cooper.

Another old saying popped into Gwen's mind: *It's always the quiet ones you have to watch out for.*

But wait a minute. If Billy was high on drugs, he could be hallucinating. Was he simply putting everything he'd overheard during the past few days into one story and pretending he was the center of it all? Alone with him in the deserted bookstore, either of these scenarios did not bode well for Gwen. Billy was either a delusional maniac, or worse, an unrepentant murderer.

Though Gwen considered running, the younger Billy could surely catch up with her before she reached the door. She had to keep him preoccupied until Ben showed up. Or Tess returned. Or Liz got back from the bank. *Where are they?*

To distract Billy, Gwen continued her purposeful movements from one section of the bookstore to another, holding tight to the trash bag. Even if there was nothing on a shelf, she reached up and shook the bag, pretending she'd added a new piece of litter. All the while, her unwanted companion hovered only steps away.

Mindful of her quest to keep Billy talking, Gwen figured it wouldn't hurt to probe for the truth. At least Billy's truth. She swiveled to face him. "Are you claiming those fingerprints are yours?"

Assuming a prideful stance, Billy grinned and nodded, but did not speak.

"So you're the one who struck Farley Cooper? Why did you attack him?"

Billy spoke with a distinct cockiness. "Guess you're not as smart as you think. Mrs. G's store, Mrs. Andrews. Her store! That bastard Farley tossed her out. Never cared that he crushed her. Oh, sure, she's trying to be brave. But I heard her crying in the bathroom at night. Farley Cooper didn't deserve to walk the same planet as Mrs. G."

"So you think the world's a better place without him?"

"Damn right. You met the cigar man last Tuesday. You heard him yelling at Wade about not buying Mrs. G.'s space when he had the chance."

Billy giggled and slapped his thigh. "You should have seen your expression when the smoke from his cigar blew in your face!"

Just as quickly, he sobered. "And Mrs. Phillips almost lost this bookstore from that fire. She was lucky only one window broke. You all should thank me for getting rid of the cigar man. I did everyone a favor."

Keep him talking. The mantra played over and over on a never-ending loop. "How did you get into Farley's place after the fire?"

Billy grinned and flipped his hand. "Easy. He was so cocky. The fire chief told him not to go inside until it was cleared. But as soon as the fire trucks drove off, he went in anyway. Damn fool didn't even lock his door."

"Did you walk in behind him?"

"Nah. I waited about ten minutes. He went upstairs for a while. Didn't know I was there."

Gwen backtracked to keep Billy's actions in sequence. "How did you explain to Wade and Mrs. G. why you weren't going home with them that night?"

"Oh, I said I was meeting a high school buddy on the pier to watch the fishermen catch spring flounder. Told them he would give me a ride home."

Gwen had no desire to hear any gory details about the actual attack on Farley, so she skipped that part and forged ahead. Allowing Billy to brag about his misdeed would no doubt flatter his ego and keep him from doing whatever he was there to do. "How did you get into Liz's bookstore to hide the bloody ashtray?"

His laugh was haunting. "The old connecting door. Banged on the frames. The latches sprung open like they always did. The cigar man was too cheap to buy a new door. Didn't even bother to change the hardware."

"How did you know about the door, Billy? It's camouflaged on this side." She pointed at Liz's heavy curtain covering the door panel. Even Gwen had been unaware of the pass-through.

Smirking, Billy supplied the answer. "Wasn't hidden on Mrs. G.'s side. She put a rack of kid's coats in front of it. On Wednesdays when she stayed open late, Wade and I brought her supper. I'd wait until they were eating and pop the latch." He waved around the bookstore. "Easy peasy."

Gwen continued to fill the trash bag. She hadn't figured out Billy's reason for wanting time alone with her, but nothing good came to mind. If he intended to do her harm, as she suspected, the flimsy plastic bag would do little to protect her. "Wade and Penelope never missed you as they ate their dinner?"

Billy shook his head, his smile demonic. "Nah. I went back through before Wade was ready to leave."

"How about Liz? She never saw you sneaking in this side?"

"Never seemed to." Billy stepped even closer to Gwen. "I knew I could stash the cigar man's ashtray in here." He glanced at the register counter as he tapped his temple. "But I remembered she had the security camera. Ha! Lot of good it did her! After I hit the cigar man, I opened the old door a little bit. Pushed that big chair out of my way."

Those scratches on the wide-planked wood floor. Liz probably assumed a shopper had moved that chair.

Billy continued to brag. "Used the cigar man's grabber stick for reaching boxes on the top shelf. Took me a few tries but I moved the camera to point at the ceiling."

Billy didn't seem concerned about being caught on Liz's security system this time. With his poor eyesight, maybe he'd never spotted the other three cameras. *Is there a backup tape?* She didn't recall Ben asking when he first explored the equipment.

"Didn't it bother you that Liz might be suspected of your crime?"

"Nah. I knew the police could never arrest her. Like I said, those are my fingerprints, not hers. And they'll never catch me."

Billy didn't seem to be hallucinating. Too many details appeared valid. Gwen could no longer deny Billy was the one who'd clobbered Farley and hid the ashtray. Disturbingly, Billy harbored not even a twinge of regret for his actions.

But why is he confiding in me? Bragging at his cleverness. He'd never want the police to hear the minutia he was sharing. No question: Billy was there to get rid of her.

To Gwen's credit – and her detriment – her quest to find the most likely suspect for the police to pursue had brought her too close to the truth for Billy to risk exposure.

Gwen continued to circle the bookstore, attempting to distance herself from Billy, but he was never far away. Time slowed as she collected a plate here, a cup there. She doubled back into spaces she'd already cleared, pretending to find another piece of trash, repeatedly shaking the bag as though she'd added to the contents. Her fingers approached numbness. The stickiness of sweat drenched her armpits, the smell of fear unmistakable.

"I admire you, Mrs. Andrews," Billy commented from behind her.

He surprised her with his statement. "You do?"

"Sure. You're a clever lady. Asked a lot of good questions.

Talked to people who might know something. But your instincts are way off. Not your fault."

"You mean checking on a stranger was a waste of my time?"

"Don't know if I'd call it a waste, but that Jeremy fellow didn't attack Farley." Again, Billy's laughter bounced around the bookstore. "It was me, Mrs. Andrews. It was me."

Gwen tilted her face upward to look at him. He was standing with both hands behind his back, rocking on the balls of his feet. "Why are you telling me, Billy?"

"You're getting too close. I heard all about your Sunday brunch. Mrs. G. told me and Wade at supper." His wide-eyed stare was nothing short of terrifying.

Unless Gwen found a way to fend him off, her life was doomed. She hugged the bulging trash bag as if the flimsy plastic would protect her from whatever Billy had in mind. *Keep him talking.* "I'm not following you."

He harrumphed. "Sooner or later, you'd ask Mrs. G. what time I came home the night of the fire. She always waits up for me, you know, even after Wade goes to bed. I like it that she worries."

"She's very fond of you." Gwen wished that someone would please walk in the door of the bookstore and put an end to this verbal sparring. "If I ask Penelope about that night, what will she tell me?"

He waved one hand in dismissal. "Oh, she'll say my shirt was bloody."

"She didn't ask you why?"

"Sure she did. I told her it was fish blood from the pier. She made me take off my shirt so she could wash it in cold water."

"But it was Farley's blood, wasn't it?"

"You know, Mrs. Andrews, I thought he was dead after I smashed that ashtray into his skull. Blood splattered everywhere. I couldn't believe he was still alive the next morning. Guess he had a hard head." Billy giggled at his joke.

261

How much longer could Gwen delay Billy's attack? He carried no weapon that she could see. Maybe he'd hidden something in his jacket pocket. Then again, his unexpected touch in the stockroom revealed his strong hands. He could simply choke her to death.

If no one arrived to interrupt, would he leave her lifeless body for Tess, Liz, or Ben to find?

Damn it, where is everyone?

Billy moved in her direction. "You deserved to know why I did it before you die. I hope you go easier. I don't wanna think you suffered." From behind his back, he raised one of the glass hurricane globes.

Chapter Forty-Four ... early evening, Tuesday

When had Billy picked up the heavy piece of glass? He seemed to be moving in slow motion as Gwen backed toward the register counter, thinking to put an obstacle between them. Her focus never strayed from Billy's face.

Is this the way my life is going to end? At the hands of a disturbed young man who couldn't control his impulses?

One name came to mind: Parker. Would he hear her if she called his name? Would she save herself or was she about to join him on the other side?

Instead, Gwen yelled, "No, Billy. Stop. You'll only get into more trouble if you hurt me. Liz and my sister and the detective are due here any minute."

And then she saw it. Liz's fire extinguisher reflected in Billy's oversized lenses. It hung on the wall only a few feet behind her. All Gwen had to do was get to *it* before Billy got to *her*. She inched backwards.

Her backbone bumped into the extinguisher. All thoughts of summoning Parker vanished. Her firefighting training kicked in as it had the other night. She swiveled sideways, jerked the canister from its base and pulled out the pin. Swinging around, she aimed the nozzle at Billy and squeezed the trigger.

When his hands flew to his face, Billy dropped the hurricane globe, the glass so thick it didn't break when it landed with a thud. He screamed and screamed and screamed again.

Gwen kicked him in the shin. Then stomped on his toes.

Billy lost his balance and landed hard on the unforgiving wooden plank floor.

Men's voices boomed in unison. "What's going on here?"

Gwen was so relieved someone had finally walked through the door. "I was only protecting myself. Billy was about to hit me with the glass globe." The fire extinguisher dropped from her grasp. When it bounced, the metallic sound reverberated before it rolled away from her.

Writhing on the floor, covered with white powder, Billy squealed, "I can't see."

Ben rushed to Gwen. "Are you all right?" His hands grasped her shoulders as he scanned her face.

"I think so." Gwen stammered as her near-miss hit home.

Detective Mike Brown tapped his shoulder mic, calling for an ambulance and a patrol car. Unclipping handcuffs from his belt, he strode toward Billy while sending a piercing glare at Gwen. "We've got to stop meeting like this, Mrs. Andrews. Is there an eye-washing station in here?"

"I don't know, but I'll look around." Despite her shaking, Gwen hurried into Liz's office with Ben on her heels. He searched the desk while she rummaged in the cabinet. Finding nothing useful, they returned to the main bookstore.

"We didn't find anything eye-related," Ben said.

Gwen glanced at the still-writhing Billy. His eyes, now red, blinked in rapid succession. Tears streamed down his face. Nevertheless, he sent a look of pure hatred in her direction.

Mike lifted the cuffed Billy to a sitting position and leaned him against the register counter. "Keep blinking, son. I've called for an ambulance. Try to stop screaming."

With Billy cuffed, but still howling, Mike addressed Gwen. "I can't believe you've done this again. When are you going to learn to stay out of police business?"

Gwen raised her shoulders as a non-answer, hugging herself as she switched her gaze to Ben. "I've been leaving messages on your cell phone since this morning. Didn't you get them?"

Ben tossed her a sheepish look. "Battery totally wiped. Need to buy a new one. Sorry. I'm here now."

A siren's wail added to the cacophony of Billy's non-stop yelping. Two EMTs rushed in with a stretcher, took one look at Billy, and began the process of washing his eyes.

From the doorway, Liz's voice shouted the question of the day. "What's going on here?"

Before Gwen could answer, Tess appeared at Liz's side and scanned the area. "My god, what happened?"

Gwen managed to answer. "Billy was going to attack me, just like he attacked Farley."

Tess's face paled. "Did he hurt you, Sis?"

"I sprayed him before he got close enough to hit me."

Liz stared at the fire extinguisher and pointed. "With that?"

Gwen couldn't tell if Liz was appalled or relieved. "It was the only weapon I could find."

Tess drew Gwen into a hug. "Good thing you're resourceful."

Within her sister's warm embrace, Gwen's shaking subsided.

"Why was Billy going to hit you?" Liz's eyebrows lifted.

"Hold up there, Mrs. Andrews." Mike Brown pulled a tattered notebook from his pocket and moved to Gwen's side, jotting notes as she relayed Billy's confession.

A few minutes later, Tess uttered. "Wow. Who would have guessed that shy young man could do such a thing?"

Gwen flashed to a list of reasons for murder she'd read in a novel at some point over the years. "I'd say crime of passion. He couldn't control his anger at Farley for upending Penelope's life. I don't know how she and Wade are going to react to this."

"Don't worry about them." Mike Brown tucked his notebook into a pocket. "We'll send an officer to explain what happened before we bring them to the hospital."

Gwen caught Ben's eye. "If you didn't get any of my messages, why are you here?"

"Mike and I were finishing up our beers when he got a phone call, so we rushed over to share the good news with Liz."

Liz's head jerked up. "Me?"

"Yes, you," Mike answered. "The fingerprint analysis is completed. You're not a match." His gaze moved to Gwen. "Now that we know those prints are Billy's, we'll take a set at the hospital for the official match. I'll have your statement typed up, Mrs. Andrews. Stop at the station sometime tomorrow and sign it." Mike turned and followed the EMTs as they carried Billy on a stretcher to the ambulance.

When Liz began to tremble, Gwen supported her around the waist. "You can relax now, Liz. You're not going to be arrested."

"I'm so relieved." Liz wiped at a tear, her mood lifting. "I'm not happy about Billy sneaking up on you, Gwen, but I'm thrilled to be out from under Chief Upton's microscope."

"There's one more piece of news, ladies."

The three of them turned to Ben.

"Chief Upton's wife visited the station this afternoon. He's been diagnosed with a brain tumor. Tomorrow morning, she's taking him to Mass General to discuss the treatment options."

The women gasped as the gravity of the news sunk in.

Gwen was the first to speak. "That's tragic. But it does explain his recent personality change."

"That's how I'm seeing it," Ben agreed. "It was so unlike him to ignore my opinions when it came to criminals."

Liz added her own ordeal. "And the way he treated Gwen and me when he stomped over here from Farley's cigar bar last Tuesday." She paused for a beat. "Poor man. I hope his treatment is successful."

"What happens now at the police department?" Gwen asked.

"Hard to say. I'm going up there now." Ben was out the door before they had a chance to react.

In the quiet that followed, Tess held up her cell phone. "Found it, Gwen. Took forever. I walked up and down the boardwalk several times. I finally asked a young woman if she'd come with me and dial my number. We heard it ringing when we reached a spot near where you found me napping. It had slipped under the boardwalk. This girl reached under the slats and placed it in my hand. I handed her a twenty dollar bill and my effusive thanks."

Chapter Forty-Five ... mid evening, Tuesday

The sisters carried glasses of wine to the Adirondack chairs. Tess placed her goblet on the deck railing. "Be right back. I need to get something from my car." She hurried along the rear deck and reappeared in a few seconds. "There's someone here to see you."

Behind Tess, Hal carried Gwen's tray of flowers. As he came nearer, he nodded toward the smiling pansies. "Maggie asked me about these. I told her I'd deliver them."

Gwen set her goblet on a deck table and reached out to take the tray. "Thanks. My front window boxes need a shot of color."

Tess waved to get Gwen's attention. "Hope you don't mind my meddling, Sis, but I called Hal a little while ago and told him to get over here. It's high time the two of you work things out. I'm going to take a stroll around town and give you some privacy."

Even after Tess had left, Gwen clutched the tray of pansies, her arm muscles beginning to quiver.

"Let me set those down for you." Hal gripped the tray and lowered it to the deck boards. "I'm here to apologize, Gwen."

A weight that had plagued her since she'd caught him smoking that damn cigar lifted like an early morning fog. She stopped short of assuming his as-yet-unspoken apology would salvage their friendship, but his intention was at least a beginning. She rubbed her aching arm muscles, searching for words. "Would you like a glass of wine?"

"Sure."

Gwen plucked her goblet from the deck railing and led Hal into the kitchen where he settled on an island stool and watched her pour raspberry Zinfandel.

"Are you angry with Tess for inviting me over?"

Gwen handed him the glass of wine. "Never angry. With Nathan gone, I think Tess needs someone to be happy."

He stretched his glass toward hers, clinking for unspoken luck. "So do I, Gwen. When you caught me smoking Farley's cigar, the look on your face broke my heart. I felt like the biggest heel in the world. I've been miserable ever since."

Gwen had been equally miserable but didn't say so.

Hal sipped his wine. "Jenna told me she stopped by."

"I was thrilled to see her, but I'm surprised you dragged her into the middle of our spat."

"Spat?" His eyebrows flew upward. "More like a life-altering parting of the ways. I'm here to apologize, Gwen. I'm sorry I broke my promise."

The advice from both Tess and Liz whispered. *Ease up, Gwen. Allow Hal this one weakness. Forgive his betrayal. Resurrect your friendship.*

Beneath it all, Gwen wasn't sure she could set aside her memories of Great Uncle Gus and sever his hold on her. Although she suspected she'd always hate the stench of a smoldering stogie, maybe she could get past her pre-teen trauma. She crossed her arms, cupping her elbows in her palms. "I've been so angry with you."

"I noticed. You're an expert with a cold shoulder."

"We had such a pleasant friendship, Hal. I saw it all going up in smoke, if you'll excuse a bad pun."

He chuckled. "I've missed your bad puns. Should I get down on one knee and beg?"

When he made a move to get off his stool, Gwen's hands flew up. "No, no. That's not necessary."

He resettled. "Then what do I need to do, Gwen? I can't imagine my life without you."

She studied him a moment longer. His weathered face, his deep blue eyes, his puppy dog expression. "You need to answer one deal-breaker question, Hal."

"What's the question?"

"Do you intend to continue your cigar-smoking habit?"

Hal roared with laughter and hopped to his feet, rushing around to her side of the island. "If I have to choose between you and a cigar, I choose you. So my answer is a big emphatic 'no.' I'll never touch another stogie, and I mean it."

Gwen reached out and stroked his cheek. With him standing so close, she caught the scent of his spicy aftershave and mint toothpaste. Despite her conviction that he'd never eradicate the stench of Farley's cigar, he'd managed to do it. Time for Gwen to relent. "I forgive you, Hal."

In less than a split second, he eased her to her feet and wrapped her in his strong arms. She relaxed into his embrace, nuzzling the crook of his neck to breathe him in.

When his lips found hers, she did not resist.

Hal pushed her to arm's length, his intense gaze roaming her face. "This feels so right."

Amber meowed at their feet. When the cat rubbed against Hal's pant leg, smile lines radiated from the corners of his eyes. "Does this mean we have her approval?"

Gwen grinned. "Either that or she's hungry."

Chapter Forty-Six ... mid evening, Tuesday

A loud car engine roared outside. Seconds later the front doorbell chimed.

"Let me guess." Hal's tone was only slightly sarcastic. "Your detective friend?"

Gwen opened the front door. "Right you are, Hal. Hello, Ben."

Hal reached around her and extended his hand. "I owe you an apology, Detective Snowcrest. Actually, two."

"I'm no longer on the police force, Mr. Jenkins. Call me Ben."

As the two men shook, Ben nodded toward Gwen. "You've got a special lady here."

Hal placed his arm across Gwen's shoulders and squeezed gently. "It'll be a long time before I risk losing her again."

"Good plan." Ben shifted his weight and tossed Gwen a glance she couldn't decipher. *Was Tess right that his interest went deeper than sleuthing buddies? Is that disappointment in his gray eyes or is my imagination once again working overtime?* She ignored the heat working up her neck. "Where are my manners, Ben? Come in and have a glass of wine."

At the island, Gwen filled another goblet and handed it to him.

Ben settled on a stool. "I stopped over to make sure you're all right."

"I'm fine. Billy never touched me."

"I feel bad that your phone messages never reached me. Luckily, your firefighting skills are first-class. You've been getting a lot of practice lately."

It was Gwen's turn to laugh. "You never know when something you learned years ago will come in handy."

Hal looked from one to the other, his expression quizzical. "What are you two talking about?"

Gwen eyed him. "I haven't had a chance to tell you."

Ben jumped in with the explanation. "At the bookstore earlier this evening, Gwen came face to face with Farley's attacker."

Hal blanched. "Tell me you're kidding."

"Not kidding at all. You'd better fill him in, Gwen."

For the next few minutes, she went over every detail of her confrontation with Billy.

When Gwen paused to take a breath, Ben took over. "Gwen sprayed Billy with the fire extinguisher. She's quite a woman." Ben treated her to a megawatt smile.

Hal's eyes widened as he stared at her. "My God, I hope this is the last time you involve yourself in a murder investigation."

"You sound like Detective Brown. Believe me, Hal, I didn't plan this. I was only trying to help Liz out of trouble."

Hal opened his arms, inviting Gwen into his embrace.

Behind them, Ben cleared his throat. "I guess I'll get going. I'm feeling like a third wheel."

Gwen pushed herself away from Hal. "You don't need to go, Ben. We're acting like a couple of teenagers. Tell me, is there any news about Chief Upton's condition?"

"He'll be on medical leave at least a few months, depending on his treatment. There's no way of knowing if he'll come back to the department or opt for retirement."

"Like you did?"

"Not quite the same. I was planning to retire. The chief wasn't."

Hal took another sip of his wine. "What happens now?"

"Mike Brown is acting as interim police chief."

Gwen wasn't surprised. "How are the dominos falling for the rest of the officers?"

Ben pursed his lips. "You don't disappoint, Gwen. I knew

you'd suspect there was more. The chief hadn't finalized my retirement paperwork. Mike asked me to un-retire and take over as the lead detective."

Hal rubbed Gwen's back. "Are you going to, Ben?"

"I told Mike I'd give him an answer by tomorrow morning. We always worked well together, so I'm thinking I'll do it."

"What a relief." Tension fell from Gwen's shoulders. "Better to have a level-headed detective chasing the criminals in Harbor Falls. I sensed you were frustrated being an outsider."

"You're right. Nothing like having all the tools at your fingertips to track down the bad guys. Not that we have a lot of them in our quiet college town, but strangers arrive all the time, and you never know what trouble they're bringing with them."

Ben pushed himself from the stool and stretched. "If you ever need my help, Gwen, give me a call. You still have my card?"

"I do, Ben. Thanks for trying to clear Liz."

He laughed. "You get all the credit, Gwen. You two lovebirds have a nice evening. See ya."

The Corvette engine roared to life and the newly-reinstated Detective Benjamin Snowcrest zoomed around the village green.

Hal linked arms with Gwen. "Are you free for a late dinner?"

"I think I can make time. The Wharf?"

"Of course. I'll call and make a reservation." Hal kissed her squarely on the mouth before pulling out his cell phone and punching numbers.

Tess rushed through the front door. "I'm back. Was that Ben driving away?"

"Yep. He stopped by to check on me."

Tess tossed Gwen and Hal a mischievous grin. "I see my little plan to get you two back together was a success. If those smiles are any indication, that is."

Hal gave Tess the okay sign of thumb and finger. "Worked like a charm. Thanks for setting it up. I'm taking Gwen out for a late supper. Want to join us?"

"Nah, you two go ahead. I think you need some alone time. Besides, I feel like watching another old movie. Is there any mac and cheese left in your freezer?"

"I think so."

"I'll check. See you in the morning, Gwen. And goodnight, Hal. Glad you're back in my sister's life."

Chapter Forty-Seven ... late evening, Tuesday

Although their favorite table at the window was occupied by a younger couple, Gwen could still spy the harbor lights twinkling in the distance.

Hal clinked his scotch on the rocks to her glass of Amaretto, the ice cubes tinkling when the rims touched. "Here's to my favorite lady, now safely back in my life."

"Again with the favorite lady. How many are there?"

"Only you, my dear. Only you."

***

Two hours later, Hal walked Gwen up the granite slabs to the thick oak doors of the converted village library. He paused one step below so their heads were on the same level before leaning in to capture her lips.

Gwen threw her arms around his neck, kissing him deep and long until she ran out of breath and broke away.

"Does that mean we're back to where we were before Farley Cooper came to town?"

She gave Hal her sweetest smile. "We're in a better place now, don't you think?"

"I *like* the way you think." His grin matched hers. "Listen, I don't want to ruin our new beginning and move too fast, so I'm heading home. Can I call you tomorrow?"

"If you don't, I'll be disappointed."

Gwen didn't go inside until Hal's taillights disappeared around the other side of the village green. With a backward shove of her foot, she nudged the heavy door closed until the antique latch snicked shut behind her. She leaned against the door's hard surface, giddy as a teenager.

Her euphoric stupor evaporated when the carved marble slab on the narrow table caught her eye, its black color a reminder of the damage it had done to Farley Cooper's skull. *Had only a week passed since Billy attacked the cigar man?*

Pushing the incident from her mind, Gwen picked up the picture of Parker walking Duxbury Beach and traced his handsome face with her forefinger. He smiled back at her.

"Hal and I are finally moving in a positive direction, Parker. But no man will ever take your special place in my heart."

Then her mouth formed a pout and she shook her finger at his image. "I have a bone to pick with you. At Liz's bookstore this afternoon, I thought about calling your name, but things happened so fast, I never got the chance. Have you figured out how to materialize somewhere other than our library home?"

Not surprisingly, he didn't answer. He just kept smiling.

Gwen kissed her fingers and touched his handsome face before resting the photo in its place of honor.

"Guess I'll ask you that question next time you drop in for a visit. Good night, Parker."

THE END

Made in the USA
Columbia, SC
25 May 2021